# EMPTY
# CUP

# ALSO BY SARAH PRICE

### THE AMISH CLASSIC SERIES

*First Impressions* (Realms)
*The Matchmaker* (Realms)

### THE AMISH OF LANCASTER SERIES

*Fields of Corn*
*Hills of Wheat*
*Pastures of Faith*
*Valley of Hope*

### THE PLAIN FAME TRILOGY

*Plain Fame*
*Plain Change*
*Plain Again*

### OTHER AMISH FICTION BOOKS

*An Amish Buggy Ride* (Waterfall Press)
*An Amish Christmas Carol*
*Amish Circle Letters*
*Amish Circle Letters II*
*A Christmas Gift for Rebecca*
*Priscilla's Story*

For a complete listing of books, please visit the author's website at
www.sarahpriceauthor.com.

*An*

# EMPTY
# CUP

## SARAH PRICE

**Waterfall**
PRESS

Published by Waterfall Press, Grand Haven, MI

www.brilliancepublishing.com

Amazon, the Amazon logo, and Waterfall Press are trademarks of Amazon.com, Inc., or its affiliates.

ISBN-13: 9781477824856
ISBN-10: 1477824855

Cover design by Kerri Resnick

Library of Congress Control Number: 2014955037

Printed in the United States of America

*To all the people impacted by the hardship of depression, whether it is consuming a friend, a family member, or even you. For those who are personally affected, may the black cloud lift and the glory of God shine down on you.*

*S. P.*

*I have shewed you all things, how that so labouring ye ought to support the weak, and to remember the words of the Lord Jesus, how he said, It is more blessed to give than to receive.*

—Acts 20:35 (King James Version)

# About the Vocabulary

The Amish speak Pennsylvania Dutch (also called Amish German or Amish Dutch). This is a verbal language with variations in spelling among communities throughout the United States. For example, in some regions, a grandfather is *grossdaadi* while in other regions he is known as *grossdawdi*. Some dialects refer to the mother as *maem* and others simply as *mother* or *mammi*.

In addition, there are words and expressions, such as *mayhaps*, or the use of the word *then* at the end of sentences, and, my favorite, *for sure and certain*, that are not necessarily from the Pennsylvania Dutch language/dialect but are unique to the Amish.

The use of these words comes from my own experience living among the Amish in Lancaster County, Pennsylvania.

# PROLOGUE

Rosanna sighed and leaned against the white pillar holding up the sagging roof of her wraparound porch. She felt as weary as the house and porch looked—both of which were in desperate need of fresh paint. The fence also needed to be painted and fixed—the horse kept wandering into the mules' paddock. Given that it was already autumn, she knew Timothy wouldn't get to any of the repairs this year. She was as resigned to this as she was to the fact that she lived in a loveless marriage.

Staring at the two-story red barn across the driveway, Rosanna watched as the sun rose behind it, the sky slowly transforming from dark blues to hues of red and orange. She heard the dogs bark from their kennel. A stray cat ran around the back corner of the barn, the likely cause of the interest from the dogs. It disappeared down the driveway in the direction of the road.

Unlike most Amish farms, their property was long and rectangular, the driveway cutting the land almost in half. The fields were closer to the road, while the house and outbuildings were tucked far in the back. The horse and buggy had to travel down the long driveway, which cut through the middle of two crop fields, in order to get to the house and barn. Bordering the back of the property were the paddocks for the horse, mules, and cows, facing south, and the family's garden behind the house. On the western side, another road ran behind the fields and barn.

It was a strange layout for a farm, and Rosanna wasn't particularly fond of the garden's location. She felt it was too close to the main entrance of the house. As a result, every time she hung laundry or helped with morning chores, she was constantly passing it and reminded of how much work she had to do: tilling, planting, weeding, harvesting. At least now with the growing season behind her, she only needed to spread manure to prepare the dirt for next spring.

The barn, however, gave her some comfort. The gray river stones used for the foundation dated back to the mid-1700s, according to her husband. It was a pretty building, and with the red paint and white trim, it stood out as a landmark for anyone traveling past it on the back road. Unlike the rest of the property, the barn was in perfect shape; there was not one warped board of siding nor one shingle in need of replacement.

That's Timothy, she thought emotionlessly.

Because the large red barn could be seen from the road, her husband kept it in immaculate repair. The windows were washed on a weekly basis, and no excuses for even one cobweb were accepted, harsh winters or illness included. Timothy was fastidious when it came to appearances. No one was going to talk about his family or his farm—at least not the people who mattered. In Timothy's mind, the people who mattered meant everyone in the *g'may* . . . everyone except her.

Rosanna knew better than to complain to anyone about the truth. Her mother had always told her not to hang dirty laundry where other people could see it. The metaphor wasn't lost on Rosanna. She knew that if she talked to one of the preachers, Timothy's reaction would be worse than anything she'd already faced. She knew that he'd never change, so what was the point in confiding in anyone? Amish women didn't get divorced. They just worked alongside their husbands and learned to keep a stiff upper lip even when sorrow dominated their lives.

"Rosanna!"

Hearing his voice call her name was jarring. While she shouldn't have been surprised that he was up, she had to dig deep to find the strength to face him. She dreaded returning to the kitchen and navigating the chaos of life, a life that felt increasingly out of control and overly demanding to Rosanna. The calm before the storm, she thought, was over. Every morning she rose early to find some time to reflect and pray—and be alone without Timothy's presence hovering nearby.

It was still early morning, and that meant only one thing: the day was ahead of her, and like all of her days, it was going to be a long one. If she were lucky, Timothy would need to leave the farm to work with the Englische.

"Rosanna!" He flung open the door, the upper hinge squeaking.

Just one more thing to fix, she thought.

"Are you deaf?"

His voice shot through her, his harsh words cutting and mean. He was in a mood; she could tell that without even turning around to greet him. Taking a deep breath, she willed herself to remain calm. It was a method of coping that she had taught herself years ago. Deep breath in, hold it, exhale slowly. For some reason, it helped.

"Was just enjoying the sunrise," she answered, careful to avoid speaking with an edge to her voice.

One look at her husband, and she knew that the morning wasn't going to start well, despite the fact that he was dressed and ready to begin his day. As always, his clean white shirt was wrinkle free, and his trousers bore not a single spot to indicate they were his work pants. No, his clothing indicated nothing was amiss in the Zook household. After all, appearances mattered to him. It was only on the inside that the secret of his shame was apparent. Freshly laundered clothing couldn't hide the real problem: it was written all over his face, even if she was the only one who recognized it.

Last night, as she did on most nights, she had retired early, putting the children to bed before retreating to the bedroom that she and Timothy shared. She read by her lantern light for a while, preferring the soft flickering of the kerosene lamp to the harsh brightness of the battery-operated lights that more and more Amish families were now using. The gentle shadows that danced on the pale-blue walls helped her relax, and after reading two pages of her devotional, she set the book on her nightstand and blew out the lantern's flame.

She awoke alone.

Again.

She stole quietly into the kitchen, suspecting that she would find Timothy there, still in his clothes and fast asleep. Before she struck a match to light the propane lantern over the kitchen table, she looked at the large sunroom that opened to the kitchen. Sure enough, she saw his form sprawled out on the sofa along the back wall. He was still wearing his work clothes from the previous day, and Rosanna suspected he wouldn't change. Again.

She found him there most mornings. It was a routine that was becoming increasingly difficult to live with. She knew divorce was not an option, but she secretly thought about it from time to time.

Now was one of those times.

"There's no coffee brewing!" Timothy said, running his hand through his uneven dark hair. He had insisted she cut it last weekend, even though he had refused to sharpen the scissors. Luckily, he hadn't noticed—or simply didn't care—that the haircut was lopsided and his bangs were cut on a diagonal. He stood in the doorway, holding it open with his arm as he glared at her. "Is it too much to ask for coffee when I wake up?"

Rosanna dipped her head in silent acquiescence as she hurried past him. "I'm sorry," she said quietly.

"And don't burn it today," he grumbled. "If that's at all possible."

The criticism would have stung if she weren't so used to it. She had heard the complaints a hundred times: she couldn't cook, she couldn't sew, she couldn't even make a good cup of coffee. The list of her flaws seemed endless when Timothy began criticizing her.

She wished she could lash out at him and point out that his constant criticism and belittling of her was driving a huge wedge between them. And it was affecting the children, too. They were beginning to see what was happening, especially Aaron, who had just turned thirteen.

It was a given that Timothy favored Aaron over Cate. After all, he hadn't wanted a little girl. He'd wanted a farm full of boys. When Cate arrived, his reaction had been astonishing: "I didn't know I was capable of making girl babies." And then he'd left Rosanna's bedside, never even pausing to hold his newborn daughter.

At nine years of age, Cate seemed immune to her father's constant rejection. She preferred being with Rosanna anyway. Whether Cate was clinging to Rosanna's dress or sitting on her lap, she didn't seem to notice that her father paid no attention to her. However, every time Rosanna heard Timothy reference their daughter as "it" or "that thing," it felt like a knife into her heart.

Initially, Aaron had been oblivious to the disparity in their treatment and to his father's behavior. He delighted in Timothy's attention. But more and more, Aaron was noticing his father's erratic behavior in the evenings as well as his extreme grouchiness in the mornings. Coupled with his puffy face and bloodshot eyes, there was no denying the fact that Timothy Zook had a problem, even if he felt that it was under control.

"Moderation," he had told Rosanna one day. "Even Jesus drank wine." He had tried to make light of the situation. "Everything in moderation. It's fine."

But it wasn't fine. Not by a long stretch of the imagination.

As she stood at the stove, turning on the gas so that she could heat the water for his coffee, she realized that moderation was something Timothy might preach but demonstrated no ability to practice. And she wasn't certain how much more of his "moderation" she could take.

Timothy was seated at the head of the table drinking his cup of coffee when Aaron bounded down the stairs. At thirteen their son was the spitting image of his father. His curly brown hair flopped over his greenish-blue eyes, and he brushed it aside as he stumbled over the last step.

"Easy there, Aaron," Timothy said, his voice tense. "Where's the fire anyway?"

"Thought I was late for chores!" Aaron grinned at his mother as he took his place at the table, sliding onto the bench and reaching for the glass of water by his plate. "Reckon not if you aren't angry."

Rosanna glanced at the clock. It was almost seven. The cows should have been milked much earlier. They needed to be milked on a regular schedule. Otherwise they produced less milk, and there was the risk that the older ones might turn sour. Rosanna didn't like it when Timothy overslept and got a late start on his chores. These days, it was happening more and more frequently.

Noticing her glance at the clock, Timothy frowned. "What difference does an hour or two make, Rosanna?" He shook his head and looked at Aaron, giving his son a wink. "Women don't know anything about livestock anyway. Tending livestock is a man's job, ain't so?"

Rosanna clenched her jaw tight, but did not respond. While on the surface his words seemed innocent enough, she knew from the cutting tone that he was putting her down. He believed that women should only work in the house and claimed they were too weak to handle barn chores. It didn't matter. She had enough on her mind without worrying about his sarcastic jabs at her. Her skin had thickened long ago. She just wished he would contain his ridicule so that the children wouldn't be exposed to it.

"Whatcha doing today, Daed?" asked Aaron as he reached for the bowl of scrambled eggs Rosanna had made after brewing Timothy's coffee.

"Well, Aaron, got some farm work to do today," Timothy began, accepting the bowl from his son. As he took it, he reached out to tousle his son's hair with his free hand. "Need to work in the back pasture while you're at school. The hay's been drying for three days now, and it's ready to be baled."

Aaron lit up at the attention. Rosanna watched, amazed how the moment that Aaron, "his" son, walked into the room, Timothy's attitude completely changed. Gone were the criticism and reproach. He greeted his son with warmth and pride. But it shouldn't have surprised her. He constantly reminded her that birthing Aaron was the only thing she had ever done right.

"Aw shucks," the boy said, "I wanted to help. Couldn't I stay home today? Just this once?" Aaron had a bad habit of skipping school, with Timothy's permission, to do the farm work. With just one year left before he was finished with his education, Aaron continually pressured his parents to allow him to cut school.

To Rosanna's relief, Timothy shook his head. "*Nee*, son. It's the last haying of the season, and I can handle it. Besides, last I heard, you were having trouble with your numbers, ain't so?"

Aaron hung his head in disappointment.

"Mayhaps if your *maem* would pay more attention to helping you with math, rather than visiting those sickly widows, you'd learn faster."

Stunned, Rosanna lifted her head and stared at him. Sickly widows? One was her *aendi* and the other was her own *maem's* best friend. They weren't just random strangers that she visited in the afternoons. They were extended family to her. Although she herself had seven siblings, none of them wanted to be around Timothy; they had long ago recognized that something was amiss in the marriage. For Rosanna, those "sickly widows" were the closest thing she had to relatives in the *g'may*, and she valued the time she spent with the two older women.

"And how about all of that applesauce you canned for charity last weekend?" Timothy said.

Now he was on a roll. Rosanna took a deep breath and braced herself for the impeding storm that brewed at the end of the kitchen table.

"Taking better care of others than your own son, who needs help with his schoolwork, ain't so?"

Ashamed, Rosanna looked away, not wanting to see Aaron's expression, aware that it would break her heart. She couldn't tell what he felt, whether it was disgust at his father's suggestion that she didn't take care of her son or discomfort at his father's insulting words. Did it matter? she wondered. Their son already knew that his parents had a dysfunctional marriage. Long ago, and despite the pain it caused her, she had stopped trying to shield him.

Her relationship with Timothy hadn't always been this way. Not when they were courting. Timothy Zook had been the picture of a perfect Amish man. He spoke of spiritual things, he praised her for her goodness, and he never said an unkind word about her. His reputation among the *g'may* was well known, even if he was from a different church district. After a year of courting, it was only natural that she had said yes when he asked her to marry him. She had spent the next five weeks feeling like the most blessed woman in the world. She was twenty-two when they married.

After the wedding, everything changed. Rosanna noticed that Timothy acted differently on the weekends than he did on week-days. Their farm was small, just enough to keep a dozen dairy cows and plant a decent-size crop of corn in one field and hay in another. But it wasn't quite enough to sustain them. To augment their income, Timothy worked part-time for an Englischer who did construction.

After work on Friday evenings, he would come home a little bit later than usual, and his eyes would be red. She thought she smelled tobacco on his breath. Two months after their wedding, she realized it was not cigarettes but something else. The bittersweet smell that lingered on his clothing and his squinty eyes clearly indicated that Timothy was not just drinking. Her best guess was that he had begun to dabble with drugs.

And then she found the bag of crumbled marijuana.

With that single discovery, her world shattered around her. She took the plastic bag to the bishop, who confirmed her suspicions and approached Timothy. She never knew what, exactly, had been discussed between the two of them. For a while, Timothy stopped misbehaving at home, clearly thankful that he hadn't been shunned by the bishop. But the longer he stayed sober, the more Timothy began to act angrily toward Rosanna.

He blamed her for ruining his reputation by telling the bishop. And with this new accusation against her, Timothy no longer pretended to be kind to her, not even in public. It was as if she didn't exist.

She was stunned by the change in his personality, and it didn't help that she was pregnant with her first child and feeling sickly. But she ignored the changes in her husband.

Until six months later, when it happened again. She found him in the morning, asleep in the barn with an empty bottle of vodka nearby. She wasn't certain he had smoked marijuana, but she suspected as much. This time, however, Rosanna said nothing. She knew that the community would not be so forgiving, and she also knew that she could not deal with additional verbal abuse from him. Besides, with a newborn infant to tend, she couldn't handle the emotional stress of living with a shunned husband.

After that, things began to spiral out of control.

Eventually the marijuana smoking stopped, but it was replaced, full force, by alcohol abuse. At first Timothy tried to hide it from her, stashing it in the barn and hayloft. After Cate's birth, however, he stopped caring if she knew. No one else in the *g'may* seemed to suspect anything was amiss. They had no reason to. After all, he continued working and was genuinely considered to be a good man. Little did they know that, once the sun set, the bottle came out and the nights became a dark nightmare.

"Best get started on your chores," she said to Aaron and motioned toward the barn.

Rosanna listened as Aaron bounded down the porch steps. Standing by the window, she watched him hurry toward the barn, and a few seconds later, the dogs ran free. Any time now, Cate would get up and demand Rosanna's attention, so for the moment she enjoyed watching the three dogs play in the small patch of grass before darting back into the shadows of the barn.

Timothy had already left the kitchen, his breakfast barely eaten—the eggs were too runny and the potatoes undercooked. There was always something not good enough in everything she did. At least his complaints stung less and less each day. Perhaps she was just numb from hearing so many of them.

Aaron was in the barn, milking the cows at last. They had only a dozen cows, so the morning chores didn't take very long. He'd bring her a pail of fresh milk so that she could make cheese or butter, depending on what they needed. The rest of the milk would be canned and sold to a local store that catered to the Amish who were not fortunate enough to have access to their own fresh farm produce.

Leaning forward, Rosanna cast a glance in the direction of her garden. The back edge of it ran along the property line of the neighbor's house, an elderly non-Amish woman, Gloria, who lived with her adult daughter in a more contemporary neighborhood. Years ago the family who had previously owned the Zooks' farm had sold half of it to a developer. That land now housed several streets of Englische houses, the first of which had backyards that bordered the Zooks' fields.

Rosanna thought that some of their problems stemmed from the isolation of their property from the rest of the *g'may*. Because the back of their farm bordered an Englischer neighborhood, there was little risk of the Amish witnessing Timothy's behavior. After the sun set, no one stopped by to visit, and that gave Timothy enough opportunity to lose himself at the bottom of a bottle. He only drank at night, long after the risk of detection by the community.

Rosanna always tried to get Aaron and Cate to bed early so they wouldn't see their father when he was in really bad shape. When he was, his behavior often became erratic.

Once, when he had been drinking, he took the hoe into the garden late at night and began digging more rows along the back. The neighbor, Gloria, came out of her house and began screaming at him about the hour and that he was too close to her property. Timothy responded by spitting at her. The battle between Timothy Zook and Gloria Smith hadn't let up since.

Rosanna was still standing by the sink, lost in thought after having washed the morning dishes, when he snuck up behind her.

"Mayhaps I'll go check on those rows of horse corn I planted at the back of your garden," he said, more to himself than to her. He had that special gleam in his eyes when he said this, and Rosanna knew exactly what he would do: drop a few ears of corn along the property line in order to attract rodents to Gloria's yard.

"Timothy . . ."

If there was one thing that Gloria complained about constantly, it was that the fence behind the Zooks' garden was on her land. Timothy always responded by insisting on planting crops right up to the fence, which then led to complaints about the increase of field mice and wood rats on Gloria's side.

Now Timothy turned his head to look at Rosanna. There was anger in his eyes, a look that she had long ago recognized as his feeling of superiority over others, especially her. She knew that the truth was that he was an angry man, angry at everything and nothing at the same time. And when he felt angry, anyone could be a target for his rage. Today it was Gloria.

"She's an old crankpot, Rosanna. No wonder her husband up and left her!"

"Isn't it better to just ignore her? Not instigate her?" she tried to reason, but he cut her off with a swift gesture of his hand. He always cut her off, as if to prove the point that her opinion did not matter very much to him.

"Her daughter is just as bad as she is," he said without any sympathy. His eyes seemed to gleam with delight at his next statement. "Why, I heard she was arrested for drunk driving not once but twice in a two-week period of time! And that's why she was away for so long." He laughed when he said this, but the irony of the gossip was not lost on Rosanna.

Even on the nights that Timothy did make it to bed, he would shuffle in after the clock chimed midnight, often knocking into the dresser or dropping his flashlight—Rosanna had taken to hiding the kerosene lanterns when she went to bed, realizing the danger of one in his hands. Other nights, he slept in his clothes with his leg tossed over the arm of the sofa. Who was he to mock Camille Smith? The only difference between the two of them was that the authorities hadn't caught up with Timothy Zook.

"And from the looks of her belly," he added with a sneer, "she breeds, too!"

Lowering her eyes, Rosanna turned away from the window. "Best finish your coffee," she whispered, not wanting to hear any more of his evil gossip. She heard him laugh as she moved to the stove, hating the ugly feeling that welled up inside of her chest.

*Please God*, she prayed, *give me the strength to follow Your will.*

# CHAPTER ONE

The small brass bell jingled as she opened the glass door to the shop. Inside, Rosanna inhaled deeply and shut her eyes for just a moment. Leather. It smelled warm and welcoming. For some reason, the scent reminded her of her father and growing up on the farm in Pequea. Perhaps it was from the many Saturday afternoons he had spent cleaning the horse's harness, rubbing leather soap on the reins and collar, wiping them clean until there was not one speck of dirt left on any of the equipment. Her parents still lived there, but in the smaller *haus*. Her oldest brother and his family managed the farm; their *daed* was now too old for such manual work.

The wide-plank floorboard creaked as Rosanna walked past a tall rack of saddles. Most of them were western-style, with funny-shaped horns in front of the rider's seat, although she did notice two smaller used English saddles for sale on consignment. Most likely children's saddles, she thought. Two Amish men stood in the aisle, their backs to the saddles as they stared at a rack of products: dewormer, equine shampoo, hoof polish. Rosanna imagined that for an Amish man, the shop evoked a similar feeling to the one she felt at the fabric store.

She loved going to the Troyer Harness Shop. Besides the smell, she loved the sounds: the soft murmur of men talking, the distant noise of machinery, and the hissing of the propane-powered lamps that cast bright light throughout the shop. It was so different from her home, which, these days, was quiet.

It was mid-May, and school had ended just last week for Cate. Rosanna was surprised that everything still seemed so quiet, but Cate had made herself scarce during her first week of summer vacation. She spent long mornings playing with the dogs in the freshly cut hayfield. Aaron had scolded her on more than one occasion, reminding her to avoid running through that field so that she didn't damage his crops. However, she rarely listened to her older brother, merely waiting until he was working in the barn or the cornfield before grabbing an old tennis ball, whistling to the dogs, and heading in the exact direction Aaron had told her not to go. Rosanna had grown tired of telling Cate that whistling was definitely not ladylike.

However, with her own chores finished and both *kinner* occupied—Aaron with his work and Cate with the dogs—it was the perfect time for Rosanna to slip away from the house and venture into town. She had used the kick scooter to go quietly down the long driveway to the road, hoping that neither Aaron nor Cate would see her and ask where she was going. Cate would surely have insisted on accompanying her. But this was a journey that Rosanna wanted to take alone.

With the kick scooter, it had taken only ten minutes to navigate the back roads to the center of town. The harness store was on Jasper Road, on the other side of town. Although it was just two blocks off Main Street, Jasper was a winding road that, once past Main, was surrounded by farmland. There were no other businesses near the harness store.

A customer stood at the counter, his back to Rosanna, settling his bill. One hand was wrapped around two brand-new reins for his horse's harness. Rosanna stood nervously in the shadows waiting. Her heart pounded, and she felt a sudden wave of guilt. Had she made a mistake to come in the middle of the day? She had never done this before, and despite how innocent the deed seemed, she felt as if she might be engaged in a terrible transgression.

Once the customer moved toward the door carrying the reins, Rosanna saw him. Her husband, Reuben Troyer, stood behind the counter, a frown on his face as he squinted through his glasses to read the piece of paper he held in his hand. He picked up a pencil and made some annotations in his thin ledger book. The creases in his forehead deepened, and Rosanna made a mental note to pick up stronger reading glasses the next time she shopped at Walmart.

As if sensing her approach, he looked up and, upon seeing Rosanna, smiled. His blue eyes twinkled, and he immediately removed his glasses and set them on top of the counter.

"What a *gut* surprise, *fraa*!" he said.

Rosanna practically glided across the floor toward him, her black sneakers making no sound. She'd worn her plain navy-blue dress because the color was one of her favorites, and before leaving for the store, she had changed her apron to make certain that there were no traces of flour or dust from her morning chores. Her chestnut-brown hair was freshly brushed, and it shone from beneath her white prayer *kapp*.

"Thought I'd wander down here to say hello and see how your day is going," she said lightly. She hoped that her presence was not a distraction for him.

To her relief, he appeared genuinely pleased. "Why, I'm glad you did!" He stepped from behind the counter and, after a quick glance over his shoulder at his workers, reached for her hand. No one looked up; their heads stayed down as they worked the leather cutter and the industrial sewing machines.

Squeezing her hand gently, Reuben led Rosanna through a swinging door into the back room. "Come, I want to show you something."

She would have followed him anywhere. Reuben Troyer—the man who had saved her life. As far as she was concerned, he was an angel who had swooped down and rescued her when she was in the depths of despair.

"What is it, Reuben?"

He glanced at her and smiled a mischievous smile that lit up his face. "It's a surprise."

Still holding her hand, he led her through the inventory room, past the shelves lined with boxes and crates. Everything smelled like new leather, and Rosanna loved it. She inhaled deeply, savoring the scent of the bridles and collars hanging on the walls.

On the other side of the room was a door that led outside. Reuben guided her through a small breezeway and toward a three-stall stable. His horse stood in the first stall, rubbing its nose on the side of the door. It was a dark bay Saddlebred, one that had seen Reuben through two marriages. Rosanna often wished that the horse could talk; she would have loved to hear what it had to say about Rachel and Grace, Reuben's previous wives.

Reuben led her to the stall next to his horse's. It was usually empty, but now it was occupied by a sandy-brown Standardbred horse. Reuben leaned against the door and reached over to brush his hand along the horse's neck. "What do you think, Rosanna?"

She stared at the creature, admiring the way its ears pointed forward, slightly arched, but not as much as an Arabian's. They twitched ever so slightly, as if listening for her response. "She's beautiful!"

"He," Reuben corrected, his hand resting on the horse's shoulder. There was a gentleness in his touch, his fondness for the animal more than apparent. "And he's for Aaron."

Rosanna caught her breath, and she felt a flutter rising in her chest and a lump forming in her throat. A horse for her son? She lifted her hand to her mouth, covering it as she fought the tears that were beginning to form in the corners of her eyes. "Oh, Reuben!"

He nodded, delighted with her reaction. His blue eyes moved over the horse again, a look of pride on his face. She knew what he was thinking—they had that type of relationship. He was picturing Aaron's expression when Reuben brought the horse home and handed the boy the lead rope.

Actually he wasn't a boy anymore. Sixteen. He was a young man now and one who had just started his *rumschpringe*, the period of time after Amish youths turned sixteen and were given freedom to explore the world before deciding to take the kneeling vow and become baptized members of the church. Most of the youths did make that commitment. Some did not. Rosanna had no doubt that Aaron would follow in the footsteps of their ancestors and accept baptism within a few years.

Regardless of that choice, every young man needed a horse. Under normal circumstances, his father would have given him one for his sixteenth birthday or shortly thereafter. The Amish didn't generally associate birthdays or holidays with large gifts, but a young man needed a horse to get around with during the rumschpringe.

Because Timothy had died three years before he could bestow that gift on Aaron, it was only right that Reuben should have the honor of gifting his stepson his very first horse. And what a magnificent horse he was!

Rosanna felt a familiar tugging of emotion in her chest. Reuben constantly did special things like this to please her and her *kinner*. She bit her lower lip and reached out a hand to touch the horse.

He snorted and lifted his head, causing her to laugh. "Spirited, is he not?"

Reuben nodded. "*Ja*, he's still young. Four years old and not quite broke for the buggy yet. But he'll be a right *gut* pacer—once Aaron breaks him."

"Oh help," she mumbled. "Must have been expensive."

She couldn't help but worry about money. After Timothy's death, she had struggled to keep the farm. That first year, the *g'may* had helped her as much as they could, but they needed to tend to their own crops and farms first. Barely thirteen years old, Aaron had stepped up to the responsibility, and between the two of them, the fields were plowed, the seeds planted, and the crops harvested. Luckily the farm was small enough that they managed it. Cate had also had to step up to help with some of the house chores.

For two years, they had struggled. At one point, her parents tried to talk her into selling the farm. "It's too much for you, Rosanna girl," her *daed* insisted.

"*Nee*, Daed," she replied, shaking her head. "I can't sell it. I need to hang on to it, if only for the *kinner* . . . for Aaron. If we sell it now, we'll never be able to afford another farm. He'd have to learn a trade, and his heart is in farming. You know that. And without the farm, I'd have to work at the market or in a store. That's just not for me."

It was just after the two-year anniversary of Timothy's death when Reuben Troyer had stopped by the house after a worship service. He was clad in his best—and as she later learned, only—black suit. His graying beard hung down to the second button on his white shirt. She knew him from church as a kindly middle-aged man. He had married twice before, but neither marriage had produced any children. His first wife had died after falling off a horse, and his second wife had died from brain cancer. Reuben remained alone for a long time after the death of his second wife, working in his harness store and attending church every other Sunday.

Rosanna had always thought Reuben's light-blue eyes and neatly trimmed graying beard made him stand out from the other men. While he was respected by the g'may, he also had a reputation of being a rather tough employer. Not unfair, but demanding. Because of this, and the fact that he was so much older than her, Rosanna had never seriously considered Reuben as an option. She had barely spoken to him. To be truthful, she really hadn't thought about getting remarried at all since Timothy's death.

But on that sunny June day, his hat in his hand and his broad shoulders straightened, Reuben had knocked on her door. When she answered it, she was more than surprised to see him standing there. Politely, he took a step backward on the porch and asked if he might have a word with her. Six months later, they were married.

"Not too expensive," Reuben finally said, interrupting Rosanna's thoughts. "Besides, he's a good horse that will see Aaron through many years." He paused, and she could tell that he was thinking about something *powerful important* to him. She gave him a moment. When he blinked and looked at her, he smiled his gentle and kind smile. "I'm his *daed* now anyway," he said. "It's the least I can do for him after all he's been through."

She didn't compliment him on his sensitive handling of her son. It was not necessary to speak the words to him. Instead, she thought them silently and sent a prayer of thanks to God for sending this amazing man to her doorstep that Sunday afternoon just over a year before.

Reuben took a deep breath and removed his hand from the horse. "Now that I've shared my surprise with you, mayhaps you'll share yours with me?"

"My surprise?"

He nodded and began to walk toward the door. "You are visiting for a particular reason?"

She shook her head as she fell into step beside him. "I wanted to enjoy this beautiful day," she said. "And to see my husband."

She glanced at his face and could see he was pleased. Her adoration of him often seemed to catch him off guard, a fact that made her love him even more. She knew that he had deeply loved his first wife, Rachel. Rosanna had been told that he had mourned her death for several years. But Grace was a different story. Rosanna knew very little about their short marriage.

"The haying?" Reuben asked.

That morning over breakfast, Aaron had announced that he planned to cut the hay, the second cutting of the season. The back field wasn't overly large, and haying didn't really require two people. But Rosanna wouldn't leave Aaron home alone while he worked in the fields. Anything could happen—and sometimes did—on farms in the different Amish communities in Lancaster. One year a woman had fallen under the wheels of the baler. Another year a child was kicked in the head by a mule. No, Rosanna was not about to leave her son alone while he worked the fields. She made it a rule to stay nearby whenever Aaron used the mules and equipment. He was still young, after all.

"He finished it just after dinner. I helped a bit."

Reuben tugged gently at his beard, staring at Rosanna as if he anticipated more to her story. When none came, he lifted an eyebrow. "Any issue with Gloria, then?"

The neighbor. No matter what Aaron, Rosanna, or Cate did outside, the woman watched. Often she stood on her property line, a cigarette in her wrinkled, age-spotted hand, her dark, beady eyes watching them surreptitiously while they worked. Whenever they came close to the back of the property, the part that bordered hers, she would suddenly begin her tirade about how the fencing was too close and against zoning regulations. Then she would toss her cigarette butt into the crops.

"No more than usual," Rosanna sighed.

Reuben placed his hand on her arm and gently rubbed it. "You've tried your best to be a good Christian, Rosanna. We all reap what we sow. She reaps unhappiness, for that is all that she plants throughout her life."

Rosanna didn't want to talk about Gloria—not now, not ever. Whenever she dealt with the woman, Rosanna's heart palpitated and her chest felt tight. Gloria was a miserable person. Over the years, it had grown increasingly hard for Rosanna to deal with her. And while God continually gave Rosanna the strength to ignore her, recently Gloria seemed to be attacking the family more often, which puzzled Rosanna. When Timothy had been alive and battling with the older woman, the conflict made sense. Now, however, it seemed as if Gloria were intent on being a nuisance to Rosanna and the children. But Rosanna knew that Reuben was right: both Gloria and her daughter appeared to live miserable lives in their small, unkempt house. Rosanna just wished they'd keep their suffering to themselves and not try to spread it around so much.

Changing the subject, Rosanna smiled as she said, "I missed you at dinner."

Several times a week Reuben returned to the farm—usually unannounced—to surprise her for dinner. After a nice meal shared with Aaron, Rosanna, and Cate, Reuben would sit outside or walk down the lane with her to enjoy the beautiful spring air. Today had not been one of those days.

Reuben shook his head, an indication that he, too, had been disappointed. "Rosanna," he said, his deep voice low and gentle, "we're backed up here. Orders are two weeks out at this point. I fear I won't be home for dinner during the week for a while."

She knew better than to complain about prosperity. Reuben employed four Amish men and one woman from the *g'may*, all of whom needed well-paying jobs because farmland was scarce. Without Reuben's business, five families would be struggling to put food on the table. And after Timothy's issues with alcohol while he was employed by the Englischer, Rosanna was not a big supporter of Amish working outside of the community.

"I should be here helping you," she said, looking around the breezeway between the shop and the stable. If only it were possible. The truth was that there was work to be done at home—that was where she needed to be. Between milking the cows, cleaning the dairy, tending to the house, washing the laundry, and doing her share in the fields, she didn't have time to help out at Reuben's harness store. At least she could take comfort in knowing that someone else was able to make a living because she could not work by her husband's side.

"*Nee*, Rosanna," he replied. "You do enough for everyone else. You don't need this burden."

She made a face. "That's not true at all!"

He laughed, a sound that carried in the still air. "Not true, eh? I know you visit the widows on Wednesdays. And Ben Lapp was in here last week and told me that you stopped in to help his wife after she took ill."

"Her allergies are dreadful this year," Rosanna said.

Reuben nodded his head, his lips pursed as if trying not to smile. She knew what he was thinking. He teased her dreadfully about how much she helped so many in the community. She always had a reason—an *excuse*, he liked to say. But his teasing was only that. Unlike Timothy, Reuben took pride in her role as the giver of the community, the one many turned to in times of need.

"Well, they are!" she insisted.

"*Ja, ja*, Rosanna," Reuben said kindly. "I'm sure they are." He placed a hand on her shoulder and smiled. "And you are the one to help whenever anyone's allergies are bad or *kinner* are sick or parents are aging."

He paused, tilting his head as he studied her face. She wondered whether he was noticing the wrinkles at the corners of her eyes or the streaks of gray that were forming at her hairline. It didn't matter. She knew that he loved her just the way she was. "God blessed me with being one of those wounded birds that you happily take in, didn't He now?"

Heat flooded her cheeks, and she averted her eyes. Kindness was something she didn't think she'd ever get used to receiving. "I never saw you as a wounded bird," she managed to say, still avoiding his eyes. He made her feel twenty again, an age when life seemed so innocent and free, the future laid out before her.

Unfortunately, her vision for the future had turned out quite different in reality. Growing up, she had dreamed of marrying a godly man and bearing lots of children. She wanted to surround herself with the love and laughter that she had felt in her parents' house as a child. In her dream, there was a farm with a white fence and purple martin birdhouses on tall poles that lined the driveway. Each night, the sun would descend in the sky behind the barn, the rays of light shining like beacons of God's glory.

As it turned out, God had different plans for her.

"I was wounded, Rosanna," Reuben said softly, his hand still on her arm. "You just didn't know it."

As was I, she thought.

"Now let me get back to my orders and try to wrap up early tonight. I want to bring this horse home to Aaron. Surprise him after supper, *ja*?" With a final squeeze of her arm, Reuben dropped his hand and started toward the store.

"You're sure you don't need my help here, then?" She wanted to be a part of his work life so that she could share his burden and contribute to his success.

He turned back to her and shook his head, chuckling softly. "There you go again," he said. "Offering to give of yourself to help others. *Nee*, Rosanna. Go home and enjoy your afternoon. Work on that quilt you started but never finished. Make me one of your delicious corn pies. This is your time, my *fraa*."

With that, he lifted his hand and slipped through the door, disappearing back into the shop.

She glanced at the sky, wondering for a moment how she could just leave and head back to the house. With finished chores, she really had nothing to do. Could she truly just sit down and revisit that quilt she was making? That seemed selfish, time spent doing something she liked rather than helping others. After everything that Reuben had done for her, she wanted to do something for him to show her appreciation.

If he wanted a corn pie, she would certainly make that for him. It was a simple enough request. But she wanted to do more to say *danke* to the man who had single-handedly swooped down to save her small family from a future of despair and hard labor, to the man who had brought laughter and love back into her life, to the man who had built her up after thirteen years of being beaten down.

# CHAPTER TWO

With the dishes cleaned and a cool breeze blowing through the fields, it was the perfect night to sit outside—just the two of them. Reuben sat in one of the white rocking chairs, the floorboards on the front porch creaking under its runners each time he pushed with his feet and rocked backward. The sound was a perfect rhythm for Rosanna to keep track of her stitches. One, two . . . creak. Three, four . . . creak.

She lifted her eyes from her embroidery, taking a moment for her vision to adjust. She was embroidering a linen cloth to sell at the local Amish store. She loved to embroider, creating sweet designs of irises and sunflowers. Even better, the tourists loved to buy anything embroidered: tablecloths, napkins, handkerchiefs. By selling her handicrafts to the local Amish-owned stores, Rosanna was able to further contribute to both her family and the community. It not only helped attract tourists to the area, it also enabled her to provide small donations to families in need when a crisis emerged. Last year she had donated money to hurricane victims. While she prayed that no disasters would happen this year, she knew it was God's will, not hers, that would decide that outcome.

As she began to see clearly, Rosanna let her gaze drift to the barn, where Aaron was in the paddock, working with his new horse. Aaron's surprise when he received Reuben's generous gift had nearly made her cry. She had never seen her son so choked up with emotion. He hadn't expected something so extravagant. Rosanna knew from past experience that an unexpected gift was the best kind to give.

Since Reuben had given him the horse, Aaron spent all of his free time with it. Every night he groomed the horse, currying the dirt in its coat with the hard, round rubber currycomb before brushing it down with a hard brush until all the dirt came to the coat's surface. He did not voice his pride in the horse, but his eyes shone when he finished grooming and led it into the paddock.

Reuben had spent the first few nights showing Aaron how to work with the horse, lungeing it in big circles using a long line and whip. Rosanna had watched, her heart swelling at the sight of her son and her husband, both such gentle souls, training the horse together. Rosanna had listened as Reuben explained to Aaron the importance of making the horse alternate between large and small circles as he lunged, first at a walk and then at a trot. She noticed that Aaron hung on to every word that his stepfather spoke. His attentiveness to both the horse and to Reuben spoke volumes about his character as a young man.

Timothy would never have spent so much quality time with their son—time spent teaching him to be a man. *An Amish man*, Rosanna had corrected herself. For a moment, Rosanna had felt tears at the corner of her eyes, but she had known better than to cry.

Now, as they sat on the porch while Aaron worked with the horse in the paddock, a calm sense of peace descended on the farm. Rosanna felt the warmth of happiness fill her.

"So, I have an idea," said Reuben suddenly.

"What's your idea, Reuben?" she asked, turning her dark eyes in his direction.

He stopped rocking the chair; the floorboard was silent as he placed his hands on his knees and leaned forward. Whatever was on his mind was something he had been pondering for a while. "You got me thinking last week when you stopped by the store," he began, choosing his words carefully.

"I did?"

Reuben laughed. He always laughed at her reactions, especially when she was surprised that she might have offered something of value to him. After years of being told that she wasn't good at anything, not cleaning or cooking or even raising the *kinner*, she always felt amazement whenever Reuben thought she was useful. Compliments had been few and far between in the years preceding their marriage.

"Indeed you did," he affirmed, a tender expression on his face. "And during worship yesterday I made a decision about the shop."

Intrigued, Rosanna tilted her head, resting it on the back of the chair as she watched him. "The bishop might say you were supposed to be thinking about God, not work."

He laughed at her jest. "You mentioned about helping out at the shop."

*Helping out at the shop?* Stunned into silence, Rosanna dropped her embroidery onto her lap and stared at him. Had he really been listening? Did he really want her help? There was nothing she would like better than to work with her husband at his store. Not only would it be nice to get away from the farm, but she knew she would enjoy interacting with other people during the day. For the past few years, she had felt increasingly isolated at the farm.

As if reading her mind, Reuben held up his hand, weathered from years of working with rough leather. "Hold on there, Rosanna Troyer. I can see what you're thinking already."

Her hopes dashed, she exhaled sharply and picked up her embroidery once again.

"Now I know you wanted to help out and all. And I sure do appreciate that offer." He smiled, as if that could mend her hurt. "But I don't want my *fraa* working down at the shop. Besides, you have enough to do here with the farm and house."

She tried not to show her disappointment. She focused her eyes on the needle, thread, and material, hoping that her expression didn't give away her emotions. It usually did.

"Now if the shop was located here on your farm," he said, tugging thoughtfully at his beard, "I might have considered you helping out a bit. You could run in and out as needed. But we have a most unusual setup."

No further explanation was necessary. She understood what he meant. When she had agreed to marry him, they had had a sit-down discussion about the living arrangements. She didn't want to get rid of the farm, and he certainly wasn't going to get rid of the shop. He did, however, understand that her house was a better place for them to reside, and without any argument, he agreed to move there instead of uprooting Rosanna and the children.

"So I decided to hire an office manager," he said slowly.

That wasn't what she had anticipated. In fact, it didn't even make sense. With the quantity of orders increasing, he needed more workers in the back of the shop to fulfill them. "An office manager?" She tried to hide her disappointment with this unexpected announcement.

Oblivious to her thoughts, he nodded, his eyes glazing over. She always called that his business mode: his mind completely focused on work. "*Ja*, an office manager. I'm getting tired, Rosanna, but I'm not ready to sell my business. Not financially or mentally."

This was the first complaint she had ever heard from him about working. In fact, his reputation among the *g'may* included a high level of respect for his work ethic. That was one of the things that had so impressed her about him. Now he was saying that he was tired? Turning her attention to her embroidery, she knotted the thread she worked with and snipped the end with a small pair of scissors.

"You're too young to retire," Rosanna said.

He raised his eyebrows at her comment, but he did not contradict her. "I just wish I didn't have to be there so much."

She exhaled sharply again. "I thought you liked being there."

For a moment, Reuben studied her while she worked. The sudden silence caused her to look up again. There was a shy expression on his face. "I'd like to spend more time here, Rosanna. Helping you and Aaron around the farm, *ja*?" He paused. "I never had a family before, and I'd like to enjoy it a bit." Another pause before he added, "I'd enjoy being with you in particular."

She blushed at his words and lowered her eyes, staring at the floor. Timothy had done everything in his power to avoid spending time with her, especially after Cate was born. He had wanted sons, lots of sons. When their second child was not a boy, he had said it was her fault. He had even accused her of praying to God for a girl instead of a boy. The image of Timothy refusing to hold his baby daughter still lingered in her memory as if it had happened just a few days ago.

Now she sat beside a man who wanted to spend time with her? She wondered if she deserved such a man and such happiness.

He watched her with anticipation, waiting for her response. She felt the emotion welling up inside of her. "Well, that would be right *gut*, Reuben."

"There's a young brother and sister who just moved in the area," he said slowly, and Rosanna suspected that this was what he really wanted to talk about, not the fact that he hoped to spend more time at home.

"Alone?" It was unusual for Amish people to move away from their families unless it was to marry. "Where are their parents, then?"

"They're from New York state. Their parents died in a car accident." He paused, his eyes watching for a reaction from Rosanna. She felt him staring at her, but she refused to meet his gaze. "A drunk driver hit their buggy."

The tightness in her chest returned, and she fought the urge to catch her breath. Accidents happen, she reminded herself. It wasn't as if Timothy's death was unique in that regard. Only in this case, the man driving the buggy had been drunk, not the people in the car. "Go on," she said, hoping that her voice didn't sound edgy. She did not want to sound like that, not with Reuben.

"They're older. She's in her midthirties, and he's in his late twenties," he said. "They've rented my *haus*."

At this announcement, she lowered her embroidery one more time. Since their wedding in December, his own house next to the harness shop had stood empty. It was smaller than the one here on the farm, with just two bedrooms upstairs, and Reuben had said he had only painful memories there. Moving in with her and the *kinner* had been a welcome change for him.

When she had walked through it for the first—and only—time, she completely understood why he wasn't attached to it. The rooms were large, but he barely had any furniture. An old Formica table and a simple folding chair were the only things in the kitchen. While she had not ventured upstairs, she assumed he had a bed to sleep in.

Reuben had noticed her surprise at the lack of furnishings and quickly explained that his second wife, Grace, had not wanted any reminders of his first wife, Rachel. Grace had insisted that everything be sold and replaced with something new. Reuben had bought a table for the kitchen and a sofa for the adjoining sitting area, but when Grace died, her family claimed that those items belonged to them. Rather than argue, he had permitted them to move out whatever they felt was their due. As a bachelor, he didn't need much anyway.

The fact that someone might rent the house was a good thing, and Rosanna felt as if it was just one more divine message regarding God's plans for them.

"I'm speechless," she confessed. "How *wunderbar*!"

Reuben nodded. "*Ja*, I thought so, too."

"I am, however, a bit surprised you didn't tell me beforehand," she said, keeping her voice even so that she didn't sound critical.

"It must've slipped my mind, Rosanna," he responded. "It's been so busy down there."

"*Ja, vell* then, it's *gut* to have the house occupied." She swallowed her irritation that he had kept something so important from her. Instead, she focused on sharing his excitement. After all, the little house sat upon a small plot of land that was of no particular value to an Amish family. The two acres were barely enough for a large garden. Because the store was set up in the stable, an Amish family would be limited as to how they could use the property. To be able to rent it was most fortuitous. "He has started already, I take it?"

At this question, Reuben cleared his throat and leveled his gaze at her. "The brother, Samuel, is a carpenter and will be apprenticing for Jonathan Lapp."

Rosanna was familiar with the Lapp family, even though they worshipped in a neighboring *g'may* due to the odd borders of the two church districts. Jonathan had a large farm down the road a spell from Reuben's business. His two brothers ran the farm while he operated a shed-making business on the rear quadrant of the property.

"It's the woman I was considering hiring," Reuben said.

*The woman?* Rosanna frowned, wondering at the announcement. "As your office manager?" She didn't want to question her husband's judgment, but she would have thought he would hire a man to help take charge of the business.

"I know it sounds a bit off," he admitted. "But apparently she ran a similar shop in New York. She knows a lot and would not require much training."

Something about the idea didn't sit well with Rosanna. She mulled over her feelings before speaking. Her husband seemed genuinely excited, and of course Rosanna liked the thought of having him help out more around the farm.

"Why did she leave the business in New York?" Rosanna asked.

"Her brother was moving to this area, and she wanted to accompany him. The New York business was in a smaller community, and she felt . . . stifled." He laughed when he saw Rosanna's reaction. "That was her word, not mine."

"Indeed."

*Stifled?* The word sounded strange when Reuben said it. It sounded even stranger when he laughed about it. Stifled was not a word that Rosanna heard very often . . . not from her Amish circle of friends. Stifled was an Englische word, a word that smacked of ambition and drive, the desire to achieve more than others—to *be* more than others. No, she did not have a good feeling about this. But she certainly was not about to share her doubts with Reuben. This was, after all, his business, and he knew what was needed to run it properly.

"When the parents died, an *onkel* took over the shop, and they felt it was best to move on," he added.

"I shall look forward to meeting her, this . . ." She paused; she didn't know the woman's name.

"Nan. Nan Keel."

Rosanna nodded her head. "Nan, then. I reckon we might want to invite both of them to supper one evening? Perhaps after worship on Sunday?"

Reuben leaned over and placed his hand on her knee. His blue eyes sparkled with pride at Rosanna's offer. "I knew you'd understand. You always do."

The door slammed open, and Cate bounded outside, a glass of water in her hands. "*Maem*," she said, interrupting the moment. Instead of excusing herself for barging in on them, she thrust the glass at her mother and made a horrible face. "Something's wrong with this water! It's gross!"

"Oh help!" Rosanna muttered, more about Cate's interruption than the water. Taking the glass, she held it up to the light. "Let's take a look-see here." The glass was clear, but the water wasn't. Tiny particles floated in the glass, the water tinged the color of urine. A woman's work never ends, she thought. "Appears the filter needs to be changed."

Reuben frowned. "I just changed that the other month, *ja*?"

Despite knowing that his *other month* was actually over two months ago, Rosanna kept the thought to herself. "The well's only thirty feet deep, and with the underground springs, it muddies up quicker than usual, I reckon. Needs to be changed every four weeks or so."

He shook his head but made no movement to get up. "That's not *gut*, Rosanna. Not healthy to drink bad water."

With a sigh, she handed the glass back to her daughter and stood up. "Then I best go change that filter," she said. "Not going to change itself."

"Old houses," he mumbled as she disappeared inside.

She hated the basement. No matter how many flashlights she used, it remained dark with dancing shadows that hid spider webs and the sharp corners of shelving. There were old glass jars containing who knew what haphazardly tossed in crates scattered over the floor. They had been there for years, probably used by Timothy's *maem* when he was a child growing up in the house.

On more than one occasion, Rosanna had wanted to clean out the basement. Timothy had called that woman's work and refused to help. The one time she tried to carry out some of the crates, she tripped on the narrow wooden stairs, dropping the box and twisting her ankle. The smell from the broken glass jars was rancid, causing Rosanna to vomit before she managed to crawl up the rest of the stairs.

For once, Timothy had displayed his softer side and retrieved some ice for the swelling. He even washed up the mess at the bottom of the basement stairs. Nonetheless, she never attempted to clean it again.

Occasionally, on days of inclement weather, she hung the laundry down there, knowing that it was warmer and dryer than outside. The only other time she went down there was to replace the water filter, the one task that Timothy had always done, once a month on the first Saturday, until he passed. He was like clockwork, never forgetting.

Rosanna had to admit that this was one of the few things she missed from her previous marriage.

Since moving into the house back in early December, Reuben had changed the filter twice. The first time, he complained about the terrible situation with the water at the house. His mumblings and dark comments had made Rosanna feel guilty, as if it were her own fault that they had remained at the farm instead of moving to the smaller house next to the shop, which had public water.

The second time he changed it, he accidentally stretched out the rubber washer. Without a tight seal, water spewed everywhere, making a mess of the basement. She'd had to shut off the water main valve for over three hours. Reuben had already left for work when Rosanna had realized the problem, and so she'd had to call a driver to fetch her to the nearest plumbing store, which was in Lancaster proper.

She never again asked him to change the filter.

"Need help, *Maem*?" Aaron didn't wait for an answer as he hurried down the steps.

"I should be all right," she said. But she wasn't. The blue plastic casing covering the filter would not budge, and she was not strong enough to loosen it.

"Here," Aaron said, gently pushing her aside. "Let me."

Three tugs, and the casing shifted. He grinned at her and flexed his arm. Then, with much bravado, he continued loosening it until it fell free, the top tipping over and the dirty filter spilling out, along with leftover water, onto the floor.

"*Danke*, Aaron," she said as she unwrapped the new filter and handed it to him. "It's an awful lot of work maintaining this place. Couldn't do it without you, that's for sure and certain."

The compliment pleased Aaron, and he straightened his shoulders. Every day Rosanna noticed the ways in which he was becoming a man. A real man, she thought. Without Timothy around to poison Aaron, the sixteen-year-old had a chance to live a godly and righteous life, one that was free from verbal abuse and alcoholism. And although Reuben wasn't one to work much around the house and farm, he had a strong work ethic and commitment to the community. Aaron could learn a lot of positive things from his stepfather.

"How's that horse coming along, then?" she asked as they headed back upstairs.

Aaron beamed. "Oh, he's a right *gut* horse! And once he's used to our buggy, Reuben said he'd give me an old harness to use."

It would be good for Aaron to have mobility once again. Their old horse could barely make it to worship service or the store.

Timothy hadn't shod its feet often enough, and one of its rear hooves was cracked, which caused it to limp after walking for more than a half mile. The fact that it had survived the accident had been a miracle and a blessing during the time before Rosanna and Reuben married.

"If anyone can break that horse quickly, it'll be you, Aaron!" Rosanna said, a smile on her lips.

He gave her a grin, his light-blue eyes twinkling. With his brown hair brushed over his forehead and the freckles dotting his nose, Aaron was a handsome young man. Over the past few years, he had seemed shy and withdrawn. In hindsight, Rosanna realized he had suffered more than she knew from observing his *daed's* bad habits and harsh words. Now, under the gentle guidance of his stepfather, Aaron was slowly emerging from his shell.

Given enough time, he'd make someone a right *gut* husband, Rosanna thought.

"You going out with your friends later, then?" she asked as she shut the basement door behind them. The door stuck, and she pushed it with her hip.

"I'll oil that tomorrow," Aaron said.

He didn't answer her question. She knew that probably meant he was staying home. Although he was sixteen and on his *rumschpringe*, Aaron was not one to take advantage of it like some other Amish boys. He seemed quite content to work on the farm during the day and get a solid eight hours of sleep each night. Unlike his father, Aaron tended to keep himself busy all day, even going so far as to weed whack the fence line and clean the pastures of manure on a weekly basis.

Last weekend, however, after the worship service and the evening chores had ended, he had slipped away. When Rosanna heard the horse and buggy headed down the driveway, she had looked at Reuben, who was contentedly reading his paper. Aaron had apparently decided to attend the youth singing and asked Reuben if he could borrow his horse.

This Sunday there would be no worship service and, therefore, no youth singing. Like many Amish *gmays*, church was held every two weeks. Off-Sundays were spent doing family-related activities such as visiting sisters or cousins or even good friends. With farms spread throughout the county, an entire day might be needed to reach more remotely located family.

It was an "off-week," the week in between church. While Rosanna loved going to worship, especially when it was slow time and they didn't have to leave an hour early, thanks to the bishop not observing daylight savings, she also enjoyed the Sundays when she could visit with friends or simply sit outside and enjoy nature. Sometimes she went for a walk, usually with Cate and occasionally with Reuben, although she always avoided walking down the road around three thirty, which was when Gloria often took her grandson for his daily stroll. Rosanna treasured those Sunday afternoons when she could spend quiet time with her family; she wasn't certain how she felt about entertaining this new woman Reuben had hired.

"Gotta fix the fence between the mule paddock and the garden tomorrow," Aaron said. He ran his fingers through his hair and sighed. "Sure hope that ole Gloria Smith isn't out there on the prowl." Everyone in the family dreaded dealing with the neighbor.

Reuben walked through the door, overhearing his stepson's comment. "What's this about Gloria bothering you again?" he asked as he removed his hat and set it on the counter. "What's she up to now?"

Rosanna clicked her tongue and shook her head disapprovingly while Aaron scowled. "Aw, now she's after Cate and me. I was checking on the corn the other day, and when I walked along the back of the field, she was out there yelling about seeds on her property. Said it attracted mice." He snickered. "Mice!"

Even Reuben chuckled. "Farmland and field mice go together, seems to me." He opened a cabinet door and pulled out a clean glass, pausing before he turned on the faucet. For a moment, it sputtered and gurgled, and then a burst of fresh water came out. He let it run while he returned his attention to Aaron and Rosanna. "Best to just ignore her," he said thoughtfully. "No sense in feeding the beast with any commentary."

"Honestly, she's just an unhappy old woman," Rosanna sighed. "Reckon she needs our prayers more than anything else."

"That's for certain," Cate added from the top of the stairs.

"Cate Zook!" Rosanna leaned back and stared up the stairwell. Her daughter sat on the second step, peering down at her. "Eavesdropping is sinful!"

"So is screaming at a twelve-year-old girl who's minding her own business," said Cate.

Both Aaron and Reuben tried to hide their laughter at Cate's sassy rebuttal. Even Rosanna fought the urge to smile. Still, she knew she had to set an example. "I think it's time for bed," she called up the stairs. "And when you say your prayers, mayhaps you'll reflect on the Golden Rule: 'love thy neighbor.'"

"Oh, I'll reflect on my neighbor all right," Cate mumbled just loud enough for everyone else to hear as she stomped down the hallway toward her room. A few seconds later, the sound of her bedroom door closing convinced Rosanna that Cate had followed her instructions at last.

"That girl!" She clicked her tongue twice and shook her head. "Willful! I just don't know where she gets that from!"

Reuben shut off the water and turned around, smiling as he leaned against the counter. "Speaks what she thinks, that's all." He winked at Aaron. "World needs all kinds of folks. Guess there's a place for willful children, too."

The usually silent Aaron snorted and rolled his eyes, nodding his head in agreement with his stepfather. The unspoken bond between the two men touched Rosanna. She had a warm feeling in her heart, despite Cate's misbehavior. It had taken a while, but after all the ups and downs since Timothy's death, things seemed to finally be headed in the right direction. Now they needed to just keep it that way, Rosanna thought. She'd do anything to ensure that happened.

# Chapter Three

When Nan walked into Rosanna's kitchen, her hands were tucked into the pockets of her front apron as if she were afraid to touch anything. Her dark eyes scanned her surroundings as if scrutinizing every detail. With a pinched expression, Nan moved around the room, either not taking notice of Rosanna or merely not caring that she walked right past her.

Feeling uncomfortable, Rosanna said nothing. She stood by the counter, waiting for Nan to make a proper introduction. None came. Reuben was still outside in the stable, tending to Nan's horse. Apparently letting Reuben take care of unharnessing the horse from the buggy hadn't bothered Nan. Instead of helping, which most horse owners would do, she had chosen to walk straight into the house. She was empty-handed, another surprise.

Rosanna wasn't certain whether the woman was simply rude or just socially awkward, but she took the opportunity to make her own assessment of this odd guest.

Nan was a pretty woman, with tanned skin and almond-shaped eyes. Despite her attractive face, there was something cold about her. Her jet-black hair was arranged in a bun beneath her crisp white prayer *kapp*, the part down the middle pulled so tight that she already showed signs of balding, a common affliction among elderly Amish people, but something not usually seen in a woman in her thirties. Unlike the heart-shaped *kapps* worn by the women in Rosanna's *g'may*, Nan's sat upon the back of her head like a stiff cup, which only added to her uptight and rigid appearance.

Nan didn't seem to notice that while she inspected the kitchen and attached sitting room, she, too, was being scrutinized. Without looking at Rosanna, she took a few steps, her black sneakers shuffling on the clean kitchen floor. With pursed lips, she examined everything, her curiosity so great that Rosanna looked around as well, wondering what Nan had seen that was so interesting.

"Well," the younger woman finally said. "This is pleasant enough!"

Rosanna frowned, wondering at the meaning of this curious comment, but she was too well mannered to ask. Instead, she stepped forward and extended her hand in greeting. "I take it that you are Nan, then."

Nan stood with complete confidence, her feet spread apart and her posture straight and tall. For a moment, Rosanna wondered if her hand would be accepted. Reluctantly, it was.

"I am," Nan said simply.

Uncertain of how to proceed, Rosanna glanced out the window, hoping to see Reuben walking toward the house. She knew it didn't take that long to unharness the horse from the buggy. Where was he? "Did your *bruder* come with you, then?"

"*Nee*," Nan said. "He's with Jonathan today. He couldn't make it."

Out of the corner of her eye, Rosanna finally saw Reuben walking across the driveway toward the house. She felt relieved that he would be joining them. She wasn't certain what to think of Nan. Her words and actions were too abrupt and forward for Rosanna's taste.

"Your *bruder* is working with Jonathan, *ja*?" Rosanna said. "He must be a skilled worker if he's been hired all the way from New York."

Nan didn't have time to respond before the door opened and Reuben entered the room, a smile on his face.

"I see you've met!"

Rosanna wanted to respond that she had indeed met Nan but that Nan had not really met her or even asked who *she* was. Instead, Rosanna smiled and gestured toward the table. "I have supper ready, if you'd care to sit a spell."

The table was set for five. Aaron was still outside working, and Cate was upstairs in her bedroom. From the sound of it, she had snuck one of the dogs upstairs, most likely Jack, who was Cate's shadow. Rosanna didn't want to say anything while Nan was here, but she made a mental note to speak later to her daughter about the "No Dogs in the House" rule.

Nan took a seat adjacent to Reuben, not offering to assist Rosanna with the meal, as any other Amish woman normally would. At least Amish women around here, Rosanna reminded herself. Different communities of Amish behaved in different manners. Mayhaps Nan came from a community that was more abrupt and less giving.

Rosanna walked to the stairs and called for Cate to join them. Once Cate bounded down the stairs, she paused and stared at Nan.

"Nan, this is my *dochder*, Cate," Rosanna said as she began to set dishes on the table: fresh green beans, corn, beets, fried chicken, meatballs, and homemade pasta.

"I didn't know you had *kinner*!"

"My son, Aaron, will be joining us momentarily," Rosanna added. "Cate, will you go fetch him, please?"

Her eyes still focused on Nan, Cate walked toward the door. Perhaps it was the way that Nan had said the word *kinner*, or maybe it was just Nan's general lack of enthusiasm meeting the child that had turned off Cate, but something hadn't sat well with her. Rosanna knew her daughter well enough to know that Cate immediately disliked the woman.

After the silent prayer, Rosanna stole a quick glance at Reuben, hoping that he would start a conversation. When none came, Rosanna cleared her throat and looked across the table at their guest. "Reuben said you moved here from New York," she began. "That's a long way to move without any family in the area."

Nan shrugged her shoulders. "I wanted a change," she explained. "My parents' store in New York is rather small, and Samuel told me about this opportunity here." Nan smiled as she said her brother's name, and for the first time, Rosanna caught a glimpse of emotion in her. "It's *gut* that he's not alone here while learning the trade with the Lapps."

"I'm sure he's glad for your company," said Rosanna.

"And I for the chance to run my own business," Nan blurted out, too proudly for Rosanna's taste. "Reuben told me that once I learn the office portion, he'll let me run the shop while he's away."

Knowing better than to question her husband in front of someone, especially a stranger, Rosanna merely shifted her eyes to look at him. He had mentioned wanting to spend more time with her, but going away? She hadn't heard any mention of that.

"Pinecraft," he said, as if reading her mind. Located on the gulf coast of Florida, Pinecraft was a popular destination for Amish couples during the colder months up north. "Winters here are downright brutal as of late. Sure would be nice to head south for a few months and not worry about the store."

Rosanna bit her lower lip, willing herself not to speak. Aaron was sixteen and finished with his schooling, but Cate was only twelve. Cate was far too young to be left alone for such a long period of time. And Rosanna did not want to leave Aaron by himself to shoulder the work on the farm. *This* would definitely be a discussion she and Reuben would need to have in the privacy of their room.

"I see," Rosanna finally responded.

Nan seemed to relax. "I have enough experience with my *daed's* shop." She paused, a dark cloud passing over her expression. "My *onkel's* shop now." She emphasized the word *onkel* as if it left a bad taste on her tongue. "It's a small enough shop. I reckon he can handle it without me."

"Surely he could have used your help," Rosanna said, uncertain how to address the fact of Nan's parents being deceased. "It must have been upsetting when your community was hit by such tragedy."

With a little prodding, Nan began to talk about New York and her father's store. Although he had made harnesses for the Amish in the community, a lot of his goods were purchased premade. At Reuben's store, everything was custom made per order to ensure top-notch quality. It was one of the reasons why the Troyer Harness Shop was so popular with the Amish as well as the Englische.

Reuben didn't seem concerned about the differences in the two shops, either in regard to size or product. On the contrary. He seemed relaxed and content, as if the weight of the world had been removed from his shoulders. He sat at the head of the table, beaming as he listened to Nan talk about her experience.

"My *daed* always resisted change," she said. "I told him that he should put in more advanced ordering systems. He didn't listen to me."

Reuben seemed interested and nodded his head. "Oh *ja?*"

"And marketing! He refused to listen to my ideas about expanding the business." She stared at Reuben, ignoring Rosanna. "He would have grown his business if he had listened to me."

"Business is not all about growth," Reuben said lightly. "Unless you're an Englischer!"

Nan didn't take his joke lightly. Instead, her eyes darkened. "If it's not about growth, then what is it about?"

He leaned forward and tapped a finger on the tabletop. "Providing a service. A good, reputable service that people can count on." He gestured toward Aaron. "No different than what a farmer provides to the community. Fresh produce and good milk, right?"

Aaron nodded. "It's true. Make enough money to pay your bills and put a dollar or two in the bank."

Nan scoffed at Aaron's remark. "Mayhaps that's true, Aaron, until such a time as you have to expand your farm and have no money to do so!" She looked back at Reuben, a fierce determination in her expression. "My ideas will expand your business, Reuben. Expansion. That would have made the difference with my *daed's* shop, if he had only listened to me." She paused. "That *is* why you hired me, *ja*?"

Growing weary of listening to Nan's steady stream of self-inflated praise and purpose, Rosanna looked for an opportunity to redirect the subject. "Nan, tell me . . . have you moved into the house already, then?" While Rosanna knew the answer, she wanted to change the subject, not caring for the direction in which the conversation was headed.

"*Ja*, we did," Nan affirmed without any enthusiasm in her voice. "Don't have much furniture as of yet."

"Oh?" Rosanna was surprised.

"Too expensive to ship our furniture from New York," Nan stated flatly. "Just Saturday last, we went to the thrift store in New Holland. We bought a few things . . . plates, pans, mattresses." She looked up and forced a smile. "The essentials, *ja*?"

Despite being in her thirties, Nan was unlike other Amish women who dreamed of home and hearth. Most Amish women, Rosanna knew, wouldn't move far from their family, church, and community. Instead, they'd remain near the people who could support them in times of need, both emotionally and financially. Nan, however, didn't seem very concerned about moving so far away and living among strangers, even if she was clearly unhappy that Reuben's house had not been furnished. Rosanna wondered if Nan's lack of desire to stay in New York had anything to do with the loss of her mother. The thought struck Rosanna that sitting in front of her was another wounded bird.

"Perhaps we have extra furniture that you might use, Nan. What are you missing?" asked Rosanna.

"Well, the kitchen doesn't have much of anything," she said, sounding a bit disdainful. "And Samuel's room is fine enough, but I'm not too keen for my mattress being on the floor." She lifted her eyebrows as she met Rosanna's gaze. "Mice, you know."

"Oh my." Rosanna caught her breath. A mattress on the floor? Mice in the house? "Why, I could certainly see if our neighbors have extra furniture to borrow, Nan. And I know that they have an abundance of cats. I hadn't realized that mice had taken over." The words popped out before Rosanna knew what she was saying. She fought the urge to wince. She knew that fulfilling such an offer would take more time than she had to give.

"It wasn't very clean," Nan responded. She wrinkled her nose when she spoke, her disapproval obvious. "But if someone has any extra furniture, might be nice. A sofa and decent table would help, I reckon."

If Reuben took offense that Nan didn't mince her words about the state of his house, he didn't show it. Rosanna, however, was surprised by Nan's criticism.

At least they have a place to live, Rosanna thought. Still, she couldn't fight the urge to help the younger woman. After all, Nan was miles away from home and apparently living in a house with nothing in the way of comfort.

If only Reuben would have told her earlier. Perhaps that was why Nan seemed abrasive and unhappy, especially when she saw how tidy and neat their house was.

Putting aside her initial feeling of disapproval, Rosanna took a deep breath and swallowed her pride. Whether or not she liked Nan as a person, she knew the proper thing to do. "Mayhaps on Thursday," she heard herself say, "I could come and help clean the place. I'm sure a good cleaning with Murphy's oil would fix it right up!"

Something changed in Nan's expression. Her fierce eyes softened, and she pursed her lips in a near smile. "I would like that, Rosanna," Nan said. "It's a daunting task to consider on my own."

Rosanna smiled back. For the first time during the visit, Rosanna caught a glimmer of what her husband saw in the young woman. Perhaps her strong personality would be an advantage for him at the shop. And giving was a Christian thing to do, after all. "I'd be more than happy to, Nan. Let me get the little one off to her *aendi's haus*, and I'll come right over."

Reuben nodded, appearing pleased with the connection between his wife and his new employee. While he didn't say much, the sparkle in his eyes spoke of his gratitude for Rosanna's kindness.

During the meal, Nan asked Rosanna a few questions about her family—where they lived and what they did for a living.

"My parents live in the *grossdaadihaus* at my *bruder's* farm in Pequea," Rosanna said as she passed the bowl of corn and beet salad to Cate. Cate wrinkled her nose and shook her head. Rosanna dished a spoonful onto her daughter's plate, ignoring her look of dislike. "They're older now and don't travel much. My two *schwesters* married into families farther out that way, too. None of my other immediate family lives nearby," she admitted.

Rosanna stopped her story there. She wasn't willing to share any more about how she had met Timothy at a youth gathering and come to live so far from family. Timothy had been staying with cousins for a while. He had told Rosanna that he was helping out on their farm while his uncle was sick. In hindsight, Rosanna knew that he might have had an ulterior motive: looking for a bride. It was good for the young men to marry women from different church districts. After all, up to half the people in any given *g'may* were related to each other.

Their courtship had been quick, just three months of buggy rides home after youth singings. Rosanna had been smitten right away, at first with his big brown eyes that seemed to dance when he spoke to her, and then with the idea of living in another town, the wife of a farmer on their own farm. With the diminishing amount of farmland in the area, many men were taking jobs among the Englische to provide for their families. The fact that Timothy had saved up enough money to buy a house on thirty acres spoke highly of his work ethic and ability to save money, even if it was located fifteen miles away from Pequea.

Her family, however, were not as enthusiastic about the union. Of course, they hadn't expressed such an opinion—not in so many words anyway. But Rosanna noticed the difference in her parents' behavior toward Timothy. They were less warm and talkative than they were with her older sisters' husbands. The lack of favor created a divide between Rosanna and her family, and, combined with the physical distance, Rosanna had lost touch with everyone over six years ago. In fact, only one of her brothers bothered to show up at Timothy's funeral, and he hadn't even stayed for the meal.

"Pequea?" Nan looked at Reuben. "We took an order from there the other day, *ja?*"

Reuben wiped at his mouth with the back of his hand. "*Ja*, Pequea. They hired a driver to come out here to bring their broken collar and harness."

Rosanna clicked her tongue and shook her head. She disliked hearing that—not from the perspective of the extra business, but because fewer Amish were providing quality leather repair or making new items that didn't break after just one season. In her opinion, quantity sales and quality products did not need to be mutually exclusive. Focusing on the former over the latter was the Englische way of thinking.

"It's a shame you don't just have all the Pequea customers drop everything off at James's farm and pick up or drop off once or twice a month. Save them the driver and help them all time-wise."

Ignoring Rosanna, Nan kept her attention on Reuben. "What you need is a computer in the shop."

Reuben waved his hand, dismissing the suggestion. "Bah! Already have a telephone," he said. He glanced at Rosanna, and she smiled. After all, she had been the one to convince him that the shop needed a telephone. He'd been reluctant, telling her that his store was busy enough without the hassle of answering phone calls. However, when she pointed out that he'd be able to take in more orders from far away, even out of state, he had relented.

Nan lit up. "That would be even better! Why, with your own web page, you could accept orders from all over the country! And, of course, with a computer, you could simplify your accounting and manage your inventory!"

Reuben laughed and set down his fork. With his elbow on the edge of the table, he pointed to his temple with one finger. "This, Nan," he said. "This is my inventory. I keep it all up here. Ask me how many items we have on the shelves, and I can tell you."

There was no doubt that he spoke the truth. Rosanna had never met anyone with such an ability to recall facts. During their courtship, Reuben had impressed her with his recitation of Bible verses. He always seemed to know an appropriate quote for any situation. After they married, she was further amazed at how Reuben remembered everything that happened at the store. Each evening, he'd recount who bought what during the day. And she noticed that, despite so much increased business, she never saw him with a calendar or a list of reminders. Instead, he just remembered every order and made certain to deliver the goods as promised and on time.

If Rosanna was impressed by Reuben's powers of recall, Nan was not. "It's the twenty-first century, Reuben," she said sharply. "Every business has a computer. It's archaic that you don't. Besides, you are the only one who knows what's in your head, ain't that so?"

Rosanna bristled at the use of the word *archaic*.

"We use the office phone for orders, Nan," he replied, clearly unconcerned by her comments. His patience was endless and impressive. Rosanna wasn't certain she would have remained so calm. Her own heart pounded, and she felt the muscles in her neck twitch. "And we have more than enough business, ain't so?" He winked at Nan. "Enough to hire a new office person anyway."

And with that, the discussion over installing a computer in the shop ended.

After the meal, Aaron offered to take Nan back to her house. Rosanna was surprised when Reuben agreed, suggesting that her son take his horse and buggy. "No sense bothering your old horse with the round trip," he explained to Nan. "Besides, my mare needs some extra work. Hasn't been worked in a while, *ja*?"

Aaron seemed equally as surprised with the offer. "Why, *danke*, Reuben." Given that it was Sunday and Reuben's horse was a steady ride, Rosanna knew that Aaron wouldn't be back anytime soon. He would certainly take the opportunity to visit some friends on his way back home.

To Rosanna's relief, Reuben escorted Nan outside, keeping her company while Aaron harnessed the horse to the buggy. From the kitchen window, Rosanna could see that they were deep in conversation. Nan's hands moved in the air as she spoke. Several times Rosanna thought she noticed Nan interrupt Reuben, cutting him off with her own thoughts and opinions. When the buggy finally rolled down the long driveway, Reuben stood and stared after it for just a moment before he wandered into the barn, probably to make certain everything was settled for the evening.

When Reuben finally returned to the house, Rosanna was standing at the sink, washing the plates and glasses. Cate was at her side, drying them. Rosanna glanced over her shoulder at the doorway. Reuben looked pleased as he stood there, a smile on his face. He watched her work with Cate for a long moment before he finally stepped into the room.

"That was quite nice, Rosanna," he said.

She forced a smile as she returned her attention to the dishes. "*Ja, vell*, Nan seems pleasant enough."

Cate didn't hesitate to offer her own thoughts. "Didn't like her. She's too loud and talks about business too much."

"Cate!" Rosanna rebuked her.

Reuben laughed. "She does have a point, Rosanna."

Encouraged, Cate continued. "Why, I didn't even think she was going to pray before we ate!" She looked at her stepfather. "Did you see how she picked up her fork before we gave our thanks?"

This comment caused more laughter from Reuben and another horrified gasp from Rosanna. "Cate Zook! I won't have any more of that gossip talk now!"

Cate made a face and returned her attention to drying the dishes, mumbling something under her breath.

"Honestly!" Exasperated, Rosanna looked at Reuben, who was still smiling. "And you spur on the child!"

"I reckon there are worse things than speaking the truth," he said, a teasing tone in his voice. "The truth shall set you free."

"A little filter on her word selection wouldn't hurt." Although she had reprimanded Cate, Rosanna agreed with her daughter. Nan *had* talked an awful lot about the business, asking probing questions and not showing much interest in anything else. On more than one occasion, she had offered suggestions for improvement at the shop—all of which Reuben shot down, gently but without any hint of budging.

Rosanna thought that given Nan's short tenure as a shop employee so far, her suggestions to change everything were inappropriate. After all, Reuben's business was already successful. He hadn't hired Nan to improve the business, something that he was much more qualified to do. No, he had hired her to manage the incoming orders while he worked with the clients and, hopefully, had more free time to spend at home.

Still, openly criticizing another person was not kind, and Rosanna didn't want Cate to think that it was all right to say such things. It was difficult, but Rosanna knew that sometimes it was better to keep observations and thoughts inside. Speaking the truth aloud could hurt a person's feelings as well as make other people wonder what was being said behind their backs.

And nothing good would ever come of that.

# Chapter Four

By Thursday, Rosanna's curiosity outweighed her dread of spending a good portion of the day cleaning someone else's house. After more than a week of working together, Nan and Reuben seemed to get along well enough. He talked about her take-charge attitude with an amused look on his face while Rosanna sat in her rocking chair and embroidered her linens and smiled. She would reserve her comments until she knew Nan better.

Rosanna did know one thing, however. Reuben seemed more relaxed and at ease. He had offered to help Aaron with his new horse on Saturday. It would be the first time that he would leave Nan alone in the store to manage incoming orders and deal with the customers picking up their items.

"That would be great," Aaron had responded to the unexpected offer. To Rosanna, Reuben's offer was music to her ears. Aaron had needed a positive male role model in his life, especially after the hardship of the last few years. As a young man, he still had a lot to work out regarding his father's alcohol abuse and sudden death. Reuben seemed to be more than willing to step into that role of guiding Aaron as a proper father should have.

But that was not the only surprising event of the week. On Wednesday Rosanna had visited with Mary King and Barbara Glick, two elderly cousins to each other who lived down the road. For an hour they had sat together on the breezeway outside the kitchen door.

"Your garden growing well, then?" Mary asked.

Rosanna nodded. "Oh *ja!* I should have thought to bring you tomatoes." The truth was that with Gloria constantly watching them, Rosanna didn't particularly care to tend to the garden anymore, and she was hesitant to delegate that chore to Cate.

"That neighbor still giving you trouble?" asked Barbara.

"Barbie!" Mary snapped, quick to reprimand her cousin. "No need to bring up troubled pasts!"

Rosanna wondered if she was so transparent that they were able to read her mind. Had it been her tone or her expression that indicated she had not told the truth? Rosanna tried to make light of the situation. "God loves unpleasant people, too, I reckon."

Barbara chuckled, despite Mary's disapproving look.

"Heard wind that Reuben's *haus* is occupied," Mary said, obviously changing the subject. "Right *gut* that someone's living there."

Rosanna welcomed the shift in conversation. Eagerly she shared her stories about Nan and Samuel Keel. It felt good to finally have something new and exciting to discuss, not just which person planted what crops or went to market that week. However, to Rosanna's surprise, Mary King had frowned when she mentioned the newcomers to the district.

"Keel, eh?"

"That's right. The Keels. They're from New York," Rosanna said.

"Not the Keels from that community in Conewango Valley, I suppose?"

Rosanna shook her head. "Frankly, I'm not certain of the town," she admitted. "I hadn't thought to ask."

Clicking her tongue and shaking her head, Mary looked displeased. At seventy-eight, Mary was a year older than her cousin and one of the oldest women in the *g'may*. She commanded a high degree of respect from the others. If she was displeased, she would certainly let it be known.

To Rosanna's surprise, however, Mary volunteered no information.

Curious, Rosanna probed. "Are you familiar with the name, Mary?"

She waved a weathered hand. "I know plenty of Keels. Don't know no Samuel or Nan." Still, she shook her head again. "It's that particular community of Amish. They're different, you know." She lowered her voice and looked around the breezeway as if to ensure that there was no one else who might overhear her stories. "Those smaller districts have trouble keeping their young people, and you know what that means."

No further explanation was needed. It was well known how hard it had become for the smaller Amish communities to thrive. That often meant that the families worked harder and also had fewer children. With limited youths, a lot of the children either moved away when they were of age or married distant cousins. As a result, genetic disease was prevalent.

Barbara Glick made a face at Mary. "Oh hogwash, Mary. That's an old wives' tale and you know it."

"And old wives' tales are often true," Mary replied. "Anyway, I wouldn't be marrying one of my *dochders* to that Samuel."

"Your *dochders* are all married already!" said Barbara.

Mary pressed her lips together, and she narrowed her eyes in the other woman's direction. "You know what I mean, Barbie!"

Rosanna quickly changed the subject, not wanting her visit with the two widows ruined by bickering. Despite the back and forth, Mary and Barbara were the best of friends. They were only cousins, but their closeness in age had strengthened their bond during their youth. In fact, Mary and Barbara were more like sisters. Even now, with both of them widowed, they lived together in the *grossdaadihaus* on the King property, part of Mary's life-right when the farm passed down to her son, Abram.

Now, with Thursday upon her, Rosanna dutifully went to her husband's former house to fulfill her promise to help Nan clean.

The front door had been left open.

"Hello?" Rosanna called out as she opened the screen door. No one seemed to be home.

Rosanna walked through the large, empty sitting room. The once white walls were gray, dark soot streaking from the wall heaters toward the ceiling. The dirt on the floor shocked Rosanna. Clearly Nan had not bothered to even sweep it since they moved in.

Avoiding the staircase, for she was afraid of what she'd find on the second floor, Rosanna made her way to the kitchen. The old laminated table remained pushed against the wall, leaving a wide, gaping emptiness in the middle of the room. Dirty plates and glasses covered the counter, and one of the cabinet doors hung open.

"Oh help," Rosanna muttered, suddenly wondering what she had gotten herself into. The house needed more than just a cleaning. It needed a complete overhaul, from top to bottom.

She wandered out the side door and made her way to the shop entrance. Two buggies were in the driveway, their horses hitched to the post outside the door. Quietly, Rosanna walked around the buggies, noticing that one had a black top while the other was gray. Team Mennonite, she thought as she passed the black-topped buggy, immediately recognizing them as the Old Order Mennonites, who chose to still use horses and buggies. It was easy to tell the difference between the gray-topped Amish buggies and the all-black

Mennonite buggies. She hadn't seen many of them in the area. It was a good sign that they were beginning to frequent Reuben's store instead of driving to Jonas Hostetler's harness store, which was located across town and much closer to their community.

Nan was standing behind the counter, talking with two of the men. Her natural ease in conversing with them surprised Rosanna. Unlike the other night at the Troyers' house, Nan appeared much friendlier and more relaxed. Gone was the rigidness. Now she seemed like a warm, happy young woman.

"Rosanna!"

Rosanna turned around at the sound of Reuben's voice.

He smiled as he greeted her. "What are you doing here today?"

"It's Thursday," she reminded him. "I'm to help Nan clean the house, remember?"

"Ah!" He snapped his fingers. Clearly it had slipped his mind. "I did forget," he admitted. He glanced over at Nan dealing with the customers at the counter. "Why don't you get started, and I'll send her along when we have a break?" He leaned over and lowered his voice so that no one else could hear his words. "It's been so busy all day! And I learned that the Mennonites in Leola aren't happy with Jonas's goods."

"I saw one of their buggies out front," she said.

"A shame for Jonas," Reuben said solemnly. "I warned him about that material from overseas. Just doesn't hold like good quality leather."

Rosanna knew what that meant. Some of the Amish who made trade items found it increasingly difficult to compete with the products sold by Englische companies. The increasing use of the Internet hadn't helped, either. As a consequence, some Amish tradespeople were using cheaper inferior materials to make their products in order to lower their costs. Reuben often complained that they were only hurting themselves since low-quality materials led to low-quality work and, as a result, damaged reputations. Apparently Jonas Hostetler was slipping into that category.

Upon returning to the rental house, Rosanna stood in the middle of the kitchen and turned around, taking in the mess. "Best start here," she said out loud. After all, the heart of every home was the kitchen, especially among the Amish. The kitchen was more than just a place to share meals. It was where everyone gathered to tell stories, read the paper, study Scripture, can foods, bake bread, and pray in the evening. Without a clean kitchen, the rest of a person's life would also be disorganized and untidy.

She began by washing the dishes that were in the sink and on the counter. Clearing her mind of any complaints, she felt herself slipping into a zone; Bible verses floated through her mind as she silently repeated her favorite Psalms. Just as she did at home, she began to forget that she was working and felt a sense of serenity wash over her. When she was cleaning and in this place of peace, she knew that she was with God. Giving to others, helping them when they would not even help themselves, was her way of honoring God and His love for her.

Two hours passed before Nan flung open the door and rushed inside, breathless, her prayer *kapp* slightly askew on the back of her head. "There were so many customers at the store!" she said as an explanation for her late arrival. "I couldn't get away for a minute."

"I understand," Rosanna replied, although she wasn't one hundred percent certain that she did. Had it truly been *that* busy that Nan could not slip away to help her? Certainly Reuben had plenty of experience handling customers on his own. Why would Nan think that now that she was working there, he was incapable of handling them? She suspected that she knew the answer, but decorum kept her tongue silent.

Already the kitchen was transformed from chaos to order. While there was still much to be done, it was clear that Rosanna had spent the past two hours working hard. She hadn't wasted any time rolling up her sleeves and focusing on the task at hand.

"Looks like you didn't need my help after all," Nan commented as she walked around the room. "Surely there's nothing left to do!"

"Oh, we aren't finished yet," Rosanna said. Her voice was soft but firm. She wasn't letting Nan off the hook. A job half done was not good enough for her. And despite the happy glow on Nan's face, Rosanna knew that there was plenty more to do. For a moment she wondered about Nan's parents and what type of house her *maem* had kept given how willing Nan was to accept mediocrity rather than live in a clean house. "I just poured some Murphy's oil in that bucket of warm water. The cabinets should be washed down and dried before we scrub the floor."

To Rosanna's surprise, Nan didn't argue. She hurried over to the bucket and dipped a rag in before wringing it out. She seemed content to help. Rosanna wondered if she had been mistaken. Perhaps the shop truly had been busy and Nan wasn't hiding behind work to avoid cleaning.

While Nan washed down the cabinets, Rosanna began scrubbing the floor. She started in the corners where the most dirt usually accumulated. Certainly Reuben had not cleaned very much when he lived here after Grace's death. Still, it surprised her that no one from the *g'may* had come to help him tend the house. She knew that Reuben's sisters lived farther away, having married Amish men from different church districts, but not to help their older brother?

"What does your other family think of you having moved here, Nan?" she asked to break the silence. She didn't mean to pry into Nan's private business, but she had to admit that she was curious.

There was a long pause. Too long. Rosanna looked up from where she knelt on the floor and turned her eyes to Nan, who stood by the counter. The rag hung in midair. She had stopped wiping the front of the cabinet, her back to Rosanna and her arm motionless. It was only for a beat, but long enough for Rosanna to know that something was amiss.

"Nan?"

The younger woman shook her head, just slightly, as if erasing something from her memory. "I'm sorry. I was just thinking about something."

Rosanna remained silent, waiting for Nan to answer the original question.

"My parents only had my *bruder* and me. *Maem* couldn't have more *bopplies.*"

That caught Rosanna off guard. Two children? Most Amish families had many children. And while she had always wanted a large family, her relationship with Timothy had been too strained to consider having more babies.

"Oh my," she whispered, wondering what type of relationship Nan's parents had.

"*Ja*, just the two of us," Nan said, her voice soft and distant. "Samuel was to take over the shop, but his interest wasn't in leather. He liked building things."

"Nothing wrong with that," Rosanna said. "Jesus was a carpenter for a while, *ja?*"

Nan laughed. "Never thought of it that way. Not so certain that my *daed* would agree."

Something in her tone told Rosanna that there was more. But whatever it was, the story held sorrow and pain for Nan. She did not offer further information, and Rosanna assumed Nan did not want to discuss it. Some matters were private and best left that way. Rosanna knew better than to pry. A person's business was personal and not meant to be shared until such a time that opening up hurt less than keeping it to oneself.

They lapsed back into silence as they worked. Rosanna glanced at Nan a few times, making certain that the younger woman was, indeed, working. While her wiping motions on the cabinets were not as thorough as Rosanna would have liked, at least Nan was helping with the cleaning. Rosanna had learned long ago not to criticize when someone was trying. People seemed to respond better to positive praise than negative observations.

"There!" Rosanna said finally, sitting back on her knees and dropping the scrub brush into the bucket of dirty water. "I'd say that this floor is worthy of being called clean!"

Nan dropped her rag into the sink. "Cabinets done, too!"

While Rosanna was tempted to disagree with her, she chose to say nothing.

"Finished, then? I need to return to work," Nan said, drying her hands on the dirty black apron that covered the bottom part of her dress.

Finished? Rosanna almost laughed until she realized that Nan was serious. "We haven't even started on the bathroom or bedrooms," Rosanna responded in disbelief at having to explain what needed to be done. Hadn't Nan used the bathroom recently? How could she be satisfied showering with that yellow stain on the bottom of the porcelain tub?

"*Ja, vell*," Nan said, starting toward the door, "I should at least check and see how the shop is doing."

Rosanna took a deep breath and wordlessly pressed her lips together. She wanted to remind Nan that the shop had run smoothly for years before her appearance just two short weeks ago. She wanted to tell her that no one was indispensable there, except perhaps Reuben. While these thoughts floated in her mind, her tongue held still, and she exhaled as Nan darted out the kitchen door.

Two hours later, she had just finished mopping the floor in Samuel's bedroom when she heard footsteps in the kitchen. Setting the mop against the wall, she hurried to the stairwell to see who was there. "Hello?" she called out.

"Rosanna!"

It was Reuben. He smiled when he saw her and held up a glass of what looked like meadow tea. "Wanted to see how you're doing. Rebecca brought in some tea today. I thought you might be thirsty, *ja*?" He glanced around. "I know how much you like meadow tea."

Always so thoughtful, she told herself. "Why, *danke*, my husband!"

He laughed as he held out the glass for her to take. As she sipped it, he looked around the kitchen and sitting room. Whistling under his breath, he nodded his approval. "I don't think I ever saw this place shine like this!"

She blushed at the compliment. "Nothing a good scrubbing won't do," she replied modestly, although she was secretly pleased that he had noticed her efforts.

"You and Nan must have worked quite hard." He took a few steps into the room, peeking through the open doorway into the sole bathroom, which was under the staircase. "Afraid you had your task cut out for you, I reckon. Never was much for housework," he admitted.

"Shop must be busy," she responded, choosing her words carefully. "Nan left to see if you needed help a while ago."

If she thought that Reuben would be upset at this news, she was disappointed. Instead, he lifted his eyebrows and merely said, "Did she, now?" He reached up and tugged at the end of his beard, nodding his head. "Good thing she did, *ja*? I got called over to Melvin Beecher's farm. His mules' harness broke, and I had to leave the shop." He glanced around the room once again. "Looks like you're finished anyway. Why don't I take you on home? I'm sure you'll be wanting to start preparing supper and finishing your own chores."

A dull pain throbbed at her temples. There was plenty more to clean, but she wasn't about to offer her services. Not today. Instead, she finished the meadow tea and handed the glass back to Reuben. Then she went upstairs to grab the cleaning supplies. The two bedrooms were clean enough, she reasoned, although deep down she felt guilty that she hadn't washed the windows or the linen closet. She carried the bucket down the stairs, careful not to spill any of the liquid. Slowly she poured the water into the sink before rinsing both the bucket and the mop.

Reuben had already returned to the shop. By herself, she wrung out the mop and placed it inside the bucket. Her shoulders ached from scrubbing so much, she realized as she carried the cleaning supplies to the small closet next to the bathroom.

It was as clean as she could make it in one day. She felt as though she had given enough to Nan, who clearly had little interest in doing more than complaining about the dirty condition of the house. Rosanna should have known that Nan would stick her with most of the work. Rosanna made a mental note to not let herself get in that situation again, although, deep down, she knew she would. It was just how things happened: when someone needed help, Rosanna stepped up.

Sighing, she turned to leave the house, but just as she opened the door, she noticed the empty tea glass that Reuben had brought her sitting on the counter. Her shoulders drooped, and she shut her eyes for a moment. *Give me strength, Lord,* she prayed. The thought crossed her mind to leave it there and let Nan wash it later. Just as quickly, she knew that thought was not godly, and whether or not it was deserved, she would not sleep that night if she walked away with the glass sitting there.

With a heavy sigh, she took the glass to the sink and quickly washed it before she finally escaped the house and tried to banish the heavy feeling in her chest.

## CHAPTER FIVE

Seated on the bench at the kitchen table, Cate let her legs swing, her bare feet brushing the linoleum. "I don't understand why I have to help Aaron today," she whined as Rosanna pulled a hairbrush through the girl's long brown hair. It hung down to her waist, the ends frayed and split. Some nights, Rosanna rubbed coconut oil in it, because cutting Cate's hair was not permitted. After all, a woman's hair was her glory, according to the Bible.

As Rosanna ran the brush down the length of Cate's hair, it snagged on the ends, and the girl's shoulders twitched. Usually she cried out, making a big scene. Today, however, she was more focused on the prospect of having to work in the fields.

"Just clearing the brush along the fence line, Cate," Rosanna said, trying to keep her tone pleasant and her brush strokes soft. "And mucking the mule paddock."

Rolling her eyes and sticking out her tongue, she balked. "That's a man's job!"

"Cate Zook!"

Ever since school had let out, Rosanna had noticed an increasing reluctance in her daughter to help with the outside work. Instead, Cate much preferred to stay inside and help with the cleaning and cooking. Even when Rosanna asked her to weed the garden, Cate lingered in the house, finding excuse after excuse to not leave her mother's side. Finally, Rosanna had given up and gone out with her. Together they had weeded the garden.

The only time that Cate seemed to be truly happy was when she played with the dogs. Jack, Pepper, and Trigger loved to run and chase her through the front fields. She spent hours throwing sticks for them or wandering along the fence line, happy to pick up rocks and other debris, which she tossed into a small wagon that Pepper was trained to pull. The three dogs were mixed breed rescues from the local animal shelter and loyal to Cate.

Unfortunately, clearing the fields was not a job that needed doing every day. And there was too much work on the farm to permit Cate an endless amount of time to play.

When Rosanna had mentioned her concern about Cate to Reuben one evening, he had paused before responding. That was one of the things Rosanna loved about him. That gentle pause indicated that he did not respond rashly or without thought. He reflected upon every situation before he gave his opinion. This time was no different.

"It's her *daed*," Reuben had finally said.

Rosanna grimaced at the mention of her first husband. She had tried hard to block him from her memory. "You thinking that she still misses him?"

The idea was unconceivable to her. Most days Rosanna avoided reflecting on those years. She was more than happy to keep those memories locked up in a mental box tucked far away from her consciousness.

But Reuben knew better. While Rosanna had borne the brunt of Timothy's negative behavior as a projection of his own poor self-image, Cate had also suffered greatly. Her *daed* had not been kind to her. Aware of this fact, Reuben had worked hard from the beginning to gain her trust and respect as the new man in the house.

"*Nee*, I'm sure that's not it," Reuben responded. "But she's clinging to you for fear that something might happen. Her love for you is great, and she would be lost without you."

There was a lot of truth to that statement. Rosanna did not need to be told twice that she had an extra shadow. Ever since Cate was born, she had seemed glued to her mother's side. As a baby, she rarely cried—except when she was taken from her *maem's* arms. Then Cate would fuss and make known her unhappiness. As a toddler, she clung to Rosanna's dress. When she was older and had to start school, Cate had cried daily, not wanting to leave home or her mother. Rosanna had thought that Cate was starting to mature out of this maternal attachment, but now she realized that it had, indeed, recently resurfaced.

"I'd let it pass for a while," Reuben suggested. "Give her a little more time."

Rosanna promised to try. Still, Rosanna's patience in the face of Cate's willful behavior often seemed to be in endless demand.

Now, however, Cate was flatly refusing to help Aaron in the fields. Rosanna knew that doing the chores alone would be hard on her son.

"I'm asking you to help your *bruder*," Rosanna said, inwardly counting to ten. It would do no good if she lost her temper. "We all must pitch in to help, *ja*?"

Pressing her lips together, Cate shook her head. "It's not fun, *Maem*."

Despite her vow to be patient, Rosanna tugged at Cate's hair, immediately cringing when her daughter winced. "Work is not always fun."

Cate remained silent for a long moment, her narrowed eyes searching an empty space on the wall, her lips pressed together.

Rosanna knew that something was going through her daughter's mind. From the intent look on Cate's face, she was clearly scheming. Knowing Cate, it could be about anything.

*"Gut mariye!"* Reuben called out cheerfully as he walked through the kitchen door. Most mornings he tried to rise early to help Aaron feed the animals. Setting his battered straw hat on a hook near the window, he smiled at Rosanna and winked at Cate. *"Wie gehts?"*

*"Maem* says I have to work in the field today!" Cate blurted. If the look on her face did not express her feelings, the tone of her voice certainly did. She was pleading with her stepfather to save her. Rosanna clenched her jaw. Cate never was one to hide her feelings.

Reuben glanced over Cate's head at his wife, questioning her with his eyes. She lifted an eyebrow but did not speak as she put away the hairbrush and continued preparing the early morning meal. The scent of coffee, scrambled eggs, fresh bread, and breakfast potatoes filled the room. The table, set with fresh linens and pretty place settings, welcomed her family to fellowship before they went their separate ways. Unfortunately, Rosanna felt as if Cate's mood was ruining one of her favorite parts of the day.

Reuben, however, did not seem flustered by his stepdaughter's complaint. He walked to the sink to wash his hands before taking his place at the head of the table. Rosanna held her breath, waiting to see how Reuben would handle an obstinate twelve-year-old. As a man with little experience with children, Reuben's patience was sometimes tested as he adapted to his new role. Fortunately, he seemed to take most things in stride.

"Mayhaps," Reuben began slowly, "you might prefer to come to the shop to work a spell today?"

This unexpected invitation surprised them both. Rosanna caught her breath. With Aaron already working as hard as he possibly could, that left only her to do the rest of the chores if Cate went with Reuben. Rosanna wished he had conferred with her before extending the offer.

While Rosanna stared at Reuben in disbelief, Cate's face broke into a joyful grin. "Really?" Reuben had never invited Cate to his store.

*"Ja,"* he replied, ignoring the increasingly annoyed look on Rosanna's face. "I could see if Daniel might help Aaron if you promise to help me with the shop."

The Troyer Harness Shop was a new environment for Cate. When she had first visited it with Rosanna a few months ago, Cate had wandered around touching the bridles and harnesses. Rosanna had watched her, wondering what her daughter thought as she paused at each item, admiring the quality and inhaling the smell of new leather. Cate had examined everything with glowing eyes, even the back area where Daniel and Martin made the shop's custom-ordered products.

"What on earth would she do?" asked Rosanna. Cate could not work on the big industrial sewing machines, and she certainly couldn't cut the leather. Either task would be dangerous for an untrained person, especially a child. But as soon as the words slipped out of her mouth, she regretted them. Did it sound as though she was questioning her husband?

But Reuben didn't seem bothered. He shifted his weight in his seat and looked at her. "She could help man the front desk, and when it's slow, I could start training Nan on the equipment."

Rosanna frowned when he mentioned his newly hired employee. "Nan?"

Nan had only worked at the store for a short while. Rosanna was surprised that Reuben felt comfortable having her learn the equipment. Daniel and Martin usually ran the machinery with a younger woman, Rebecca, who helped part-time during busy spells. But Nan? From what Rosanna understood, Nan had some experience helping her own *daed* at his store. While Nan might have hoped to take over the business, his focus had been on her older brother. Samuel, however, had plans of his own, and they did not include harness making or working with leather.

"She's a right *gut* worker and is eager to learn everything," said Reuben.

For some reason, Rosanna doubted that Nan was as eager to learn as Reuben thought. It wasn't just that the younger woman had barely helped with cleaning the house. No, there was something else that bothered Rosanna about Nan Keel. She didn't know whether it was Nan's sharp tongue or the lack of work ethic she displayed, but Nan tested every ounce of Rosanna's resolve to love her neighbor. As soon as the thought crossed her mind, Rosanna said a quick prayer to God asking for forgiveness and realized at the same time that it was a prayer God heard far too frequently from her.

She poured coffee into a green mug and handed it to Reuben. "I reckon I might be able to bring her down to the shop after she finishes her morning chores," Rosanna offered, trying to soften her tone despite having so much to do. The buggy ride to the shop would take at least thirty minutes of her morning, between harnessing the horse and driving there and back, but if it helped Reuben and calmed down Cate, she was willing to sacrifice that precious time.

Reuben sighed and smiled at his wife. "That would be *wunderbar!*"

Cate perked up, excitement and joy written on her face. Positive attention did that to the twelve-year-old. Despite really needing her daughter's help with the gardening and field work, Rosanna's heart swelled with happiness to see Cate brighten at the thought of spending the day at the shop with her stepfather. This would be good for her, Rosanna told herself.

"Can we go yet?"

Rosanna looked up from the far side of the bed where she was tucking the thin quilt under the mattress. Cate stood in the doorway, a hand on her hip. Her dark skin glowed from having been in the sun all morning, and her hazel eyes flashed. Without a prayer *kapp* covering her head, she almost looked Englische—most certainly too worldly to be Amish.

"Did you check on the bread?" Rosanna asked.

Cate nodded.

"Did you hang up the laundry?"

"*Ja,*" Cate sighed, leaning her cheek against the doorframe as she rolled her eyes. "We just did laundry on Monday anyway. Why do you insist on washing the clothes so much?"

Smoothing down the quilt, Rosanna's fingers paused to touch the pattern near her pillow. She assessed her work. The bed was readied and everything else tidied; the main bedroom was finished. "Because everyone dirties them," Rosanna said as she straightened up and moved toward the door. "And cleanliness is next to godliness."

Cate made a face. "I like getting dirty."

Rosanna smiled as she walked past her daughter, pausing to gently touch Cate's cheek in a rare gesture of affection. "I noticed."

With most of the morning chores finished, Rosanna gave in to Cate's enthusiasm. It wasn't often that Cate was so excited about something, and working at the shop would be a wonderful experience for her.

Rosanna opened the stall door to groom the mare before harnessing her to the buggy. Although she knew she had a long afternoon of work ahead of her, there was something peaceful about working outside—especially when she didn't have to worry about what mischief Cate was up to.

"Can Jack come with us?" Cate asked.

Rosanna sat inside the buggy, holding the reins. Both side doors were rolled open so that the fresh air could blow through. "*Nee*, Cate," she said. "Not today. See how it goes and then ask Reuben, *ja*?"

Her answer didn't please Cate, but the girl didn't argue. Instead, with an overly exaggerated sigh, she jumped into the buggy and sat next to her mother.

When Rosanna clicked her tongue and gave a gentle slap of the reins onto the horse's back, the buggy lurched forward and started rolling down the driveway. The wheels hummed along the pavement, and the buggy swayed, just a little, back and forth. The front windows were open, hooked to the roof of the buggy, and small strands of the mare's hair fluttered inside.

"Too much in your mouth, Cate?"

Cate nodded, licking the back of her hand to remove the horse hair from her tongue. Rosanna laughed softly as she reached up and shut the narrow window.

It only took ten minutes to get to the shop. When they arrived, Rosanna was surprised to see a car parked outside the front door. Englische rarely visited the harness shop, although she knew it was not unheard of. Still, she eyed the car with curiosity as she tied the horse to the hitching rail. Turning away, Rosanna saw a young man walk down the steps of Reuben's small rental house. Surely that was Samuel.

Gesturing for Cate to wait a moment, Rosanna walked in his direction, a curious but warm smile on her face. "Samuel Keel?"

He looked up and studied her for a moment before extending his hand to shake hers. "Rosanna, then, *ja*?"

"Right *gut* to meet you," Rosanna said, noticing immediately how different Samuel's demeanor was from Nan's. His expression appeared softer and gentler; there was a touch of shyness in his dark eyes. And his hands were large and calloused, the sign of a man who had known many years of hard labor. Even his posture, his shoulders straight but not too squared, spoke of a reserve that was more simple and plain.

He put his hands in his front pockets and shifted his weight as if nervous. He didn't seem to know what to say—another difference between the two siblings. Finally, he moistened his lips. "*Danke* for helping Nan with the *haus*," he said.

The only response that Rosanna could give was a smile. She knew it would be unkind to point out that she hadn't actually *helped* Nan, for Nan had preferred to stay in the shop. At least Nan hadn't taken all of the credit for cleaning the house. If Samuel knew that Rosanna had been there, clearly Nan had acknowledged her contributions. For some reason, Rosanna found it difficult to envision Nan complimenting anyone other than herself.

"*Ja, vell* . . . best get going," he said, nodding toward the car. "My driver's here."

The gravel crackled under the wheels of the car as it pulled out of the shop's driveway. Rosanna stared after it, trying to understand the differences between the two siblings. Samuel seemed quiet and polite and, from what little Reuben had told her, a very hard worker. Apparently Jonathan Lapp had nothing but praise for the young man.

"There she is!" Nan greeted Cate as if they were the best of friends, but her piercing voice caught them both off guard. Then, to Rosanna's surprise, Nan came around the counter and knelt before Cate, as if she were a child of two and not twelve. "I heard I was to have a little helper today!"

Rosanna thought she saw her daughter wince.

"We just met your *bruder*," Rosanna said, attempting to change the subject in the hopes that Cate could escape to find Reuben.

It worked. Standing up, Nan glanced toward the door. "He was home, then?" She seemed disappointed, perhaps because he hadn't stopped to visit with her. "I know they were going to a new job site this afternoon. He must have brought the horse home and gone with the driver."

Cate slipped behind Rosanna and gently nudged her leg. Taking her cue, Rosanna glanced around the shop. Better to get right to the point, she thought. No need to dillydally with false niceties. "Is Reuben here, then?"

Nan gestured toward the back room. "Working with Daniel on a collar."

Not certain whether or not she should interrupt him, Rosanna hesitated. "*Vell*, I brought him some dinner," she said, holding up a red-and-white cooler. "Might you see that he gets it?"

With a broad smile, Nan nodded. "Of course!" She reached for Cate's shoulder and began to guide her toward the counter. "Let's get started. I can teach you everything you need to do while I'm helping in the back . . ."

As they walked, Cate cast a forlorn look over her shoulder at Rosanna. It tugged at Rosanna's heart but also made her want to smile. Even bad experiences helped a person grow, Rosanna told herself as she set the cooler on the counter and walked to the door.

Thirty minutes later, the horse unharnessed and hosed down, Rosanna was out in the field, working under the warm June sun. The weather had been favorable during the spring, but June had roared in with cold nights and hot days. She hoped that wasn't a foreshadowing of the summer. Without air-conditioning or fans, the house retained heat, resulting in sleepless nights on the second floor.

Rosanna wore protective glasses as she weed wacked, and they made her face sweat. She did her best to ignore the beads of perspiration that rolled down her cheeks as she walked along the fence line, cutting the weeds that had grown against it. The gentle humming of the weed whacker drowned out any other noise and gave Rosanna time to escape into her head where no one was asking anything of her.

The dirt felt dry on her bare feet, especially when she cut along the back of the garden. While she trimmed, she quickly assessed the rows of vegetables planted in the straight furrows she had plowed well over two months ago. Everything was growing nicely; the tomatoes were nearly in need of staking, and the zucchini plants were spreading their vines with a hint of yellow flower buds beginning to show. The two rows of beets were also growing well. Rosanna could almost taste the sweetness of pickled beets come late August.

Out of the corner of her eye, she noticed movement near the fence. And then she smelled it: the bitter, woodsy scent of burning tobacco. She took a deep breath and quickly counted to ten before turning to greet her neighbor. "Hello, Gloria," she managed to say with a smile on her lips. She hoped that she sounded friendly as she remembered Jesus's Golden Rule: love thy neighbor. "Beautiful day, *ja*?"

Gloria dragged on her cigarette, purposefully blowing the smoke in Rosanna's direction. "Your dogs got loose on my property again."

Resisting the urge to cough, Rosanna took a step backward. "I'll have Aaron check the fencing again," she offered. "A groundhog must be digging under at night."

Gloria had short, curly hair that was too dark to be natural and dark, piercing eyes. She stared at Rosanna, clearly not in agreement with that theory. "Groundhog? I don't think so!" she snapped. The wrinkles over her upper lip deepened as she inhaled the smoke from her cigarette again. "Camille's goin' to call the cops on those dogs. You best make certain you fix that fence!" She turned and marched back toward her ranch house, leaving Rosanna to stare after her.

"Have a good day, too," she whispered under her breath.

Her interactions with the Smith family always left Rosanna feeling a lot of gratitude for having been born Amish. If growing up Englische made people so miserable, then she found extra comfort in her plain and simple lifestyle. While she interacted with the Englische on an infrequent basis, she had never met any Amish person who so lacked civility and seemed so miserable. Even old man Weaver, who barely mumbled hello to anyone after worship service, was more pleasant than the Smith family.

The sound of a buggy in the driveway interrupted her thoughts, and she turned toward the house, wondering who had arrived. Squinting in the sun, she thought she made out the shape of a young man and knew that it must be Daniel sent from the store by Reuben to help Aaron. She retrieved the weed whacker and her hoe before heading back to the house. By the time she stepped onto the driveway, the hot black macadam burning the soles of her feet, Daniel was already there.

"*Danke* for coming," she said as she extended her hand to properly welcome him. Rosanna hadn't interacted much with him, but Reuben often spoke of him with praise for his work ethic and common sense.

The young man smiled crookedly; it gave him a warm and friendly appearance. His straw hat, battered from years of use, was as crooked as his smile as it sat cockeyed atop his curly blond hair. "Glad to help!"

Rosanna set the weed whacker on the ground by her feet. She still needed to trim the grass along the driveway and then use the hand mower on the patches of grass around the house. Despite having asked Cate to do that earlier in the day, Rosanna knew her daughter had been too excited to concentrate on any of her chores.

"How are things down at the shop?" she asked.

"Just fine. Cate's working the front desk while Reuben shows Nan how to use some of the equipment," Daniel replied. "She's a fast learner."

"Cate?" she asked, unable to hide her joy and almost beaming with pride at his compliment.

"*Nee*, I meant Nan."

Of course, she thought, hiding her disappointment. It wasn't his fault, she told herself. After all, he barely knew her daughter. Forcing a smile, Rosanna nodded her head. She knew that it was good for Reuben to have a strong person helping him in the office. It made sense that he train Nan on all of the different aspects of the business. However, Rosanna knew that, deep down, there was something not right with his choice of a possible successor. Besides, she thought, given Cate's affection for the shop, she might even be interested in taking it over herself one day.

For the rest of the afternoon Aaron and Daniel worked in the fields while Rosanna focused on the yard. From time to time, she paused and looked in the direction of the mule-pulled hay baler. Most of the time they were too far away, and she could barely make out the faces of the two men. But when she did, she could tell that they were working hard.

It was good that Reuben had sent Daniel to help. Aaron needed more male role models in his life, especially when it came to farming. Reuben had not grown up on a farm and knew little about crops and fertilizing. His family did not even own cows, although his maternal grandparents did live on a farm. The fact that he sometimes helped Aaron with the morning milking and feeding was just short of miraculous. Rosanna was thankful that Reuben had been willing to learn. The act of teaching his stepfather to handle the animals had done wonders for Aaron's self-esteem.

Now, if she could only help Cate find that same level of confidence.

# CHAPTER SIX

"He's got nowhere to go, Rosanna," Reuben said.

The sink water ran in a steady stream from the faucet, the noise muffling his voice just enough so that she couldn't read his emotions. With his back to her, he went through the motions of scrubbing the day's dirt from his hands. When he turned off the water, shaking his wet hands over the sink, she handed him a dish towel. The clock chimed five times: suppertime. The table was set and the food ready to be served; all they needed was bodies seated on the bench and chairs. But other than Rosanna and Reuben, the kitchen was empty.

It wasn't like Reuben to bring someone home for supper. He'd never done that before. So Rosanna had been more than surprised when Reuben walked into the house with Daniel in tow. While she didn't begrudge Daniel a seat at the supper table, she found herself caught off guard at Reuben's request that the young man stay overnight. As Reuben continued talking, Rosanna realized that overnight might extend to weeks or even months.

"What happened to his home?" She kept her voice low, just in case their voices carried through the open window. She could see

Aaron and Daniel leaning on the fence by the barn. They were talking and watching Cate throw a stick for one of the dogs.

Since last week's invitation to help at the harness shop, Cate had become an elusive figure at the farm. She tended to spend most of her time with Reuben. If she was at home, she was begging Reuben to let her work there the following day. While it pleased Rosanna that her daughter demonstrated such a good work ethic, she was becoming increasingly tired of doing both her chores and Cate's. Her back hurt and her feet were swollen from standing all day with nary a break. If Cate thought she was going to work at the shop all summer, Rosanna knew she had to correct that—even if it meant disappointing her daughter.

And now there was the Daniel situation. Granted, he was friendly enough. Just last Saturday afternoon, Daniel had returned to help with the barn work. Aaron had seemed right pleased, and the two certainly got along well. But for him to move into their home?

"He's willing to help Aaron with the morning and evening chores," Reuben said. "That frees me up to leave earlier in the morning and stay later when needed."

"That's all well and good—" Rosanna started.

He interrupted her. "And he can help Aaron break that horse."

She pursed her lips. The horse was fine, having clearly been used on a buggy before Reuben had purchased him. His ground manners and familiarity with the harness had been established a week after he arrived. "Something else is going on here," she said. She had a sinking feeling in her stomach.

"He doesn't have any family here," Reuben finally admitted. "I just want to help him out. He's a *gut* young man, Rosanna."

The sorrow in Reuben's voice was obvious, and Rosanna regretted her hesitation. She could tell that Daniel's situation reminded Reuben of his own lost family. With both of his parents deceased and only one sibling still alive but living in Ohio, Reuben was truly alone.

"No family?" Rosanna asked.

Reuben refused to meet Rosanna's gaze. "No immediate family anyway."

Respecting the emotion she read in his face, Rosanna softened her tone. She changed the subject, knowing that there was a reason for whatever Reuben was leaving unsaid. "Where has he been living, then?"

Dropping the dish towel on the counter, Reuben shrugged. He didn't seem to notice that she quickly picked up the towel and folded it neatly. "With cousins. But it's far from the shop, and his horse is lame."

"What about the house at the shop?" asked Rosanna.

Reuben frowned at the question, his irritation more than evident even before he spoke. "Rosanna . . ."

She knew what he was going to say. It would not be proper for an unmarried man to live with an unmarried woman, even if they were coworkers and even with Nan's brother residing there. Clearly, living on the shop property was not an option. Ashamed that she had even suggested it, she turned her back to him and tried to swallow her embarrassment.

It was not that she begrudged Daniel a roof over his head. No, that wasn't it at all. But she had just started to get used to having a family—a *real* family. Selfishly, she enjoyed the soft conversation at the breakfast table as everyone began to wake up and discuss what they would be doing that day. She enjoyed the quiet evenings after supper, watching Cate play with the dogs and Aaron work with his new horse. There was always something going on, but they were the activities of her own family and did not include a complete stranger.

Glancing out the window again, she saw Aaron toss back his head, his brown curls looking windblown. There was an expression of delight on his face as he laughed at something Daniel had said. It was more than apparent that the two of them got along well enough. For that fact alone she had to admit that it was nice to have Daniel around; it was gratifying to finally see Aaron connecting with another young man. For the past three years he had worked so hard on the farm to help her keep things under control and money flowing that he hadn't experienced much of his youth. It would be good for him to have a companion, as well as someone to lighten his load of work.

"Bear one another's burdens, and so fulfill the law of Christ," she whispered, more to herself than to Reuben. Then she turned away from the window and back to Reuben. "You know I'd never say no." Rosanna sighed and tried to smile as she glanced toward the stairwell. "And there is that spare bedroom upstairs anyway."

*For the other children I never had*, she wanted to add, but didn't.

While the house was not large, there were three bedrooms upstairs and one larger bedroom downstairs, a typical setup for an Amish home. With children sharing bedrooms, she could have had plenty more *kinner*. But after Cate came along and Timothy sank into that dark abyss, God intervened and decided for Rosanna that two was enough. So the spare room had remained unoccupied for all of these years, and both of her children had their own rooms.

Of course, if Daniel was to stay with them for a while, she'd have to get that unoccupied bedroom on the second floor ready. It would need to be dusted and swept, and she'd also have to put fresh linens on the mattress before Daniel could retire there that evening. More work, she thought. "I'll freshen it up with clean linens after the supper dishes are washed, then."

Unaware of her inner thoughts, Reuben was clearly pleased by her answer. He smiled, his expression relaxing as she relented to his request to accommodate Daniel. "It won't be for long, I'm sure," he said, reaching out to cover her hand with his. "You have a big heart, Rosanna Troyer."

The compliment brought color to her cheeks, but this time due to modesty, not shame. She lowered her eyes. "No more so than any other woman, I'm sure," she demurred politely.

Prior to marrying Reuben, Rosanna hadn't heard many compliments. Even in her youth, good grades and hard work were expected, not celebrated. During her marriage with Timothy, complaints were the norm, whether they were about her cooking or cleaning, or her appearance or demeanor. She had been criticized to the point that she had grown immune to the pain, having learned to tune it out.

She appreciated this compliment from Reuben—especially when it implied that she could have made a different decision; that she could have determined whether or not to allow Daniel to stay in that room. She took Reuben's accolade as confirmation that she had a say in this matter and that he did not want to subject her to his whim. It made her feel like a partner of sorts, and it was important to Rosanna that Reuben considered her not just his wife but his partner. This was not common within the Amish community. Large decisions were normally left to the husband.

Rosanna mused that perhaps this was due to the fact that both she and her husband had been through prior marriages, which had led him to become more permissive. Although he was older, Reuben was amazingly open-minded. "If women can work in the fields or in my store," he sometimes declared, "then, in my book, they are entitled to making their own decisions. Men do not always need to make them for them."

Ten minutes later, the five of them sat around the table and bowed their heads in silent prayer. The newcomer, with his blond hair and hazel eyes, seemed out of place among Rosanna's dark-haired family, but his manners were impeccable, and she couldn't complain about his appetite. An entire loaf of fresh wheat bread baked just that morning disappeared along with the cold cuts, a cup of cheese, and a bowl of chowchow. Working at the shop certainly gave young Daniel a hearty appetite.

When the serving plates were empty, Rosanna jumped up to refill them. Reuben and Daniel talked about the shop, and Cate seemed to listen with her full attention. It was unusual for Cate to be so interested in something, so Rosanna let her sit instead of asking her to help serve the meal.

When she finally had a chance to sit down, she reached for the bowl of chowchow to scoop some onto her plate. As she did so, there was a break in the conversation among the men, so she took advantage of it. "Reuben said you'd be needing a place to sleep for a spell," she said, curious to see Daniel's reaction.

But there was none. He did not seem surprised at her words, and Rosanna realized that, despite Reuben asking her for her permission to house the young man, he'd likely already told Daniel that he could stay. Although she'd agreed to the arrangement, it bothered her, and she felt her pulse quicken in irritation.

Daniel didn't notice. He wiped his mouth with the back of his hand and nodded. "That's right. My cousins let me stay with them, but my horse is lame and needs to be off work for a few weeks. Too far to walk to work at the shop."

His and Reuben's stories matched, not that Rosanna expected them to conflict. She just wasn't used to being expected to house other people in her home, especially for an extended period of time and without some sort of warning. Still, Daniel was a nice-looking young man, she thought, and his eyes reflected an emptiness that, despite her displeasure at being taken for granted, tugged at her heartstrings.

When the supper-meal was complete and the after-prayer said, Aaron and Daniel disappeared outside, and Reuben retreated to his recliner by the windows in the sitting room. He liked to relax after eating by reading the Bible or the *Budget* newspaper. Cate helped to clear the plates from the table while Rosanna turned on the hot water, waiting for it to steam before she began washing the dishes. Out of the corner of her eye, she noticed Cate slink toward the door.

"And you are going where?" Rosanna asked, her attention still on the dishes.

"Do you have eyes in the back of your head?" Cate asked.

Rosanna laughed, even though Cate's question bordered on insolence. "I just might, *dochder*. I just might."

"I wanted to go play with the dogs a spell."

For a moment Rosanna again felt the beat of her heart speed up. There was a pile of dishes, utensils, and cups waiting to be washed and dried. The table needed a good wiping, and the floor begged to be swept. And she still needed to clean that bedroom for Daniel. All of this work, and Cate wanted to go outside to play? But one glance at her daughter's hopeful face and Rosanna relented.

"Go on now," she said, her chest tightening. "Enjoy the good weather."

Cate beamed. "*Danke, Maem.*" Without wasting one second, her bare feet carried her across the kitchen floor.

"Just stay away from that back fence!" Rosanna called as the screen door slammed shut.

"Such noise!" Abruptly Reuben set down the newspaper and looked up, scowling. The creases in his forehead deepened, and his mouth turned down at the corners. "You know, Rosanna, if I have one rule, it's for peace and quiet after the supper-meal. That's my time to relax, not to listen to loud voices and doors slamming!"

The displeasure on his face caused Rosanna to quickly apologize. She knew that Reuben demanded peace and quiet in the house in the evening hours, especially just after eating. It was just one of the many "one rules" that had moved into the home along with him.

Rosanna watched as he lifted the paper, the unhappy grimace remaining on his face. She took a deep breath and focused on washing the dishes, trying to keep the plates from clanking against each other as she washed them.

Growing up in a large family, Rosanna wasn't used to quiet houses. On evenings and weekends, neighbors and cousins were always visiting. She was the youngest of eight, and Rosanna could remember the noise that resonated throughout the house. Her older sisters communicated with each other by raising their voices from one floor or room to the next. When chores were performed in unison, there was always a cacophony of clamoring shouts, shutting doors, and the muffled sound of little feet from the younger children traipsing across the hardwood floors.

With Timothy, noise hadn't been an issue. Alcohol caused him to sleep through most everything. Even Cate's constant colicky screaming as a baby hadn't awoken him.

She had learned about Reuben's aversion to noise shortly after they were married. While the din associated with a big family had always been music to her ears, it was the opposite for Reuben. His complaints about the noise, sometimes warranted while other times not, seemed unreasonable. But Rosanna knew better than to complain. Being quieter was a small price to pay for the love he bestowed upon her.

Five minutes passed, and the only noise in the house was the crinkle of the newspaper when Reuben turned the pages. She finally heard him take a deep breath and fold the paper, the signal that he was finished reading and would soon retire.

"Two more custom orders came in today from Ohio." From the tone of his voice, Rosanna wasn't certain whether or not he was happy about the announcement. "It's a rush job, so I'll be working late tomorrow and Saturday, I reckon."

Rosanna caught her breath, trying to mask her disappointment. Usually he came home early on Saturdays. After an early supper, they would go for a long walk down the shadowy lane leading to the main road and then continue toward the big pond at the corner of Lee's Mill and Studden Roads. Sometimes they would sit on the weathered picnic bench that had been set there way back when. Rosanna would throw pieces of old bread to the ducks while Reuben talked about work or the days of his youth when he apprenticed at a shop in Indiana. It was a bonding time for them, a time without interruptions from Cate or questions from Aaron. It was just the two of them for a solid hour or so. If he was going to work late they would not have that time together this week.

But work was work, and she couldn't argue when he needed to spend extra time at the shop. "I reckon it's good to get a head start on it, then." She was glad that he wasn't looking at her. She knew that she could never hide the emotion in her eyes.

"Could use Cate a few days next week," Reuben said.

"I was counting on her to help me with the garden," she replied. She hadn't weeded it since the previous week. Her enthusiasm for gardening had disappeared with the knowledge that every move she made was watched by the Smiths. At least with Cate by her side, Gloria was less likely to bother her.

Reuben contemplated her request and scratched at his beard. "Nan's picking up a lot of the extra work in the back, Rosanna. She's a fast learner."

Rosanna bit her tongue, promising herself that she would never tell Reuben about how lazy Nan had been the day they had cleaned the house.

He didn't notice her silence. "I really want to get these orders finished by Saturday." He sighed. "It's the distractions that waste the most time. The men bring their items in or spend awhile looking through the inventory. They need my time . . . or rather take it up. I just can't get to the back shop to work on new orders."

Had they not already talked about this? It seemed to be an ongoing problem, yet rather than finding a solution, Reuben was letting it grow into a larger one. A resolution seemed impossible down at the Troyer Harness Shop. Every suggestion was met with an excuse as to why it wouldn't work. Rosanna had almost given up trying, yet she replied, "I still think you should get the men to drop their goods in need of repair at James's farm and pick it all up once a week. Think how much time you'd save."

Reuben didn't respond.

"You could put Daniel or Martin in charge of managing that, too. Even find other farms in different outlying towns." She wondered if his silence meant that he was listening to her idea and considering it.

"Maybe Nan could do it," he finally admitted.

Nan? Rosanna tried to not grimace. She'd been hearing an awful lot about Nan for the past two weeks. She was getting tired of it. The way Reuben made it sound, Nan was the answer to all of his problems. The answer to his prayers! Yet Rosanna had seen even less of Reuben since Nan's arrival. Now, with more orders and Nan's idea for increasing the volume of repairs, Rosanna doubted that would change. So much for his plans to spend more time at home, she thought.

"She is rather new, Reuben. Around here, I mean. People know Daniel and Martin. And the men might be more comfortable dealing with them."

"Mayhaps," he said, his tone noncommittal. "Back to Cate. I'd like her to come down and work tomorrow and Saturday, *ja*?"

"Both days, then?"

He nodded, looking tired. He had been working long hours, coming home late, and going to bed early. If Cate could help him a little, Rosanna knew she should not stand in the way.

"Mayhaps just tomorrow, then?"

"Fair enough." He smiled, but even that looked forced and fatigued. "And since we don't have church this weekend, I've invited the workers to fellowship here on Sunday."

Her heart skipped a beat, and she lifted her hand to her chest. With Daniel living in the house, it was only three extra people, but it meant even more work for her. More cleaning, more cooking, more time spent pleasing others while having no time for herself. She breathed through her mouth, willing herself to be calm. "Will Nan and Rebecca bring some food? Perhaps some bread or rolls and a pie?"

Dismissively, Reuben waved his hand. "They work all week, Rosanna. I wanted this to be a relaxing day for them. No worries, no obligations. Just enjoying each other's company away from the shop."

He did not see her bite her lip. Or if he did, he did not make any attempt to investigate her reaction. She felt a tightening in her throat, and sensing the tears that welled in her eyes, she turned her back to him and pretended to dry the plates. "I see," she managed to say, her tone forced. How could he say that to her? Didn't she work all week, too? Even though she worked at home, she helped to sustain the family just as much as he did.

She could hear him get up from the chair, discarding the paper on the floor. "Best get headed to bed," he said. His voice sounded weary. "Long two days ahead of me."

Rosanna turned around, disappointment on her face, but he was already gone. She watched the bedroom door shut and listened to the noise of his feet shuffling on the floor. After a few minutes, she heard the bed creak. He hadn't even said good night, and he hadn't offered to help prepare Daniel's room. It would have been a big help for him to bring up the cleaning supplies. But none of those things had happened. In the silence of the kitchen, she stood alone, a feeling of darkness filling her.

Sighing, Rosanna headed to the storage closet. Armed with a bucket filled with rags and wood cleaner in one hand and a mop in the other, she ascended the stairs to the second floor. She tried to push all the thoughts out of her mind, preferring emptiness to the hope that someone would offer to help her. She realized that no one was aware of the weight of hardship she felt. Besides, she thought as she opened the last door in the small hallway and entered the bedroom, she was beginning to suspect that spending time inside of her head might turn into the best company for the evening.

# CHAPTER SEVEN

By Monday morning, thick air hung overhead and blanketed everything in a layer of humidity. Rosanna stood on the porch with a basket of damp clothes, looking up at the threatening clouds. While the crops needed the impending rain that was announcing itself through the distant thunder, the dreary weather of the past three days had done nothing for Rosanna's mood. She felt as drab, boring, and lifeless as the gray, overcast sky. The lack of sunshine grated on her nerves, and she wondered if there was any sunshine left in her own life. Maybe not.

The past week had seemed endless, with too much work and very little reward. No sooner did her head hit the pillow at night than she awoke to another gray dawn. She hadn't received a word of gratitude from her family for any of the chores she did, even though she didn't think a slight hint of appreciation would have been asking too much.

She barely slept at night. She tossed and turned, her mind spinning with thoughts that played over and over in her head: the chores for the next day, prayers for the sick, and pleas for God's guidance and peace in her life. It was this last one that she struggled with the most. She knew that God had everlasting kindness and the capability to show mercy. He was not quick to temper but gave love freely. That was the way she wanted to live: to demonstrate that she, too, could live a godly life and find peace. As she prayed at night, she reflected on her shortcomings of the day and vowed to be stronger tomorrow. She was sure that if she prayed enough to the Lord her God, her prayers would be answered.

But in the new dawn of another gray cookie-cutter day, she found herself faced with even more of the same chores as the one before. She knew that in all probability the next one held the same promise. Her enthusiasm for living a godly life ebbed. She wondered if He listened to her.

Last Saturday, Rosanna had again found herself alone in the house. During breakfast, Cate had eagerly offered to accompany Reuben to work. She seemed more than willing to forfeit her chores in favor of being at the shop. Before Rosanna could remind her daughter that her help was needed at home, Reuben had readily agreed.

Rosanna had sat in her chair staring at her husband. They had agreed that Cate would work at the shop only one day that week. If only she could speak to him in private so that she could express her opinion. Irritated, she realized there was no way to voice her thoughts without contradicting him. And because he looked so pleased with his stepdaughter's interest in the shop, Rosanna knew she wouldn't mention that he had forgotten—or was ignoring—her very specific request on Thursday for Cate's help on the weekend. Not only did the garden need weeding, but the tomatoes had to be staked and the patch of grass along the driveway had to be mowed again. Since Reuben had invited his employees to come visiting the following day, Rosanna also needed to prepare the food in advance.

Without Cate's help, she'd never get all of her work finished. Again.

"Rosanna, that's all right with you, *ja*?" Reuben said.

Rosanna realized that everyone was staring at her. Hiding her annoyance at both Cate and Reuben, she took a deep breath and forced a weak smile. What else could she do but give her permission? "You did say you had two big orders," she said, remembering his comments from the other evening. "If Cate can help, then it's all right with me."

She saw that Aaron was watching her with a concerned look on his face. He had always been the one who could read her emotions, who knew when something was bothering her. "You know I'm going fishing with Jacob and Eli today, *ja?*"

Another deep breath, and Rosanna nodded her head. "You have a good time," she replied. "Nothing here that can't be done on Monday, I reckon."

As she watched the buggy drive down the lane, Rosanna had stood on the porch for a few minutes, taking deep breaths to calm her nerves. She'd been surprised to feel a wave of relief in her chest as the buggy disappeared. She felt as though she'd been holding her breath. She felt a moment of peace knowing that she was going to be alone for most of the day, something she hadn't realized how much she was missing. But the moment she had recognized it, she was immediately overcome by guilt for feeling relieved to be alone. The guilt caused the tightness in her chest to return and her temples to throb. The pain in her head became so intense that halfway through her chores she had to lie down for fifteen minutes.

If Rosanna had thought the next day would improve, she'd been gravely mistaken. Despite her best efforts to remain cheerful and happy, she had felt nothing but stress. When Daniel, Martin, Rebecca, and Nan arrived for dinner, a meal that she had spent most of the previous afternoon preparing, Rosanna had a hard time keeping her composure. Although Sunday should have been a day of rest for her, at least while Reuben read his Bible, Rosanna had cleaned the breakfast dishes, set the table, and warmed up the food she had cooked the previous day: a large ham, fresh bread, a green bean casserole, and mashed potatoes. It hadn't taken long for the kitchen to release the smells of good, fresh food. Everyone but Rosanna was excited about the meal.

The weather was perfect, with only a few clouds in the turquoise sky. A warm breeze carried the scent of dogwood trees and rustled the leaves of the growing corn crops. The only problem was that Rosanna wasn't able to enjoy it. While everyone else sat outside talking around the picnic table, she was stuck in the kitchen, preparing the plates of food.

Only Rebecca offered any help, and Rosanna gladly accepted, especially since Cate was running in the back fields with the dogs. As Rebecca hurried into the house, Rosanna paused, just for a moment, as if anticipating that Nan, too, would extend an offer of assistance. None came. Instead, she sat with the men, laughing at their jokes and talking about the shop. Stunned at Nan's poor manners, Rosanna shook her head as she crossed the small yard toward the house.

After the meal, Cate had helped to clear the table, but only after Rosanna gave her a stern look and motioned toward the house with her head. The guests had been too engaged with Reuben to offer to assist her. Rosanna only heard bits and pieces of the conversation, but she didn't need to hear more; it was mostly about the harness store. However, she did notice that Nan was doing most of the talking. She spoke louder than any other Amish woman Rosanna had ever known and, in Rosanna's opinion, with an attitude of unearned authority. Her voice had grated on Rosanna's nerves.

By the time everything had been cleaned and the dishes washed and put away, the party was over. Rosanna had watched the two buggies roll down the driveway. Daniel and Rebecca were riding together to a youth gathering in the neighboring church district. Martin had offered to take Nan back to the small house on the shop's property. As the buggies disappeared, Rosanna could still hear Nan's voice in her head. The high-pitched sound seemed to carry in the air.

That was when the pain in her chest had started again. At first it was dull, an ache near her heart. She felt as if something was squeezing her, the tightness spreading down to her midsection. She had to sit for a few minutes, taking deep breaths before she was able to get up and make her way to the bedroom. Reuben and Cate were outside, helping Aaron with the evening chores. Rosanna had rested for thirty minutes, trying to calm the rapid beating of her heart in the hopes that the tension would vanish.

It hadn't.

Now she faced a new week. She tried to relax as she hung the laundry to dry. Monday was always a wash day. She never understood why clothes seemed to attract so much dirt over the weekend. The laundry seemed to breed in the baskets. In just those two days, only one of which was a workday, Aaron and Cate had seemed to go through more clothes than during the rest of the week. Rosanna disliked doing the laundry. The hand washer with the wringer caused her arm to ache afterward, but she knew it was better to stay on top of the dreaded chore than postpone it.

Rosanna grabbed two clothespins from her basket and stuck one on the sleeve of Cate's brown dress. It hung on the line, limp and dark. With the dampness in the air, nothing was going to dry. Frustrated, she unpinned the sleeve. She'd have to hang everything in the basement instead.

"*Maem!*"

Rosanna shut her eyes. Patience, patience, she repeated to herself. Some days, when she heard her name being called, she felt like ignoring it. Nine times out of ten, it was a request to locate something. Rosanna would be forced to drop whatever she was doing to investigate—and more likely than not the item was exactly where it should have been; they just hadn't bothered to look. She knew she should feel pleased that her family wanted her assistance, but it was getting to the point that just hearing someone call her name gave her heart palpitations.

"*Maem*! Come quick!"

The tightness returned to her chest, and she clutched the damp dress in her hands. Taking a deep breath, she looked toward the garden. Her irritation immediately turned to panic.

Cate was running toward her, tears streaming down her face. There was dirt on her dress, and her hair had fallen free from its bun. Cate wasn't a crier, so whatever had happened must have been bad.

Dropping the dress on top of the basket, Rosanna walked quickly down the porch steps.

As Cate approached, Rosanna opened her arms and let her daughter collapse against her chest. Cate pressed her head against her mother's shoulder as she sobbed, her cries catching in her throat.

Rosanna gave her daughter a minute to calm down before she loosened her hold and bent down to wipe the tears from her cheeks. "Take a deep breath, Cate. What happened?"

Sniffling into her sleeve, Cate attempted to hold back another sob as she stared at her mother through teary eyes. "It's . . . it's that awful Englische woman!"

"Englische woman?" When Rosanna registered her daughter's words, the palpitations immediately returned. Why couldn't Gloria just leave her family alone? Rosanna placed her hands on the girl's shoulders and looked her squarely in the eye. "Tell me what happened."

"Jack chased a stick that I threw, and it got caught in the fence," Cate said between choked sobs.

"Oh, Cate!" Rosanna fought the urge to frown. How many times had she warned Cate to stay away from the section of the fields that bordered Gloria's property?

Cate shook her head. "That's not it, *Maem*." She took a deep breath, one last tear falling down her dirty cheek. "He tried to get the stick and pulled at the fence. Gloria and her daughter came running across the yard, screaming that they were calling the police, that he's rabid and trying to attack Camille's baby."

The Smiths again? A sigh escaped Rosanna's lips. And now the woman was threatening to involve the police? Rosanna knew well enough that Amish and legal authorities did not mix well. It wasn't that the Amish had many run-ins with the law. Occasionally a teenager on rumschpringe might experiment with alcohol or worse, resulting in local law enforcement clashing with the Amish bishops. But as a rule, there were few interactions between the two powers. Like the rest of the community, Rosanna wanted to keep it that way.

In fact, Rosanna preferred to stay off the radar of any Englische. The only time she ever had any contact with Englische police officers was after Timothy's accident. With the bishop and preachers involved, she hadn't had to say much. The shock of his sudden death had kept her quiet, and there hadn't been many questions from the police. When the bishop had learned of Timothy's closet drinking, he merely shook his head and mumbled, "An accident waiting to happen, for sure and certain. The evil of the bottle is the work of the devil."

Rosanna was convinced that Cate had done nothing wrong, but the thought of possibly being reported to the police unnerved her. The last thing she wanted was any trouble. But that was the one thing that Gloria and her ill-mannered daughter seemed to seek. Although Gloria worked the night shift at the twenty-four-hour convenience store, Rosanna was uncertain if Camille worked, as her car often sat in the driveway for days. Clearly neither of them had enough to do.

"And withal they learn to be idle, wandering about from house to house; and not only idle, but tattlers also and busybodies, speaking things which they ought not," she thought, remembering the verse from 1 Timothy in the New Testament.

Pulling her daughter into her arms, Rosanna rubbed her hands along Cate's back. "Now, now," she consoled, too aware of her own pounding heart and the increasingly awful feeling of stress returning. "It's going to be fine. Jack doesn't have rabies, and he wasn't trying to attack the *boppli*."

Despite her words of comfort, she wasn't sure that everything would be fine. The dance with Satan ran deep in their neighbors' veins, and Rosanna suspected that this incident was far from over. If only she knew why they hated her!

Rosanna knew that she'd have to speak to Reuben about this. Perhaps if she could encourage him to speak to Gloria, he could find out why she was so intent on harassing Rosanna and her children. After all, she told herself, that's what husbands did: protect their families.

To her surprise, when Reuben came home at eleven thirty, just in time for the dinner-meal, he merely laughed at Rosanna's story.

"She's just an old woman," he said, chuckling. "A miserable one, I'll grant you that, but they aren't going to call the police."

His answer didn't satisfy Rosanna. With the hope of his support vanishing, she tried a different angle. "Mayhaps she won't call the police, but now Cate is scared to work in the garden."

Another laugh, but this time with a little less joviality. "Or making excuses, *ja?*"

"Excuses?"

He shook his head and gave Rosanna what could only be described as "a look."

"Isn't she helping at the shop?" Rosanna asked.

Holding up one finger, Reuben gave a pensive *ah* as if making a point. "Do you think that I haven't noticed she is skirting her chores around the house? Why, Daniel's been helping Aaron in the mornings and evenings. Might do her some good to not play with those dogs anyhow!"

Rosanna's heart began racing again. The disappointment and bitterness in Reuben's words hurt—she felt that he was lashing out at her. Regardless of whether Cate was pulling her weight around the farm, didn't her work at the shop prove she wasn't lazy? Daniel was living in their home and sharing their food—it was only proper that he help with the chores.

Rosanna realized that Reuben had not only called Cate lazy but also manipulative. She had a flashback to Timothy. Hadn't he always called Rosanna lazy? Hadn't he always complained? Rosanna's heart beat faster. What was happening to her relationship with Reuben?

"She works hard," Rosanna finally said, determined to stick up for her daughter. "And she's been through a lot, Reuben."

"She's tougher than you think," he said.

"Criticizing her is not the solution. 'Let no corrupting talk come out of your mouths, but only such as is good for building up, as fits the occasion, that it may give grace to those who hear.'"

"I hardly see where I have corrupting talk, Rosanna."

Reuben's reprimand stung. She couldn't understand how they had gone from discussing Gloria's threat to exchanging words about Cate. "I was telling you about that Gloria woman. She's not kind, and she's scaring my *dochder*!" The words came out sharper than she intended. "It would be nice if you talked with her."

The laughter disappeared from Reuben's face, and he frowned at her. He had noticed the edge to her voice. "I will not talk with her," he said without emotion. "I don't have time for such petty things, Rosanna. Nor will I give her the satisfaction of knowing that she has upset my family. Pray for the Lord to handle this."

Without another word, Reuben stood up from the table and retreated to the bedroom, where she knew he would rest for twenty minutes before returning to the shop.

The nerves in her arms tingled, and she fought the urge to cry. She didn't know why she had snapped at him. The situation wasn't his fault; it had been inherited from Timothy. But the realization that she now had to shoulder the responsibility of keeping peace along property lines felt heavy. Rosanna suspected that Cate's playing with the dogs would also demand her parental supervision from now on. All of this in addition to helping Aaron with the barn work and doing all the house chores and tending to the garden.

As Rosanna thought about this, she suddenly remembered that she had committed to filling in for Annie Yoder at market for the next two Fridays. That meant rising at three in the morning to catch the van to Maryland. She wouldn't return until almost nine in the evening. She'd have to spend all of Thursday preparing the meals so that Cate could, hopefully, warm them for the family.

Sighing, Rosanna shook her head and turned her anger toward herself. Why had she agreed to help Annie? Why hadn't she simply said that she couldn't do it? Once again, she had created her own problems by saying yes when she really wanted to say no! But that was a word that wasn't in her vocabulary. "No" was the opposite of "yes." "No" was negative. "No" created disappointment. "No" upset people. She had always learned that it was better to be disappointed than to be the one doing the disappointing.

The only problem with living that philosophy was that she often felt that the burden of pleasing others was draining her, both mentally and spiritually.

# CHAPTER EIGHT

The next Sunday the Miller family hosted the worship service. When Reuben drove the buggy down the Millers' gravel driveway, two young men hurried to take the horse's reins. Reuben climbed down and straightened his jacket before turning back to help Rosanna.

She took his hand and placed her foot on the black iron step, holding the buggy's door frame as she emerged. The buggy shifted as she stepped to the ground. She waited for Cate to climb over the seat and jump down beside her. Aaron had elected to walk, preferring to join up with his friends at the old oak tree by the Bechlers' pond rather than ride in the back of his stepfather's buggy. Despite having been given a horse, he had yet to earn enough money to buy an open-topped buggy. At sixteen, he wasn't particularly inclined to start driving one anyway. They were used for courting, and he had plenty of time ahead of him for that.

Forty gray-topped buggies already lined the fence. The horses pulling two-wheeled Meadowbrook carts had been unhitched to provide them with more comfortable rest. Those pulling the traditional buggies remained harnessed. Although these vehicles were much heavier, they were built on a four-wheel platform, so no significant pressure was transmitted to the horses' backs other than the light weight of the shafts.

The horses that had been unharnessed were tied with lead ropes to two long iron railings adjacent to the barn. Most of them seemed to be dozing, their heads drooping and their back legs cocked just slightly above the hoof. They knew from experience that it would be at least a half day before the trip back home. The position of the sun would alert them to the passing of time.

Four hours or so later, forty pairs of ears would suddenly prick forward in unison and heads would rise. Snorts, neighs, and nickers of horses eager to return to the comfort of their stalls and their evening hay and grain would announce the end of the gathering and the imminent procession of the buggies.

Cate ran off to join her group of friends by the chicken coop, leaving Rosanna to wander toward the house with her basket of freshly baked pies. Most of the women had already gathered in the kitchen. They stood in a loose circle around the periphery of the room so that newcomers could be greeted with a handshake and kiss from each woman.

Rosanna dreaded this part of the service. She felt a tightening in her chest as she walked through the open door and glanced around the room at the sea of women, all dressed in black and talking softly to each other. Despite finding this greeting distasteful, Rosanna obediently walked to each woman, extending her hand and leaning forward to kiss them on the lips. No words were exchanged, just a nod of the head. She wasn't partial to this tradition, especially in the winter months. Still, she knew that she had to take the good with the not-as-good.

Fannie Miller hustled over to her and took the basket, thanking her for her contribution to the fellowship meal. Rosanna assumed her place at the end of the line. During the summer months, worship services were often held in the barn, where the doors could be opened and more air could circulate. Rosanna preferred those services over the indoor ones, when the *g'may* crowded into the first floor of too-small farmhouses where the walls had been constructed with hinges so that they could be removed to make one large room for everyone.

She glanced at the clock over the refrigerator. Ten minutes remained before the women would leave the kitchen, walking in single file across the yard and to the barn.

"Rosanna, heard you have a new tenant." Rosanna turned to Katie Miller, Fannie's sister-in-law. They lived on a farm that neighbored Jake and Fannie's. The brothers farmed the same fields, sharing in the expenses and the profits. It was a good arrangement for them, but Rosanna often wondered what would happen when their own sons were old enough to take over the property.

"*Ja*, Reuben hired a new girl to work at the shop," Rosanna replied.

Rosanna didn't act surprised that Katie seemed aware of the details. Of course, Rosanna thought. The Amish grapevine.

Someone touched her arm: Lizzie Mast, the older sister of Annie Yoder, the woman Rosanna had helped at market. "Was wondering if you might help some," Lizzie said. "Need fabric to make tie quilts for auction. Thought you might be able to help visit neighbors and ask. Maybe some of your Englische neighbors. They always have so much extra clothing."

Inwardly Rosanna sighed. Something else to worry about, she thought. But with a smile on her face, she nodded. "Of course, *ja*! When do you need the fabric?"

"Sister Annie and Mary Hostetler are coming in three weeks to cut squares. You're welcome to join us."

She'd have to remember that date and write it on her calendar when she returned home. As far as fabric went, she'd send Cate on a mission to the Englische neighbors, reminding her to avoid Gloria

Smith's property. Maybe she'd have Cate write up a flyer and put it in people's mailboxes. That way they could just drop off the clothes at the farm. Her mind raced as she tried to figure out how to best help Lizzie.

By the time everyone began walking out the door and toward the barn, Rosanna had a plan mapped out and knew exactly how she would handle this project. Satisfied, she tabled the idea and tried to focus on the more important task at hand: the worship service.

Unlike her own life, the worship service was predictable and orderly. For three hours every two weeks, Rosanna did not need to think or make decisions. She simply sang the hymns and listened to the two sermons. The men always sat on one side of the barn and the women on the other. Sometimes after service there might be a members' meeting, and the unbaptized members would take the young children outside or, in the winter, upstairs in the house, while the bishop or preachers discussed a private matter. Sometimes the members of the *g'may* would need to vote, such as when deciding on a new rule or whether to assist someone in need.

Today, however, was just a regular worship service. To her dismay, Rosanna could barely keep her eyes open as Bishop Smucker preached after the opening hymn. Twice her eyelids drooped, and once she felt her head jerk. Embarrassed, she glanced around to make certain no one had noticed. Elizabeth Esh, who sat to her right, gave her a hint of a smile. Rosanna pushed her fingers into her palms, hoping that the sharp pressure of her nails against her skin would help keep her awake. It didn't.

When her eyelids began to droop again during "Das Loblied," the second hymn that was always sung between sermons, Rosanna felt a soft push on her arm. Elizabeth motioned with her head toward the door, a hint that she should excuse herself as if she had to use the restroom. A right *gut* idea, Rosanna thought. She quietly stood and moved between the other married women seated between her and the open door of the barn.

Outside she slowly walked toward the Millers' house. Despite the humidity, the air refreshed her. The heat in the barn, generated from so many people sitting so closely together, certainly had not helped her fight off sleep.

It had been a hard week, especially when Cate fell ill on Wednesday with a stomach bug. Without that extra set of hands to help with chores, everything had fallen on Rosanna's shoulders: the laundry, the cooking, the cleaning, and the shopping. She'd also helped Aaron during early morning and evening chores because the harness shop was swamped with new orders, and Reuben and Daniel had been unavailable.

On both Wednesday and Thursday, Reuben had left well before breakfast, taking a small red cooler packed with food to the shop. He hadn't returned home until almost seven o'clock each night. With a soft kiss on her forehead, he dragged himself to bed, politely refusing the plate of food she had left for him. She had stared at the closed bedroom door and felt disconnected from him. She wished that she could help alleviate his workload. Yet she couldn't help wondering why he kept taking on more orders if they couldn't handle them.

And then Friday morning had arrived. The driver's headlights had illuminated the driveway even before she was finished pinning her prayer *kapp* to her elastic headband. One glance at the clock, and she knew that it was going to be a long day. The driver was early, and she was barely awake. Since she was the first person to be picked up, she settled into the back of the van and rested her head against the window. The glass felt cool against her skin, and she shut her eyes, trying to steal a few more moments of sleep before the van filled up with the rest of the passengers headed to market.

Given that there were six more stops, it took over an hour to pick up everyone.

Thankfully, once they were at market, the day had passed quickly. Annie Yoder normally worked in the pickle section, so that was where Rosanna had been assigned. At first the strong smell of the vinegar had overwhelmed her. By the end of the day, she didn't even notice it. She did notice, however, the abrupt mannerisms of the Englische who visited the market. Unlike the Amish, they were pushy and forward, asking strange questions that often bordered on offensive. By the time the market closed at six, she was ready to collapse in the van and head back to the farm.

Only one more Friday, she'd told herself as she pressed her head against the window once again.

She had returned home to a kitchen sink filled with dirty dishes, a floor that hadn't been swept, and a mountain of laundry that had apparently appeared out of nowhere. Her entire Saturday had been spent playing catch-up, and sleep had not been a part of the equation.

Now it was Sunday, and she was still exhausted. She needed to stretch her legs and breathe in the fresh air outside. It was too hot inside the barn, and it didn't smell all that pleasant. Removing herself from the hard pine bench she'd been sitting on for three hours had been a smart suggestion from her friend Elizabeth.

"You all right out here, Rosanna?" She turned at the sound of her name and was surprised to see Reuben walking toward her. His brow was twisted in concern. As he approached, he reached for her arm, holding it gently in his hand. "You've been doing a lot, my *fraa*. I have no problem with you going right on home after service if you can't stay for fellowship."

Grateful that he cared enough to not only notice her absence from the worship room but to come check on her, Rosanna merely shook her head. "*Nee*, Reuben," she started. "I'm weary, but no more so than anyone in there." She smiled. "My week may have drained me, but that doesn't mean I shouldn't be here to honor our Lord and enjoy fellowship with our *g'may*."

Truth was that she always enjoyed this day, the one day when she could relax a bit and count on others to help out—some more than others. To miss it by returning home early was far worse in her eyes than experiencing a few lowered eyelids and jerky neck motions. Besides, she knew that if she had glanced around the room she would have picked out at least a half-dozen others, mostly men, dozing off during the hymns and sermons.

And then, of course, there was another reason she wanted to stay. During the ritual assembling of the worship members, the married women entered the barn first followed by the married men, both in chronological order by age. For this reason Rosanna always knew who she would sit next to at service. But when it came to the unmarried women and men, there were sometimes changes in their ranks that provided cause for chitchat on the Amish grapevine. This week the gossip was focused on Nan.

Unlike her brother, Samuel, Nan insisted on attending the worship services. She wore the stiff cuplike cap from her former New York Amish community. It made her stand out among the other Amish women with their soft, heart-shaped prayer *kapps*. Nan didn't seem to mind being different. If nothing else, it gave her the opportunity to talk to people who were curious about the type of Amish community in which she had grown up. Most people wanted to know about the differences, as if testing the other districts for their loyalty to the Ordnung as well as to the Ausbund.

To Nan's credit, she said very little that could be taken as criticism of her previous community, stating only that it was diminishing in population by the year. Young people moved away while the elderly moved home when God called them. That was part of the reason she and Samuel had relocated: it was a dying Amish community. They'd had no choice but to move.

This was not the same story Rosanna had been told.

Despite being exhausted, Rosanna wanted to stay both for the fellowship and out of curiosity.

After Reuben returned to the service, she allowed herself a few more minutes to take in the fresh air and to stretch her legs and clear her head. Her mind felt foggy, and her muscles ached with a weariness that did not come from hard work. The last thing she needed was to come down with a sickness like the one Cate had experienced the previous week. Chalking up her physical stress to her busy week, she took a last look around the Millers' farm before she headed back inside the barn.

After the service, the women carried platters of prepared food from the kitchen to the tables set up under the shade of two large oak trees near the driveway. The men had created the two long tables by putting the legs of the pine benches into trusses. Meanwhile, the younger boys collected the Ausbunds and carefully stacked them in a wooden crate for the next service.

In the kitchen, the older women directed the younger ones to work. With so many people, not all of them had a task. Thankfully, Rosanna was among them. She stood outside on the porch with Elizabeth, a few feet away from a group of older women.

"You look beat," Elizabeth said to Rosanna. She pursed her lips and shook her head. With her ruddy cheeks and bright eyes, she was a happy-looking person who always seemed to have something good to say. Rosanna needed to hear something positive right about now.

"Rosanna Troyer!" Elizabeth continued. "Why on earth would you agree to go to market?" She clicked her tongue: tsk-tsk. "That's for those young girls to do, or women helping their own family . . . not a woman who's helping to run a farm!"

"I know, I know," Rosanna admitted. "Annie needed help and—"

Elizabeth held up her hand. "Don't say it." She paused. "You just couldn't say no, *ja?*"

Rosanna forced a sheepish smile.

*"Nee!"* Elizabeth whispered as she leaned closer to Rosanna, patting her arm. "It's an easy word to say, Rosanna! Start practicing it a bit more."

*"Nee,"* Rosanna responded, and they both laughed.

The elderly and the families with younger children took the first seating of the fellowship meal. Rosanna normally helped in the kitchen, waiting until everyone was finished and the tables reset for the remaining members of the church district before eating her dinner. Today, however, Elizabeth insisted that Rosanna join the others when the first group of people ate at eleven thirty.

The women sat at one table while the men sat at the other. The segregation of the sexes had never seemed odd to Rosanna— she knew no other way. Yet she found herself searching the sea of men, all dressed in the same white shirts and black vests, in the hope of spotting Reuben. He was near the end, sitting beside one of the preachers, Elmer Weaver. They were engaged in conversation until the bishop, with a subtle motion, indicated it was time for the before-prayer.

Every head bent down, Rosanna's included, to thank God for the bountiful food set before them. Rosanna added her own prayer, silently expressing her gratitude for His grace in her life.

Once the prayer was over, the noise level rose as the women seated at the table began to pass plates of pickles, coleslaw, applesauce, bread, and cold cuts. Rosanna dished only a little of everything onto her small white plate, worrying that there might not be enough for everyone. After all, there were over two hundred people in attendance today, more than usual during the summer months.

"I met that young woman who's working at the shop," a young mother with a toddler on her lap said to Rosanna. "Nan is her name, *ja*?"

Rosanna felt that familiar tightness in her chest as she tried not to look in Nan's direction. Nan was standing near the doorway, talking with some of the other unmarried women. Rather than helping with filling water cups or cutting bread for the second seating, she was socializing and distracting the other women from their tasks.

"When did you meet her, Linda?" Rosanna asked.

"Oh, I'd say a few days back. At the food store." Linda jiggled the small child on her lap, which made the short little strings of the girl's prayer *kapp* bounce on her shoulders. "She helped me with the *kinner*, and I gave her a ride back to the shop."

The food store? A ride home? Rosanna took a deep breath as she realized that Nan must have left the harness shop during the day to walk to the food store. Even if she did that on her lunch hour, she never would have had enough time to walk there and back. Rosanna wondered if Reuben was aware of Nan leaving the shop unattended for so long. "That was kind of you," she managed to reply.

"Seemed pleasant enough," Linda said, spreading soft, homemade butter on a piece of bread for her daughter. "Although I was a little surprised to learn that Reuben plans to turn the shop over to her."

It took a minute for Linda's words to register with Rosanna.

Linda looked up and smiled. "I mean, given that she's so new to the area, that's all."

Thankfully Elizabeth changed the subject, asking the woman next to Linda about her mother, who lived in another district. Rosanna took advantage of the opportunity to escape the conversation but still look as if she were listening. In reality, she tried to make sense of what she had just heard.

Was it possible that Reuben had hired Nan with the idea of turning the business over to her? The thought seemed unlikely, although not totally impossible. Without any children of his own, what was he to do with his business? Aaron had expressed no interest in it, and Cate was only twelve. Besides, she'd most likely marry and move in with her husband's family when she was older.

Being a *maedel*—an older unmarried woman—with experience in the harness business, Nan could potentially run the shop for Reuben. He'd justified hiring Nan so that he could work less and spend more time at home, helping Aaron on the farm and enjoying Rosanna's company.

Still, he hardly knew Nan. She had only been employed at the shop for a few weeks, and they still knew very little about her. In fact, after talking with Linda, Rosanna had more questions than answers. She worried that her husband was placing too much faith on fitting a square peg in a round hole. And if it really was his intention to let Nan run the store, he had never once mentioned it to Rosanna. Was that because he was just busy or because he didn't want to involve her in the business? She needed to consider the answer to that question before approaching her husband.

# CHAPTER NINE

I don't interfere with your *kinner*, Rosanna," Reuben began, irritation in his voice and a scowl upon his face. "But I have one important rule. Outten the lanterns when leaving the room."

All week Reuben's mood had hung like a dark cloud over the house. Short-tempered and neglectful, he seemed absorbed in his own world. His work hours were not improving. The few minutes that Rosanna saw him during the early morning or late evening hours were tense, and their conversations were short and terse. When he did pause to talk with her, it seemed that all he could do was complain about Cate or his work. When Rosanna could get a word in, he merely interrupted her, arguing with her before she could even finish her thought.

Rosanna bit her lower lip, feeling the sharp sting of her upper teeth against it. She was surprised there wasn't a bruise there from the many times she bit it to keep herself from arguing in Cate's defense.

"I told her repeatedly, and she keeps doing it," Reuben complained. "I'm starting to think she's doing it out of disrespect."

Rosanna remained quiet.

He had returned from work at six o'clock. Rosanna was helping Aaron with the milking while Daniel assisted Cate with watering the garden and weeding the front section. Having Daniel there removed the burden of dealing with Gloria Smith from Rosanna's shoulders, and it gave Cate some layer of protection.

Lately, Reuben's arrival meant everyone scattered. Tonight, once chores were done, Daniel had as usual retreated to his bedroom when he heard Reuben's buggy pull down the driveway. He tended to sleep a lot, and after working all day at the shop, he knew better than to stay downstairs when Reuben was home. Otherwise he'd be sucked into a conversation about the business. Aaron had wandered across the side field to go visit one of his friends. Some nights he'd ride his horse bareback, but this night he'd walked. As for Cate, Rosanna wasn't sure where she had gone. Most likely she had retreated outside to play with the dogs, a consistent source of comfort for the girl.

"Propane and lamp oil are expensive! She has no value of the dollar. Why, she hasn't worked at the shop this past week! Now she's leaving on lights and wasting fuel?"

Unable to listen to the barrage of complaints, Rosanna must have made a noise, for Reuben stopped talking and turned to stare at her. "What? What is it now?" he snapped. His blue eyes were tired, and she could see how irritated he was.

"You do it all the time," she blurted out with no emotion in her voice. After listening to the complaints over and over again, her mouth spoke before her mind could catch up. "How can I tell Aaron and Cate not to do something when you don't set the example?"

The dark cloud hanging over his head turned black. His mouth flattened, and his nostrils flared. The wrinkles in his forehead deepened as he scowled at her. "I never leave the lantern on!"

Rosanna tilted her chin defiantly. "You did it just the other night."

"Well," he said, his voice defensive and angry, "I don't do it intentionally or consciously!" She knew that he was furious that she had dared to criticize him. It was written on his face.

Even though his words were inconsiderate and infantile, she said nothing else. His response had startled her. Until recently he had always been respectful and kind, compassionate and patient. *That* Reuben hadn't walked through the kitchen door lately. Instead, when he entered the house, he created a spiral of negativity. When Rosanna tried to soften his mood or point out what he was doing, he lashed out, and the situation became even more volatile.

Rosanna was beginning to think Reuben could not admit when he was wrong. She wondered how many other character defects her new husband had.

She stood there staring at him, a blank expression on her face. It was one that she had perfected from many years of being married to Timothy. Inside, she felt the muscles of her chest squeeze together, and she found herself short of breath. Her line of vision began to blur, as if the walls were closing in upon her. He didn't notice when she reached out to steady herself by placing her hand on the back of a kitchen chair.

With a grimace, he stormed into the bedroom, making certain to drop his shoes on the floor in such a way that she knew he was going to bed. Another night wasted, and all over a lantern that Aaron or Cate had left burning in the bathroom. The longer and harder Reuben worked, the shorter his temper grew.

Shaking her head, Rosanna pressed her free hand against her chest. She could feel her heart pounding. She wondered briefly if she might be having a heart attack.

It was moments like these that she missed her family the most. Her parents were aging and lived too far away, outside of Pequea with her oldest brother on the family farm. One sister had moved to New York and another to Ohio. She rarely saw any of them. As the youngest of the eight children in the family, she didn't have much of a relationship with her siblings. She wasn't even close to her two sisters, Anna and Susan, who lived in nearby communities in the southern part of Lancaster County. Despite being just three years older than Rosanna, Anna focused all of her attention on her own family, and Susan hadn't written a letter since a month after Timothy died.

The fact that her siblings were so indifferent bothered Rosanna. It was a poor example to set for her own children. Oh, she knew that Aaron and Cate got along well enough, but at times she worried that they were not closer in age or spirit. In some ways it felt as if she were raising two only children, a thought that bothered her when she realized that one day she would leave this place and live in God's kingdom. Just as she felt alone and without much family, so would her children.

Right now, with Reuben going through this troubled period, she felt very much alone.

*"Maem!"*

Aaron's panic-stricken voice broke her train of thought, and forgetting about her chest pains, she hurried outside.

He stood in the driveway, staring toward the garden. Pausing on the top step of the porch, Rosanna followed his gaze. Cate stood on the small patch of grass between the garden and the cornfield, one hand resting on Jack's collar. On the other side of the wire fence that edged their property, Gloria and Camille were pounding metal stakes into the grass. Each time their hammers struck the tops of the stakes, a metallic sound reverberated across the garden.

"What on earth?" Rosanna said.

"I was just coming back from Abe's. I heard the ruckus before I saw them out there." He shook his head. "Looks like they are hanging up that green tarp on the property line."

SARAH PRICE

"She's still going on about that?" Rosanna could hardly believe Aaron's words. "Didn't you drop off those tomatoes the other day?"

She only had to look at his expression to know the answer: yes. "It didn't make a difference, *Maem*," Aaron said. "They are just miserable people. Completely soulless. Let them hang their ugly tarp."

No truer words had ever been spoken. Rosanna sighed. "I should still find out what this is about." She took a few steps toward the driveway.

"Don't," Aaron said softly, blocking her with his arm. His eyes travelled to the back fence where the two women were making a big display of pounding the stakes. "There's nothing you can do, *Maem*. If anything, you should get Reuben."

That's not happening, Rosanna thought. "He worked hard today," she replied, not wanting to drag her son into her marital problems. Aaron's silence, however, told her that he already knew about them. She looked at her son, suddenly aware that he had turned into a man—seemingly overnight. She gave him a small smile, knowing that her eyes told the truth. If there were two traits that defined her, they were her inability to hide her emotions and her inability to say no.

"*Maem*!"

Rosanna turned toward Cate and saw that the color was drained from her face. On the other side of the fence, Camille was waving her arms in the air. One hand was clenched in a fist as she yelled in their direction. When Camille saw that she had Rosanna's attention, more words flew from her lips. Rosanna suspected that whatever she was saying was nothing anyone on the farm wanted to hear.

"Let me go, Aaron," Rosanna said, gently pulling her arm free from his grip. "I don't want bad blood between neighbors."

Her voice sounded stronger than she felt. Perhaps it was the sight of Cate, who was usually so strong and even sassy, but who now looked frightened. The maternal instinct in Rosanna began to rise, and she knew that she had only one choice: face Gloria and stop walking away. There was only so much turning the other cheek that a person could take, she reasoned.

Rosanna took a deep breath before she fixed her eyes on the two women on the other side of her garden. "I'll handle this."

Walking across the yard toward them, Rosanna silently counted to ten. She willed her pulse to stop beating so rapidly. Whatever the Smiths were trying to achieve by pounding stakes in the ground, she knew that it did not bode well for peace among them. But Rosanna also knew that she had always tried to do right by Gloria. She had neglected the back of the garden, choosing to let the rows of corn planted there die rather than raise Gloria's ire. She had issued a stern warning to Cate, who now played in the fields on the other side of the farm. Finally, Rosanna had asked Aaron to deliver fresh tomatoes in the hope that the gesture would calm the Smiths and cause them to retreat from their offensive attacks.

"What's this about, Gloria?" she asked, surprised that her tone didn't waver as she approached the older woman.

"I'm sick of seeing your dogs, smelling your manure, and looking at your weedy garden!"

The sleeveless shirt that Gloria wore exposed her arms. The flesh lacked muscle and flapped as she hammered the metal stake into the ground. Four feet away, Camille followed her mother's example, feverishly pounding another post. With her recently cropped hair and wrinkles around her lips, the young woman looked almost twenty years older than she was. Despite the differences in their body shapes, they looked more like sisters than mother and daughter.

"And I know what you are telling everyone! Complaining about us to neighbors!" Gloria lifted a tobacco-stained finger and pointed it at Rosanna, a fierce look upon her face. "You are a liar, Rosanna Zook!"

The accusation took the wind from Rosanna's lungs. A liar? Complaining? Certainly Gloria was mistaken. Speaking ill of others was not in Rosanna's nature. Yet Gloria's force and vehemence indicated that she believed what she was saying. Her knees buckling, Rosanna fought a light-headed feeling and somehow found the strength to remain standing.

"I . . . I don't understand, Gloria," she said, fighting to maintain a sense of decorum as she watched Camille furiously pounding another green metal garden stake. She looked at the line of them they had already forced into the ground. Around the first four, the women had attached a heavy green tarp by stapling the edges together. It looked hideous and trashy, a testament to their lack of class.

"I don't want to see you spying on us anymore," Gloria hissed, spittle flying from her lips. "I see you looking over here all the time, watching what we're doing! And I don't want to hear your barking dogs, either!"

The dogs did bark, that was true. But only when they played with Cate. Was that a crime? As for spying on them, Rosanna would have laughed if the loathing in Gloria's dark eyes hadn't warned her that this was no joking matter. "This is a bit ridiculous," Rosanna said, her nerves beginning to stretch thin. How long must I keep turning the other cheek? she wondered. "No one is spying on you."

The truth was that she was the one who always felt eyes watching her whenever she worked outside, whether it was watering or weeding the garden. She had taken to walking with her head down and her shoulders hunched, as if to shield herself from Gloria's eyes. Even now as she stood there, trying to reason with the unreasonable, she felt the heaviness of tolerance and restraint bearing down upon her.

In the back of her mind, Rosanna wished that she had followed Aaron's advice and awakened Reuben to handle this. Clearly the presence of her daughter was giving Gloria a false sense of invincibility. And the daughter's frenzied pounding of every stake made her appear even crazier than Rosanna was beginning to suspect she was. Perhaps, she thought, Gloria would be more subdued when speaking with a man. Then again, in his present mood, Rosanna wasn't sure Reuben would handle this any better than she was doing.

Suddenly Camille looked up from her pounding. Her narrowed eyes gave her a sinister look. Dropping the hammer, Camille rushed at Rosanna, her arms lifted in a threatening manner. For a moment Rosanna thought that Camille would reach over the fence and strike her. The anger and hatred in the woman's eyes caused Rosanna to catch her breath. Where had that come from? It was as though her loathing consumed her soul.

Rosanna took a step backward in surprise.

"I'm protecting my child, Rosanna," Camille yelled, her voice high-pitched and nasal. "I have that right, too!"

Rosanna remembered Camille as a young girl, no older than Cate. She had never seemed particularly friendly or pleasant, but she had never paid much attention to her Amish neighbors. Then, about two years before Timothy died, Camille's battered green car had pulled out of the driveway one day and didn't return for many months. Rosanna hadn't given much thought to Camille leaving home until she heard a whisper of drug use and jail time. Praying for the young woman, Rosanna had asked the Lord to take care of His lost sheep. Whether or not the stories were true, Camille eventually returned home—with a baby—but the hardship of life without community and faith had taken its toll.

With the gaunt and washed-out Camille standing before her and only a fence separating them, Rosanna wondered what could possibly have created such hostility and self-righteousness. What was it about the world of the Englische that created such poison among their people? That now left her facing the rancor of a woman both jaded and disgraced?

"I'm not certain what you are protecting your child from," Rosanna said.

"Your dogs!" Camille yelled, waving her arms again. "They constantly try to attack us!"

"Camille, please," Rosanna said, holding up her hands in an attempt to calm the woman's raving temper. "I've told Cate to play in the other fields. The dogs haven't been back here for days."

"I have the right to protect my child," Camille said through clenched teeth, and then, leaning forward, she grimaced and added, "Just as you protected yours!"

The air rushed out of Rosanna's lungs, and she almost reached out to steady herself against the wire fence post. She stopped herself in fear that one of the women would hit her hand with the hammer. The color drained from her cheeks, and she felt dizzy and faint. Was it possible? she thought. Did Camille know?

Rosanna swallowed as she backed away a few paces, letting the angry women continue raging as they built their ugly makeshift fence. She needed to get to the safety of the house and sit down. Actually, she needed to lie down, even if that meant facing Reuben again that evening.

When Rosanna was at a safe distance, she turned and walked toward Cate, who had witnessed the entire scene. "Come along," she whispered, placing her hand on her daughter's shoulder and guiding her toward the house.

"What's wrong with those Englische?" Cate asked, her voice wavering. Rosanna had never seen such an expression of fear on her daughter's face. It upset her almost as much as the display of anger from her neighbors.

"They're *ferhoodled*," Rosanna finally said, resorting to simply calling them confused for lack of a better explanation.

"Are all Englische like that?"

Rosanna glanced over her shoulder and saw that Camille was mocking her, imitating Rosanna's shocked expression to her mother. The thought of two people behaving in such a manner stunned Rosanna, and she felt a wave of pity for them. "I don't know, Cate. I just don't know."

It was a growing problem with the Englische, the ever-increasing importance they placed on the individual's rights, even when they conflicted with the collective whole. Rights over duty, Rosanna thought as she guided her daughter toward the house and away from those awful people. Jesus had instructed His followers to do unto others. The Golden Rule. He had clearly made it the duty of the individual to ensure that all rights were respected and that no one had more entitlement than another.

"Come, Cate," she said softly, hoping to distract her daughter's attention to something else. "Let's make those flyers for the neighbors, *ja*? The ones for Fannie Miller's clothing donations? Then you can distribute them in the morning after chores. I'll be at market, so it will give you something to do to pass the day. Something good to forget the . . ."—she hesitated, trying to find the right word—"the un-Christian behavior of others."

Cate nodded, walking faster to keep up with Rosanna.

"And we can pray for them, too," Rosanna added. "They must be very unhappy people. They need God in their life. Prayer would do them good and make us feel better, I'm sure."

At this, Cate bristled. "Won't make *me* feel any better, no how!"

Rosanna knew she should scold her, but she couldn't find it in herself. Even though Rosanna would pray for Gloria and Camille, it was only because she knew it was the Christian thing to do. Her heart would not truly be in it, but it was her duty to pray for those two misguided people.

Rosanna and Cate spent the next hour seated at the kitchen table, their heads bent as they wrote with big blue markers on white paper: Clothing Donations Wanted for Quilting. Rosanna wrote their address underneath the words, which were evenly spaced and neatly written. Cate copied the flyer, her handwriting not as smooth and her lines a bit lopsided. Still, she didn't complain once, not even when Rosanna took a moment to pray for the Smiths.

"Oh help," Rosanna mumbled. The clock on the wall had chimed eight times. "You need to be getting to bed soon, *dochder*."

"Aaron hasn't come in yet," Cate began to protest.

Rosanna capped her pen and set it onto the last flyer that she had printed. Leveling her eyes at Cate, she shook her head. "Never you mind about Aaron." She had heard the buggy leave shortly after the altercation with the neighbors. "Besides, tomorrow's Friday, and I have to fill in for Annie Yoder at market again."

Cate did not argue further, but Rosanna could hear her grumble under her breath. She got up from the table and shuffled barefoot across the floor toward the stairs. Rosanna watched her for a moment, her eyes lingering on her back.

For a short while, Rosanna sat alone in the silent kitchen, staring at the empty staircase. Cate was growing more willful by the day, something that Rosanna would have to address well before the girl turned sixteen. While she knew that Cate's behavior was a defense mechanism, she also knew that it would not sit well with others in the church district. After attending a series of baptism meetings during worship service, all potential members needed to be voted into the district. A young woman with the reputation of being strong willed risked having to take the instructional twice. And their church district, being led by Bishop Smucker and the three preachers, was particularly strict when compared to others.

Shaking her head, Rosanna returned her attention to the flyers. Cate's were scattered on the table, the marker left uncapped. With a sigh, Rosanna reached for the papers and stacked them neatly atop hers. She knew that she'd have to remind Cate to distribute them in the morning. Perhaps, she thought, Aaron might go with her.

Rosanna moved to the sofa to embroider while she waited for Aaron to come home. She wanted to speak to him. She must have drifted to sleep, because she awoke to the door opening. The needle had fallen from her hand onto her lap, and the linen rested by her side.

"You all right, then, *Maem?*"

With the pale light of dusk filling the room, everything in the kitchen and sitting area appeared dark, almost an eerie blue. "Don't turn on the light," she said. "I'm headed to bed. I just fell asleep here."

He crossed the room in four easy strides and sat down in Reuben's recliner. She didn't want him to worry, not about her. This was his running around time, the time to have fun with his friends. The last thing her son needed was to be burdened with her problems and anxieties.

"You have fun tonight?" Rosanna asked.

Aaron hesitated, as if taken aback by her casual tone. "Why are they so angry?"

Rosanna reached up to rub her temples. "*Ach*, Aaron," she sighed. "I don't want to talk about them. I'd much rather hear about your night. You're home early."

Now it was his turn to sigh. "I don't know which is worse . . . our neighbors or that Nan!"

"Nan?" Startled by the change of subject, or perhaps merely by the topic itself, Rosanna sat up and stared at her son.

"I went to the youth group," he said. "We met at Amos's place."

"Troyer?"

In the dark, he nodded. "*Ja*, Amos Troyer." He remained silent for a moment. She could sense the intensity of his emotions. When he finally took a deep breath, she braced herself for whatever he intended to tell her. "Nan showed up. At first she kept talking about the harness shop." He paused, and she could sense his anger. "*Maem*, she told everyone that she's Reuben's second-in-command and that she's in charge when he's not there. Why, you should have seen Daniel's face!"

"Daniel was there, then?" Rosanna asked.

"*Ja*, he was. He left shortly after she started bragging so much." Aaron emphasized the word "bragging" in a tone of disgust. For Aaron, her child who never complained, to comment on someone else's behavior spoke volumes about how inappropriate Nan must have been. "Why, I couldn't believe the things that she said, *Maem*! And so unappreciative of all that you have done for her."

"Me?"

In the increasing darkness, Rosanna saw him nod. "You and Reuben. She even commented on how messy the shop was. And the *haus*!"

Rosanna trembled as she tried to calm herself.

Aaron seemed to sense Rosanna's increasing anxiety and immediately softened his tone. "I know you went and cleaned that house for her and her *bruder*. Rebecca told me how Nan barely helped you." He leaned forward and reached out to touch her knee. "You need to stop giving so much to other people. Givers need to receive, too."

"Helping others is the Christian way—" Rosanna started.

Aaron interrupted her. "Jesus said to teach a man to fish is better than merely providing the fish."

"He also said to help the needy," she countered.

"Bah! She's not needy. She's boastful . . . thinks too highly of herself, for sure and certain!"

"She's been through a lot. She lost both of her parents, after all." Rosanna could hardly believe that she was defending Nan. Still, it wasn't in her nature to judge others or to speak unkindly of them. "Let no corrupting talk come out of your mouths, but only such as is good for building up, as fits the occasion, that it may give grace to those who hear."

Once again, Aaron scoffed. "I'm talking to my *maem*." He leaned back in the chair and ran his fingers through his hair. The remaining light from the window behind him hid his features, but she could see the silhouette of his wild mass of unruly curls. "But it gets worse. She started flirting with Elijah and then with Abe!"

Rosanna frowned, thankful for the cloak of darkness that hid her expression. Flirting? That wasn't something Amish women did very often. In fact, Rosanna couldn't remember witnessing one instance of anyone outright flirting with a man. "Are you sure, Aaron?"

"I'm sure, *Maem*. I was standing right there. Why, she even whispered in Elijah's ear, asking him to take her home in his buggy."

"Oh help."

"That's right! The shop and her *haus* are right next to the Troyers' farm. He didn't even know how to respond and walked away from her. That's when she moved on to Abe. I saw her hanging on his arm like . . . like . . ." Good-hearted Aaron couldn't finish the sentence. He didn't have to continue. Rosanna suspected she knew what he was avoiding saying.

"I'm not certain how to respond to this news," she admitted. While Nan wasn't her problem, she suddenly worried that if word of her behavior traveled the Amish grapevine, it could reflect poorly on Reuben. "I will confess that I'm a little surprised. She doesn't seem to be that sort of woman."

"According to Daniel, Nan acts different at the shop when Reuben's around. When he leaves, she's awful bossy and just down-right mean."

Contemptible behavior seemed to be running rampant these days, Rosanna thought.

The last thing Rosanna wanted to do was burden Reuben with this. Anyway, there was nothing she could do about it right now—she had to leave the house early for market. And on Saturday she needed to bake in the morning before she visited the old folks' home with a group of women from church in the afternoon. Even though Sunday was an off day with no worship service for their *g'may*, Reuben would use the day to rest. She certainly wouldn't want to discuss Aaron's story with Reuben then.

"Best keep this between us for now," Rosanna said. "I'll try to speak with Reuben about all this. Find a way to let him know, I reckon."

"Sooner rather than later," Aaron said as he stood up. "At the rate she's storming the youth group, the bishop will catch wind of her behavior in no time."

No doubt, Rosanna thought as she listened to the echo of her son's heavy footsteps on the hardwood stairs in the darkness. For a few long minutes, she sat alone once again. The last thing she needed was another problem to deal with. Between helping Annie Yoder and the visit to the elderly, she had enough to do over the next two days. Now, knowing that Reuben might have a problem brewing at the shop, Rosanna's heart felt overburdened. If only she could share it. She had always taught her children that a load is lighter when many hands lift it. It was just one more philosophy that she preached without practicing.

Sighing, she made her way through the darkness to the bedroom. She knew it was almost nine; the clock would certainly chime soon. But despite having to arise so early in the morning and the long day that awaited her, she knew that she wouldn't sleep. With so much on her mind, anxiety would once again rule the night.

# CHAPTER TEN

On Tuesday, after morning chores were finished, Rosanna used the kick scooter to visit Reuben at the shop. Since his workload had picked up so much, he no longer came home for the noon meal, and so she thought she'd bring him some dinner.

At first she'd been surprised by how little he'd been home recently, as this was the time of year when work was typically slower. Reuben had attributed the increase of business to the rising cost of gasoline. It hindered the Amish from hiring drivers, and the long distances they had to travel by buggy were wearing on the horses' harnesses.

Rosanna, however, had learned that someone else had laid claim to being the source of demand for Reuben's goods.

The previous Friday morning, Rosanna had been heading to the market in the van with the other Amish. As she rode in the back, Rosanna praised God several times that this was her last Friday covering for Annie Yoder. Apparently gasoline hadn't been too expensive for the Yoders to travel out west to visit family!

During the first leg of the trip, Jonah Yoder, a distant cousin of Annie's husband, had commented to Rosanna, "Met that young woman managing Reuben's shop. Sure seems lively, that one."

Rosanna was quick to correct him. "She's not managing the shop. Just working the front desk."

"That so?" Reaching up, he scratched the bare skin under his nose. "Heard it's been awful busy in there."

"Lots of orders, *ja*," Rosanna agreed.

"Heard from that woman . . . what's her name . . . yet?" he asked, trying to recall it.

"Nan," she responded drily.

He nodded. "That's it. Nan told me she's been doing extra marketing these past few weeks, drumming up the business and all." He gazed off into the distance, unaware that Rosanna felt as if the wind had been knocked from her lungs. "Shame she can't do the same for my *daed's* wood shop."

Rosanna didn't respond. She knew that it was better to silence her tongue than to speak evil.

Over the weekend, Jonah's words echoed in her ears. With Reuben working long hours, he seemed to talk less and sleep more whenever he was home. On Sunday she'd caught him asleep on the porch, his Bible on his lap and his mouth open while he dozed. She didn't wake him for supper, but covered a plate so the flies wouldn't get on his food and left it on the counter. But when he finally woke, he merely shuffled into the bedroom and crawled into bed.

By Tuesday she had decided to take a ride down to the shop to find out what exactly was happening there. If Nan was spreading stories of her grandiose business acumen and taking credit for an increase in sales, Rosanna wanted to see firsthand if it was true.

After leaning the scooter against the side of the shop, she smoothed down her freshly laundered black apron and made certain the hem of her green dress was straightened. No sense in visiting if she didn't look proper, she thought as she reached for the basket of food and headed for the shop's front door.

When she entered, the voice that greeted her was not her husband's.

"Rosanna!" Nan said with a forced smile. She walked around the counter and extended her hand. "How *wunderbar* to see you!"

Shaking the proffered hand, Rosanna returned the smile. Manners count, she reminded herself. "*Danke*, Nan. You, too." Her eyes skimmed the room, searching for Reuben. Instead, she saw Daniel bent over the cutting equipment while Rebecca and Martin worked at the loud sewing machines. Somewhere back there was Reuben's desk, but Rosanna could tell that he wasn't there. Disappointed, she returned her attention to Nan, who watched her expectantly. "Reuben's not here, then?"

"*Nee*, Rosanna." She reached for some papers, shuffling them on the countertop. The crisp noise strung Rosanna's ears, almost as much as Nan's next words. "He took a ride over to Peter Miller's farm in Strasburg."

"Strasburg!" That was too far to travel by horse and buggy. Certainly he had hired a driver. "Whatever for?"

At this question, Nan beamed. "Peter's a cousin of Jake Miller. Reuben went out to deliver a new harness."

Jake Miller? He had hosted the worship service just two weeks ago. Like most Amish, he had extensive family throughout Lancaster County. Still, any relatives that lived in Strasburg were most likely distant, both in miles as well as familiarity. "Why wouldn't Jake's cousin use a local harness maker?" And since when, she wanted to add, did Reuben deliver new harnesses?

From the expression on Nan's face, Rosanna knew that she'd asked the exact question that was anticipated. Nan lit up, and she straightened her shoulders, grinning as she did so. "I talked with Becca Miller after worship service. Was telling her about how the Troyer Harness Shop has the best harnesses I've seen, even after working at my *daed's* shop in New York! She must have told her husband."

Feeling as if she had walked into a trap, Rosanna tried not to let her emotions show. After all, it was good that Nan promoted the business, she told herself. But deep in her heart, Rosanna didn't feel like rejoicing at the younger woman's enthusiasm. Nan's pride felt dirty to Rosanna, like a pile of laundry that was long overdue a good washing. She wouldn't go so far as to call it sinister, for that implied evil, but she felt as if a foreboding cloud hung over Nan's words. Something was amiss. Rosanna just couldn't figure out what.

"That's awfully kind of you, Nan," Rosanna said, forcing each word. "And to think, it's only been . . . what? . . . four weeks?" She knew the words implied how novice Nan was, but she'd pray for God's forgiveness later. Only Jesus was perfect, she reminded herself.

Nan didn't seem to notice the undertone of sarcasm in Rosanna's voice. Instead, she grinned even wider, if that was possible. "The opportunities here are endless!" she gushed. "And I'm learning so much!"

Was it possible that harness making in New York differed so much from Lancaster, Pennsylvania? Rosanna wanted to ask, but knew that she shouldn't and wouldn't. One sin was enough for the day. "Learning is *gut*," she managed to say. She started to walk around the counter, the basket of food still on her arm. If nothing else, she could leave Reuben's dinner on his desk so that he knew she had stopped by and had been thinking of him.

Rebecca looked up as Rosanna paused by the big oak desk. Her large green eyes lit up and she smiled. "Why Rosanna!" She stopped working and sat back in her padded chair. "So *gut* to see you!" There was something joyous about her face, cherubic in appearance and angelic in nature.

Rosanna returned the greeting.

"I never did thank you for the other weekend," Rebecca said softly, her eyes flickering to the floor. "I meant to send you a note to say how nice it was to visit."

Rosanna felt a presence behind her. Without turning around, she knew that Nan stood there, lurking and listening.

"Oh dear me!" Nan said, waiting until Rosanna looked at her to wring her hands apologetically. "I've been working so much that I forgot, too!"

Her words sounded as contrived as her sorrowful expression. Rosanna forced herself to lift a hand, a gesture meant to calm both of them. "Never you mind," she reassured them. "It was our pleasure to have you." Another smile, only this one was directed at Rebecca. "Sharing fellowship with others is always a welcomed treat," she added.

She couldn't leave the shop fast enough. As she pushed the kick scooter toward home, her mind reeled. Call it women's intuition or a basic gut instinct, but Rosanna knew that something was not quite right about Nan. On the surface she seemed pleasant enough, but there was a dark and disturbing shine in her chocolate-brown eyes that concerned Rosanna—especially when Nan talked about the business. And the changes in Reuben? Anxiety welled inside Rosanna's chest, and she focused on taking a few deep breaths to calm herself.

Mayhaps, she thought as she passed by the street that led home, it was time to pay a quick visit to Mary King.

As soon as the thought struck her, Rosanna felt a new sense of confidence. Just the other week, when Rosanna had been visiting Mary King and her cousin, Barbara Glick, hadn't Mary indicated some familiarity with a Keel family from New York? While she hadn't offered any information about them, she had certainly recognized the name. Maybe Mary would feel more comfortable disclosing what she knew about the Keels from New York if Rosanna shared her feelings of discomfort about Nan.

The Kings lived two streets past Rosanna's farm. Mary King was spry and lively, quick to laugh at private jokes, but also the first one to shake her head when she heard gossip. Approaching her to disclose anything about the Keel family would not be a simple task.

"Rosanna Troyer, so right *gut* to see you," Mary said when she opened the door, surprised to see her unexpected visitor. "This isn't your normal visiting day!"

"Was riding home from Reuben's shop," Rosanna said as she entered the small house. "Thought I'd swing by to visit a spell."

"I'm right glad you did! Barbie's visiting her *dochder* in New Holland. Awful quiet around here when she's gone." She gestured toward her sitting area just to the side of the kitchen. "Go sit, Rosanna. I'll fetch some meadow tea!"

As Rosanna entered the room, she looked around. It was always tidy and clean, with the smell of furniture polish in the air. She made her way to one of the recliners and sat down, realizing that the room was hot. Without the windows open, the air hung heavy. "It's terrible hot in here, Mary. Shall I open the windows for you, then?"

The elderly woman glanced up from where she stood at the counter, pouring her homemade tea into two glasses. She seemed to contemplate the closed windows, a frown on her face as she realized that she had been suffering needlessly. "Oh help," Mary muttered. "I thought I had opened them earlier!"

She laughed, more to herself than to Rosanna. Without waiting, Mary shuffled across the floor and, with a firm hand, flung open the windows, clearly indicating that she did not need Rosanna's assistance. "Wondered why it was so stuffy in here!"

Rosanna watched as Mary hustled back to her recliner. She had been reading the *Budget* newspaper, a battery-operated light shining on the table next to the chair to help her see. A pair of reader glasses rested upon the folded paper. The lenses, smudged with fingerprints, certainly made it hard for Mary to see through them. Without thinking, Rosanna reached over, picked up the glasses, and wiped the lenses with her apron.

Mary chuckled as she sat down. "Always thinking of others now, aren't you, Rosanna?"

Surprised, Rosanna looked up. She hadn't even realized what she had done. Embarrassed, she set down the glasses and tried to shrug off her kind gesture. "No more than others," she mumbled.

"*Ja, vell*, remember one thing," Mary said, wagging a finger at her guest. "An empty cup cannot give!"

Her words caused Rosanna a moment's pause. Most days, that was exactly how she felt . . . like an empty cup. Each morning she woke up and prayed for God's blessing and to renew her commitment to live a godly life that centered on Christ as her savior. She always felt refreshed then, but slowly, throughout the day, her cup began to empty. With each request for help or demand from her family and friends, she felt increasingly hollow until, at the end of each day, she was, indeed, a shell of the woman she wanted to be.

The silence rang in her ears.

Too much time passed without a response. Mary stared at her with an intensity that made a wave of heat rush to Rosanna's cheeks. She flushed and chewed on her lower lip. Mary continued staring at her. Her face was wrinkled with age, and there was a profound sense of wisdom about her. The mother of nine children, all but one who had joined the Amish church, Mary had worked hard to raise those children and then help with her grandchildren.

As if reading her mind, Mary leaned forward and wagged her wizened finger at Rosanna. "I know a thing or two, Rosanna Troyer," she said, a mischievous lilt to her voice. "You weren't just stopping by to see me. Something is amiss, and I bet I know what this visit is about!"

That was unexpected and caught Rosanna off guard. "You do?"

"I can see it in your face," Mary said, leaning back in the recliner. "You're worried that Reuben won't make a *gut daed*!"

"He is a *gut daed*," Rosanna replied, quickly jumping to the defense of her husband. "He treats Aaron and Cate quite well. Why, just the month past he bought a horse for Aaron, and he takes Cate to work with him, which she loves."

Mary pursed her lips and shook her head. "I meant to the new *boppli*!"

At this, Rosanna made a face, worried that the older woman might be getting addled in the brain. "Whose new *boppli*?"

"Yours!" Mary laughed. "You thought you could hide it, but us old-timers can tell." She reached down and, with a swift gesture, pulled the handle so that the chair reclined and the footrest popped up. "Could see it in your eyes at our last gathering, and during the last worship service, I saw you sneaking out!"

Is that what people thought? Morning sickness? Rosanna exhaled, quickly trying to think of how to approach this new twist to her visit. Honesty, her *maem* had always told her. Be upfront and honest. "I'm not having a *boppli*," she said softly. "That's not why I came to visit."

Mary blinked as if she hadn't heard Rosanna.

"I came because I wanted to ask what you know about the Keels from New York," Rosanna admitted.

"The Keels?" Mary seemed taken aback. "That's what this is about?"

Rosanna nodded her head.

The older woman looked disappointed. Clearly she had thought she knew something that others did not.

While it had given Rosanna the opening she needed to ask about the Keels, her question had caught Mary off guard. "Why would you think I know anything about the Keels?"

"When I mentioned where Reuben's new employee, Nan, was from, you seemed to respond." Rosanna paused, watching Mary's reaction. "As if you, mayhaps, recognized the family name?"

For a long, drawn-out moment, Mary said nothing. She tapped her finger against the arm of the chair, contemplating her answer. With narrow eyes, she stared into the distance before looking at Rosanna and clicking her tongue. "Gossip is evil," she started. Before Rosanna could say anything, Mary held up her hand. "So I won't ask why you might want to know, and I won't say anything more than what I know."

Rosanna waited for Mary to continue. If only Mary would ask, Rosanna would gratefully unburden herself by telling the older woman of the pain she felt, the pain that weighed on her shoulders from worry and stress. The weight of the burden that was so heavy that Rosanna had begun to walk slightly hunched over. Between Gloria's animosity and Nan's stories of ambitious—and possibly fictitious—advancement, Rosanna knew that she no longer had the strength to suffer silently.

But she sat in silence, waiting.

Finally, after moistening her lips, Mary spoke. "I've never been to this community of Amish, but I know of them through my cousin, Susan." She looked at Rosanna from the corner of her eyes. "You know Susan, *ja*? Melvin's Susan?"

Rosanna shook her head.

"From Ephrata?" Mary seemed genuinely disappointed when she realized that Rosanna didn't know her cousin. Dropping her hand back into her lap, she frowned and exhaled sharply, a short little puff of air to express her exasperation. "*Ja, vell*, anyway . . . Susan and I were in the same youth group. Another one of the girls, Lydia Huber, married a young man from that Conewango Valley area. He had been here visiting a cousin, I seem to recall." She paused, blinking rapidly as if something was caught in her eye. "That was many years ago, Rosanna."

Rosanna nodded, understanding that Mary's memory of people and places from so long ago might be inaccurate.

For a long moment, Mary seemed to stare over Rosanna's shoulder, as if searching for details that had been long forgotten. "Ah," she said, lifting her hand and pointing her finger in the air. "*Ja*, I wouldn't have remembered anything about that girl, that Lydia Huber . . . but last winter . . . I think it was February . . . I went to a quilting bee. Not that these old eyes can see so well anymore." She laughed. "*Ja*, a quilting bee when I last saw Susan. She mentioned that Lydia had a daughter who died. An accident."

Rosanna sat up straighter in her chair.

"Said there were two grandchildren." Mary leveled her eyes at Rosanna. "I never knew their names, mind you. But Susan was concerned over Lydia's health, seeing that she was upset over the loss of her daughter, and one of the grandchildren was creating a ruckus over something. I didn't think to ask no more about it, seeing that would be gossip and all."

"What does this have to do with Nan Keel?" Rosanna asked.

Mary rolled her eyes and shook her head. "Oh, Rosanna. Do I have to spell it out for you? Lydia's grandchildren are Keels."

It took a moment for the words to sink in, for their meaning to unfold in Rosanna's mind. "I thought that Nan's parents both died in the accident . . ."

Mary shook her head. "*Nee*, ain't so. The *maem* died in the accident. The *daed* died afterward, after quite some time in the hospital."

"Oh," Rosanna said, her lips pursed. She felt as if the wind had been knocked from her lungs. Why would Nan have misguided everyone about the accident? Was there a reason to hide her *daed's* hospital stay? "I see."

"Your question answered?" Mary asked.

Rosanna wasn't certain, but she suspected that something was amiss with Nan's story. There were inconsistencies between what Nan had shared with her and Reuben and what Mary had just told her. Rosanna didn't want to say as much to Mary. "You've told me what you know," Rosanna managed to say. "That's all I can ask for, *ja*?"

"That's for sure and certain," Mary laughed, but when Rosanna didn't even smile, Mary tilted her head and studied her face. "You look tired, Rosanna. Something else bothering you, then?"

It felt good to finally have someone interested in what she had on her mind. "Been having some issues with the neighbor behind the farm," Rosanna said. "Constantly yelling and screaming at us." She paused reflectively. "Mostly me, and now Cate some."

Mary disapprovingly clicked her tongue against her teeth and shook her head. "Those Englische . . . tsk-tsk."

"And she's just so mean about everything. I even tried to make peace with them, brought over my first batch of ripe tomatoes."

"You did that?" Then Mary gave a soft smile. "Of course you did. I shouldn't even be surprised!"

"And not even so much as a thank you."

"My word!" Mary spoke in a breathless voice that indicated her disapproval.

Rosanna sighed. "I'm about at my wit's end." For a moment Rosanna felt bitter tears sting at the corners of her eyes. But she refused to shed any over that woman. "Even made Cate cry the other day."

"Cate?" Mary sounded surprised. Everyone in their community knew that Cate was not prone to fits or tears.

"*Ja*, Cate! The woman even covered the property line with a green tarp because she claimed the dog tried to chew through the fence. Her daughter was after us, too. I thought she might even try to get physical at one point."

Mary gasped and put her hand over her heart. "Oh help!"

"I just don't know what to do."

"You *are* handling a lot, Rosanna Troyer," Mary acknowledged. "Best be turning that particular situation over to God, I suppose."

Rosanna knew that she was right.

"And your Reuben sure does work long hours at the shop," Mary continued. "I heard from my sister Miriam that Reuben's been hiring a driver to go pick up items for repair at farms so that the farmers don't have to leave." She raised an eyebrow. "He went all the way to Manheim to get Miriam's son's harness that broke. Fixed it right on the spot."

Driving to Manheim to repair items? Delivering new purchases to Strasburg? Rosanna's mouth fell open. Hiring drivers was expensive because they charged by the mile. If Reuben was driving to help all of these farmers, he was certainly spending just as much as he was making, especially adding in the expense of Nan's salary.

"Bless his heart," Mary said. "Such a *gut* man to care so much about the community. Always doing so much for the sake of others. He was a good husband to Rachel and also to Grace, even when she wasn't always so kind to him, especially after she fell ill."

"I hadn't heard about this." Rosanna had not asked about his first two wives, nor had Reuben offered any information.

"Brain tumors. Made her moody and irritable." She clicked her tongue as she shook her head. "He took right *gut* care of her up to the end. Never did think he'd marry again." She smiled, a gentle smile that almost made Rosanna's cheeks turn pink.

After another fifteen minutes, Rosanna reluctantly excused herself. With a promise to visit Mary again the following week, she left for home. Time had slipped away from her, and she was leaving later than she expected. By the time she got home, she'd need to start the afternoon chores and begin to prepare supper. If Reuben had traveled so much during the day, Rosanna knew better than to expect him home much before six o'clock. But at least that would give her time to make certain that everything was especially clean and quiet for him to relax after such a long day.

The conversation with Mary had raised more questions than it had provided answers for Rosanna. As she made her way home, the rear wheel of the push scooter squeaking as it glided along the road, thoughts whirled through her mind.

Rosanna knew that Reuben loved being in the shop. Why then, she wondered, was he spending so much time away from it? His original idea to hire Nan so that he could spend more time at home seemed forgotten as he worked on new orders and dealt with new customers. From what she had seen at the shop earlier today, Rosanna suspected he was being encouraged by Nan.

As she rounded a bend on the road near the farm, Rosanna saw someone coming toward her pushing a stroller. Thoughts of Nan and Reuben immediately disappeared when she recognized Gloria. There was no way to prevent the two women from passing each other. Swallowing her fear and trying to ignore the panic that welled inside her chest, Rosanna said a quick prayer for a peaceful encounter.

*Speak to her,* a voice said in her head. *Be the good Christian.*

Rosanna somehow found the strength to cross the road and approach her neighbor. She lifted her hand in a slight wave to indicate that she wanted to talk. Gloria stopped walking and eyed Rosanna with suspicion. On neutral territory, Rosanna felt a little less threatened.

"It's a nice day for a walk," she heard herself say. When Gloria didn't reply, Rosanna took a deep breath and continued, diving right to the point. "Might I have a word with you?"

Gloria raised an eyebrow and reached into a pocket in the back of the stroller for her pack of cigarettes.

"I don't want to have disagreements with you, Gloria," Rosanna said, amazed at how calm her voice sounded. The strength she displayed was not mirrored inside her. "I'd like to have peace."

"Peace," Gloria said with no emotion. Rosanna had the distinct feeling that the older woman was playing with the word, rolling it around in her mouth in a mocking sort of way.

"I . . . we will keep the dogs away from the back garden. I'll have Aaron put up a better fence to keep them out, if that would help." She paused as if waiting for Gloria to say something. "And Cate will play with them in the other fields."

"That one dog is dangerous!"

"Jack?" Rosanna almost laughed, but her nerves were rapidly unraveling. She didn't like confrontation. Nor did she like having to defend her family, even if it was just one of the dogs. "Why, he's the sweetest of them all. Mayhaps I might ask Aaron to bring him over so you could see for yourself."

"No!" Gloria lit her cigarette and made no attempt to blow the smoke away from Rosanna. "We're trying to teach the baby to stay away from dogs. She's too curious, and it's dangerous."

Rosanna wanted to tell Gloria that teaching her grandchild to be afraid of dogs seemed overprotective, but she knew better than to speak those words out loud. If memory served Rosanna properly, over the years Gloria's daughter had repeatedly brought dogs to the house. They never let the dogs outside, except on a leash, and they usually disappeared after six months or so. No one ever asked where they went. Rosanna could only speculate.

"I haven't seen the dog near the fence as of late," Rosanna managed to say. "But like I said, we'll continue keeping them away from the garden and back pasture."

"See that you do!" Gloria flicked her cigarette so that the ashes dropped to the ground, not caring that some fell on Rosanna's shoe. Without another word, she turned and continued walking.

A hollow feeling filled Rosanna's chest.

Sure enough, when Reuben finally returned that evening, he looked tired and worn out. Rosanna had sent Cate to a neighboring Amish family to visit with their daughters and bring them a rhubarb pie. Everything was quiet and peaceful, just the way she knew Reuben liked it.

She wanted to ask him about Manheim and Strasburg, but she knew better than to say anything if he didn't offer. He'd tell her when he was ready, and like an understanding wife, she would honor that.

"I'm going to lie down, Rosanna," he sighed as he got up from his recliner. She glanced at the window. The sun hadn't even set yet. "I'm just exhausted."

In the silence of the house, Rosanna focused on her embroidery. It helped the time pass and kept her mind from racing with questions and thoughts that she didn't want to think. When the room was engulfed in shadows, she got up and turned on the propane to the overhead lamp. A loud hissing noise filled the silence. She struck a match against the strike pad on the wall and lit the lantern. Immediately the shadows disappeared, and a brilliant light made the room look as if it were midday.

Outside, one of the dogs barked at an approaching buggy. She lifted her head and looked out the window. With the sun dipping toward the horizon and the sky a mixture of red and orange, the day was winding to an end. She wondered who would be visiting at this hour. Certainly Aaron hadn't already returned from seeing his friends.

Stepping outside of the house, Rosanna squinted as she tried to see who was driving the buggy. Only when the door slid open did she recognize John Esh, her friend Elizabeth's husband. Barely pausing to hitch the horse to the rail by the barn, he hurried toward the house. Clearly this was not going to be a long visit.

"What's wrong, John?" she called out.

At the sound of her voice, he lifted his head and looked at her. "Elias Beiler collapsed, and he's been rushed to the hospital."

Rosanna gasped. One of the preachers? "What happened?"

When John reached the bottom step of the porch, he removed his straw hat and drew his arm across his brow. "Can't say yet, Rosanna." With his receding hairline and thin gray beard, he looked older than he was. He had always been a tall, wiry young man with a calm and quiet temperament, the complete opposite of Elizabeth, who was lively and laughed a lot. "Mayhaps a heart attack. He'd been having pains recently."

Stunned, Rosanna wasn't certain what to say. She knew Elias's wife, Lydia, would be with him at the hospital. All of their children were grown and married, so there were no *kinner* to tend. Still, she felt that she should do something.

"Shall I get Reuben, then?" She gestured toward the house. "He's just lying down a spell."

John shook his head. "*Nee.* Just wanted to alert you about the preacher so that you folks can pray for him."

"Of course."

"I best be going," he said quickly. "Need to tell others, *ja*?" He nodded before turning to leave.

Long after his buggy left, Rosanna stood there staring at the sky. Even though Elias Beiler was an older man, the thought that he might have suffered a heart attack was still shocking. Her hand crept to her chest, where she could feel her heart beneath her dress, beating as rhythmically as a horse's hooves on the road. The news worried her. She, too, had been feeling poorly recently: stressed, worried, and emotional. How often had she felt pain in her chest when her heart beat too fast? Her blood seemed to course so rapidly that it hurt.

## Chapter Eleven

"*Maem*," Aaron called through the screen door. His voice sounded panicky; there was a sense of urgency to it. "You best come quick."

Rosanna had just lain down on her bed, her head pounding with what she thought might be a migraine. With the shades drawn and a cool cloth on her head, she had shut her eyes and hoped for a few minutes of quiet. Now what? she thought. Removing the washcloth, she set it on the nightstand, not caring that it would leave a wet mark. She'd deal with that later. Her bare feet hit the wood floor, and she stood up. Little white lights flickered in the corners of her eyes, and she steadied herself by placing a hand against the wall.

"*Maem!*"

"I'm coming," she called back, trying to hide her irritation at being disturbed. Thirty minutes, she thought as she shuffled her feet and moved toward the door. Just thirty minutes to try to get rid of this headache.

The pain in her temples worsened with each step. She didn't need this right now. She needed to rest. Ever since her encounter with their neighbor Gloria on Monday, she had had a constant lump in her throat and felt as if she might get physically ill at any minute. Her stomach ached, and her appetite had vanished. In four days, she had lost enough weight that she had to shift the spot where she pinned the front of her dress.

By the time she made it to the screen door, she realized that Aaron was not alone. Two tall men in police uniforms stood next to him. Over their shoulders, she could see the police car parked right in front of the garden, its red lights rotating.

She swallowed hard as she realized that this was not a social visit. When it involved the police, it never was. The angle at which the car was parked made it visible to the neighbors bordering the back of the property as well as anyone passing along the road by their mailbox. She looked in the direction of the Smith house, and sure enough, she could make out the forms of Gloria and her daughter standing on their porch and watching. Rosanna felt a deep wave of nausea.

"Mrs. Zook?"

"Troyer," she corrected the officer, her voice unsteady. The only other time police had visited her property had been on the day that Timothy died. "Is something wrong?"

One officer removed his hat. "Ma'am, we have a report that you have loose dogs."

Her eyes flickered from the two officers to Aaron, who stood there wide-eyed and pale, and then back to the officers. "Excuse me?"

"A complaint has been filed about your dogs," the other officer repeated, his gaze sharp and narrow. He shifted his weight and pulled his belt over his overextended waist. "Neighbors said they've been roaming in their yard and bit their child."

Aaron snorted and shook his head, averting his eyes. "Ridiculous," he mumbled.

"I have no idea what you're talking about," Rosanna managed to say. Her head felt light, and she leaned against the doorframe to steady herself. "We don't want any trouble here. The dogs have never left the property. It's fenced all the way around."

The first officer looked over his shoulder. "Might we have a look at the perimeter?"

Rosanna's hands began to shake. "I don't understand any of this." She looked at her son. "What is going on?"

"*Maem*, go back inside," Aaron said.

He placed his hand on her arm and started to guide her, but she shook away his grip, embarrassed by his gesture. "I'm fine." She didn't want to display weakness, not to her son and certainly not to Gloria. She just wished that Reuben was home. His support and wisdom would have removed the tension she felt in her shoulders.

The four of them began to walk along the driveway toward the garden. The three dogs were in the kennel outside the barn. When Cate wasn't home and playing with them, they were always in the kennel. Rosanna just didn't have time to keep an eye on them. One of the officers nudged the other and pointed in the direction of the kennel. The dogs barked twice then wagged their tails as if expecting to be let out.

The officers walked carefully between the rows of growing vegetables, and despite the larger one's gruff attitude, this display of respect did not go unnoticed. But when the distance increased between the officers and Rosanna, she noticed the guns hanging from their hips. Catching her breath, she grabbed Aaron's arm. She'd never seen a firearm before, and the sight of it startled her.

"It's going to be fine," Aaron whispered. "She's just mad and trying to harass us."

As they made their way toward the back of the property, Rosanna noticed all the weeds. She was embarrassed that her garden wasn't tidier, and she felt the color rise to her cheeks. Under normal circumstances there was nary a weed growing between the rows. This year, however, she had let them take over.

"What's this about?" The policeman gestured toward the green poles and tarp that bordered the back of the garden.

Rosanna maintained her silence. She suspected the question was rhetorical. Clearly both men could see that it was a makeshift privacy fence. The sight of it was embarrassing, as much for Gloria as for herself.

"There's a big hole in the fence," the other officer said. "Must be where the dog got out."

Immediately Rosanna's embarrassment disappeared. "Where is it?"

He pointed behind the growing corn. Sure enough, she saw a large hole in the wire fencing as well as in the tarp. Aaron beat her to it, kneeling to study the wire and blocking her view. She peered over his shoulder and caught her breath: The hole was large enough for a dog to get through, there was no arguing that.

"I was out here cutting the weeds the other day," she said, turning to the officers. "Friday, I think it was." She neglected to mention the incident with the neighbors. "And just Monday, my *dochder* was out here playing with the dogs. There was no hole here."

Aaron looked up at the police officers. "This was cut." He pointed to the wires. "From the other side."

The police officers knelt down to look closer at the hole. With the wires cleanly cut and bent backward, it was obvious that a dog had not chewed through the fence.

"Sure does seem that way, don't it?" the one officer said while the other stood up and began walking the fence line toward the horse pasture. Occasionally he bent over to check that there were no gaps or holes in the bottom where a dog could have crawled underneath.

"If it's that old woman living there—" Aaron began.

Rosanna shot him a look that warned him to be silent.

"Can't necessarily say who complained," the officer explained; however, the way his voice dropped at the end made it clear that Aaron was correct.

Aaron shook his head in disgust. "She's been yelling at my mother and sister whenever they're out here."

"No law against that, unfortunately," said the officer.

"Reckon there's no law against my sister playing with her dogs in the fields, either!"

"Aaron!" Rosanna was shocked at her son's words and harsh tone. "We want no trouble here, Officer. Just peace and to be left alone."

He smiled at her. "I understand, Mrs. Troyer."

The other officer returned from his inspection. "Everything appears fine to me," he said.

His partner leaned over and lowered his voice. "A neighbor dispute."

Rosanna clenched her jaw. She didn't like the way the two officers made it sound as if she, too, had contributed to the situation. "There's no dispute here. I just want to be left alone!"

The first officer held up his hand. "I've seen these situations before. Like I said, I understand. Neighbors can be tough to handle." He looked disdainfully at the Smiths' backyard, which was filled with garbage. There was also a pile of ashes and blackened grass. "We have a no-burn ordinance for houses. Only farms are permitted to burn debris."

The other officer raised an eyebrow. "Seems a summons might be in order for that."

Inwardly, Rosanna groaned. Certainly Gloria would blame her for that. Nothing was ever her responsibility. Her perception of the world was that everyone else had a problem. She never considered how her own behavior and toxic personality contributed to her misery.

"And that outbuilding there," the officer continued. "Sure is bigger than allowed by zoning without a permit. Wonder if they obtained one." He scribbled something on his notepad.

Out of the corner of her eye, Rosanna caught Aaron's smile. On the surface, she felt vindicated by the fact that her family had done nothing wrong, but she also knew that trouble was brewing. Any warnings or reprimands from the authorities would not sit well with Gloria Smith. They would just cause more animosity. Knowing how much ill will Gloria bore toward others made Rosanna feel that the end to this dangerous game was not even close. Forgiveness was simply not a word in Gloria's vocabulary.

"We just want to live in peace," Rosanna whispered again as they returned to the house.

Half an hour later, Rosanna finally made it back to her bedroom. This time, however, she knew she'd never be able to sleep. In the darkness of her room, she let the tears fall from her eyes. She was ashamed of herself for crying, but the deep pain in the center of her chest was overwhelming. Her breath grew short as she tried to silence the sobs coming from her mouth. It would do no good to concern Aaron if he heard her, she told herself.

She hated crying. Her mother had always told her that tears were for nonbelievers. A person with faith—true faith—would remember Isaiah 58:11: "The Lord will guide you always." Crying felt like admitting that she had lost faith that God would handle everything. She knew all she had to do was believe. She shut her eyes and prayed, prayed for God to take care of all the things that were bothering her. She turned her worries over to Him and prayed her gratitude for the blessings in her life.

She fell asleep praying.

# Chapter Twelve

His voice echoed in her head as she picked up the dirty plate and fork from the table by the recliner: *Cate needs to learn to clean up after herself.* Just the night before, Reuben had scowled as he watched Rosanna washing her daughter's ice cream dish.

The crumbs on this plate looked like blueberry pie. Cate didn't like blueberry pie. Neither did Aaron. In fact, Rosanna had made it for one person and one person only: Reuben. He must have awoken during the night again and come to the kitchen for a midnight snack. Like Cate, he had simply left the dirty plate behind—despite the fact that he had walked right past the sink to return to bed. Left it for her to clean up, Rosanna could only assume.

At least he had turned off the light, she thought bitterly.

She didn't know what was wrong with him. Lately he would walk into the house after a long day and not even bother to greet her with a smile or a kind word. Instead, he'd bark some command at her. While she knew that he was under pressure at the harness shop, she felt increasingly disheartened by his moods. After all, she worked, too.

It didn't matter, she said to herself. Once the kitchen was clean, she would have the house to herself and could spend some time alone. She needed that time. Her head was still spinning from yesterday's discussion with Mary King, the visit from the police, and then the news about Elias Beiler. Whenever she thought about Nan or the preacher, her heart began to beat rapidly, and she felt dizzy. Sometimes she even saw little lights flickering before her eyes. More than once she'd had to sit down to catch her breath while shutting her eyes and willing herself to calm down.

A doctor, she thought. I need to see a doctor. An Englische doctor.

Of course that meant making an appointment and hiring a driver. She knew that Reuben would be concerned and would insist on coming along, but then he'd have to miss work, and it was too busy right now, especially with the influx of orders from neighboring towns. It just wasn't practical for him to take time away from the shop right now. She didn't want to bother him. Anyway, she'd found out that sitting down and taking deep breaths made the palpitations disappear.

With a sigh, Rosanna pushed the thought of a doctor out of her mind.

Her last chore of the day was to stake the tomato plants in the garden. She had torn up some old rags to use for tying the plants to the wooden stakes. With the rags shoved into her apron pocket, she headed to the back of the barn to grab a rubber mallet and her stakes. Year after year, she reused the same stakes: tall green metal rods that Timothy had purchased at an auction. Despite the fact that the rods were so heavy, she managed to carry them out to the tomato patch in only two trips.

No sooner had she started pounding the first stake in the ground—the soft thud of the mallet against the rod reverberating in the still air—than she sensed someone watching her. Without even looking up, Rosanna knew that it was either Gloria or Camille.

Ignore them, she told herself. Wasn't that what Reuben had instructed them to do? Ignore them as if they weren't even there.

Quickly she tied an almost-two-foot-tall tomato plant to the rod. She pinched off the young shoots at the bottom of the stem, knowing that this would help the plant grow faster. Then she moved on to the next one. Rosanna could still feel the presence of someone on the other side of the fence. She began to silently repeat the Lord's Prayer. *Our Father, who art in heaven,* she prayed. *Hallowed be Thy name.* The second rod was positioned properly; she tied it and pinched the stems so that she could move to the next plant. *Thy kingdom come. Thy will be done.* The mallet slipped from her hand and landed in the dirt. Someone laughed from the other side of the fence. As she reached for the mallet, she noticed that her hands were shaking. *On earth as it is in heaven.*

By the time she finished tying up the third plant, she felt a familiar tightness in her chest. Out of the corner of her eye, she saw Camille dumping sticks over the fence into the garden. Rosanna paused for a moment, but Reuben's words echoed through her head: *ignore . . . ignore . . . ignore . . .*

Why were those two women so hateful? She concentrated on her breathing, trying to slow down the increasing rate of her heart. Did they dislike her family or Amish people in general? Rosanna had witnessed many instances of Englische acting poorly toward the Amish. Just last year Aaron had been using the kick scooter to visit his cousin three miles away when a passenger in a beat-up-looking car flicked a burning cigarette at him.

Rosanna reminded herself that for every horrible person, there were a hundred kind Englische. Most tourists treated the Amish with respect and honored their wishes not to take photographs of their families. Many of the Englische who lived in neighborhoods that bordered Amish farms were caring and considerate. But something had triggered hate in the hearts of the Smith family.

"I saw what you did," Camille called out to her. From the smell, Rosanna knew that Gloria was there too, sucking on one of those cigarettes and stinking up the air with the odor of cheap tobacco.

*Ignore, ignore, ignore.* Rosanna focused all of her attention on the tomato plants.

"He was out here in the garden that night," Camille continued, her tone mocking. "Drunk as usual and yelling at my mom!"

With the fourth plant finished, Rosanna moved farther away from the fence to work on the fifth one. Only five more to do, she told herself.

"I saw you!" Camille laughed. It sounded more like a cackle.

The fact that the young woman took such joy in saying hurtful things stunned Rosanna. How could a woman who was so unclean in heart and spirit raise a child to be anything but as despicable as she was? The child didn't even have a father in the house—Rosanna wasn't even certain if Camille knew who the father was. Rosanna had never seen anyone visit the house since the child was born. It was always just the little toddler playing alone in the yard with the network of red, yellow, and blue plastic gym sets.

"He called for you, didn't he? You saw him out here, and you ignored him!" Another cackle.

Shutting her eyes, Rosanna silently willed the woman to stop speaking. You are evil, she thought. God is my shield.

"You knew he was coming after you in the buggy and that he was drunk. You could have stopped him."

The wave of tightness around her rib cage almost made Rosanna fall to her knees. But she refused to give Camille that satisfaction. Darkness crept into her vision, and she could barely see to hammer in the sixth stake. When her aim missed and she hit her thumb, she winced—both from the pain and the sound of the two women laughing at her.

153

Gloria tossed her cigarette butt over the fence. It landed in the row of vegetables behind the tomato plants. Rosanna glanced at it, worried that it would catch fire. Fire, she thought. Ignore their fire.

"You ignored him and left, knowing he would follow," Camille repeated. "You killed him as much as the car did!"

The mallet fell from Rosanna's hand and bounced once in the dirt. Turning her back to the women, Rosanna began to walk toward the house. She couldn't stay in the garden and finish her work. Not today. Maybe never. Her hands trembled and her knees felt weak. She prayed to God to give her the strength to make it the distance to the house. She pressed her hand against her chest and clutched at her dress. With Aaron at an auction and Cate at the shop, there was no one there to witness the tears that streamed down her cheeks. Her heart pounded and her throat closed. She was having trouble breathing. She wished someone were home. More cloudy darkness flooded the corners of her eyes, creating a narrow tunnel before her. She felt dizzy, and there was a ringing in her ears.

I'm having a heart attack.

Gulping for air, Rosanna stumbled twice as she made her way to the house. With uncertain footsteps, she managed to climb the porch stairs. Her hands still shaking, she reached for the railing, but her blurred vision made her miss it. She fell to her knees, and her hands just stopped her face from hitting the floorboards.

The pain shot up her wrists to her shoulders, and she cried out. Rosanna hardly recognized her own voice. The tears fell freely as she rested her forehead against the floor. For a few minutes she stayed in that position, her eyes shut as she prayed. *What is happening to me, Lord?* She took a deep breath. *If I must come home, Lord, please make it quick. The suffering . . . I need it to end.*

When she opened her eyes, it took Rosanna another minute to realize that her lungs had cleared and she could breathe normally again. Slowly she lifted her head and, moving her arms, was able to push herself so that she was sitting on her heels.

If this wasn't a heart attack, she wondered, what was it?

She managed to steady herself and climb to her feet. Carefully she made her way to one of the rocking chairs on the porch. For a long time she sat in the chair, her head resting against the back and her hands clutching the rounded arms. Her mind was blank as she concentrated on her breathing.

As she calmed down, her eyelids drooped, and she wiped away a final tear. Camille and Gloria had been there that night. They must have been smoking outside before retreating into the house to lose themselves in front of the television. Rosanna remembered that Timothy had stumbled through the garden, yelling at the dogs and throwing rocks at them. Witnessing her father's abuse of the dogs, Cate had run outside, screaming to save them from being hurt.

That was when Timothy had turned and, with a smirk on his swollen face, thrown the rock at his daughter.

Rosanna wasn't certain if it was the sting of the rock hitting her arm or the shock that her *daed* had thrown it at her that made Cate hysterical. Rosanna had run toward her and wrapped her in her arms, pressing Cate's head against her chest to shield her as she guided the girl away from her father.

Aaron had stood on the porch, the color drained from his face. With his black pants—torn at one knee—and his beige work shirt, he looked like a miniature version of Timothy. The mixture of disgust and horror in his eyes was the final straw for Rosanna.

*"Kum!"* She motioned to Aaron and began walking down the driveway toward the road.

She could hear Timothy still ranting at the dogs, but by the time she had reached the end of the driveway, he was yelling for her. His deep voice echoed across the fields. Rosanna could not help but look back . . . just once . . . and that single gesture told him that she had heard him—and chosen to ignore him.

"Hurry," she instructed her children as she walked faster. She didn't know where she was going to take them, but she knew that she would not go back into the house with that man. Not tonight, mayhaps never.

That was when he harnessed the horse to the buggy and came after her. It took him longer than usual, probably because his coordination was off. When she got to the top of the hill, she looked over her shoulder and saw the buggy turn onto the road. She knew she should go back and stop him; she could see that he was weaving onto the wrong side of the road. Instead, she walked even faster.

As she and the children rounded the hill, a car passed them, headed toward their farm. Moments later, she heard the screeching of tires and knew from the sound of the impact exactly what had happened.

You could have stopped him.

It was the thought that had haunted her ever since that night.

You might as well have killed him . . .

She awoke many nights with this thought ripping through her. Would God judge her as a murderer? She had not obeyed her husband; she had knowingly walked away. She had only been trying to protect her children and herself, but she had known.

Was what she had done a sin? Would she be judged as a sinner for not turning back and trying to prevent the accident?

Shaking herself free of the terrible memories, Rosanna knew that she needed to talk to the bishop. If she confessed to him, he would guide her on this matter. With a clean conscience, mayhaps she would finally understand what was happening to her now.

She heard a horse neigh and the gentle whisper of buggy wheels on the driveway. She looked up, half surprised and half relieved that someone was approaching. With her strength gone, both physically and mentally, she couldn't even get to her feet to greet the visitor. Her expression blank, she merely stared into space and waited.

"Rosanna!"

It was Reuben. He didn't even stop the buggy and get out. He merely turned it around. "Preacher Beiler has passed. I'm needed at the Beiler house, but I told them you would make some food to take over! They'll need bread and some salads, *ja*? Will be lots of visitors, for sure and certain."

She blinked her eyes. A moment passed before she registered what her husband had said. The preacher? Passed? She watched as Reuben lifted his hand and gave her a quick wave before guiding the horse back toward the road. He hadn't noticed that she never once moved. He hadn't even waited to hear her reaction. He had merely given her more work to do and then driven away to continue his business.

As if on autopilot, she stood up and headed to the door. Without emotion, she walked inside. The corners of her mouth were turned down and her eyes were blank. Bread and salads were needed, she told herself. He had promised them, and she would deliver. She always did.

# CHAPTER THIRTEEN

The following Sunday after worship service, a members-only meeting was held in the gathering room of the Peacheys' large farmhouse. Every piece of furniture had been moved out, and the hinged folding doors to the three main rooms had been opened, creating a space large enough to host the entire church district for this very important event.

There was tense silence as Bishop Smucker paced before the members, his hands clutched behind his back and his eyes staring at the floor. He spoke about the importance of the role of a preacher to the church, how whoever was selected would help guide the community, preach at services, and, perhaps, one day, become bishop. He talked about the family of the preacher, how they were just as important, for they supported both the man and the community.

Rosanna barely heard a thing. Since Tuesday, time had seemed to pass like a fog before her. After Reuben had left, she spent the rest of the day baking bread and cooking potatoes for potato salad. Her mind had remained blank, and she had thought of nothing. Absolutely nothing. Habit guided her through the motions of kneading bread and peeling potatoes. She didn't need to pay attention to the recipes; she knew them by heart.

When Reuben returned to accompany her to the Beiler house, her lips had remained still as he carried the box of food outside. She followed him and wordlessly crawled into the buggy. She situated herself on the front seat, and after Reuben gently slapped the reins on the horse's back, she steadied herself against the buggy's dashboard. During the short ride, Reuben told her what he knew: Elias had been in the barn and had collapsed in the hayloft. Several days later, he had died at the hospital without once regaining consciousness.

When Reuben finished speaking, Rosanna hadn't responded. She'd just stared out the window, Reuben's words filling the void between them. He didn't seem to notice her silence.

When they arrived at the Beilers' house, Rosanna joined the other women who were helping to wash walls, windows, and floors. The men had already removed the furniture from the first-floor rooms, storing some in the basement and the rest in the barn. As Rosanna worked, she listened to the other women's hushed conversations. No one seemed to notice how quiet she was. Instead, they spoke of their own surprise and grief that Elias had been called home so suddenly.

When the undertaker had returned the body to the house that evening, the bishop, the two remaining preachers, and the deacon gathered with Elias's wife and grown children. A circle of brown metal folding chairs had been set up in the room, and the walls had been removed so that more people could comfort the family. Bishop Smucker spoke for a few minutes, reminding everyone that Elias was now with Jesus and that it was a journey they would all make one day.

When he finished speaking, everyone knelt before their folding chairs with their faces buried in their hands as they prayed. Rosanna had done the same, but with her hands and face pressed against the bench of the kitchen table.

Afterward, Elias's widow, Lydia, her face pale and drawn from the shock of losing her husband so unexpectedly, rattled off names of people to invite to the funeral. Occasionally one of her children would offer a name, and she would nod her head in approval.

For the next two days, from sunrise to sunset, people had come to the Beiler house for visitation. Rosanna had known without asking that she was needed to help feed the visitors. During the day she worked at the Beiler house, and at night, back in her own kitchen, she made more salads and bread to bring with her in the morning. More than four hundred people had filed through the house to pray over Elias's body, laid out in the simple pine coffin in the back bedroom. Afterward they sat for a few minutes on the folding chairs in the main gathering room.

The funeral was on Friday. After a two-hour service, twenty-seven buggies—each marked with a number written in chalk—had followed the wagon carrying the coffin to the graveyard. Rosanna had stood quietly by Reuben's side watching as the coffin was lowered into a freshly dug hole. One of the preachers spoke while the bishop and the two remaining district preachers stood behind him.

Beside her, Cate shuffled her feet, her shoulder bumping into Rosanna. Her daughter was restless. Who could blame her? Three days of mourning seemed long to a child. It seemed long to Rosanna, too. All she could think about was finding the opportunity to speak to the bishop. That thought, and that thought alone, raced through her head, again and again.

On the road a car slowed to gawk at the gathering of so many Amish people, all dressed in black, standing in the cemetery. Without looking, Rosanna knew that they were snapping photos. A few mourners shifted their stance so that they could not be photographed. Rosanna hadn't moved although Reuben had lightly touched her arm so that she might turn to escape the intruding lenses. He didn't notice that she remained standing in the same place.

Now, once again, the *g'may* was gathered. Everyone but Rosanna listened intently to the bishop. Her mind continued to focus on speaking to him afterward. All she needed was just a few minutes of his time. A chance to tell him what had happened three years ago and confess her role. Just a few, short minutes . . .

"And now we will vote," the bishop announced.

Everyone walked outside while the bishop and the preachers set up two tables, one for the women and one for the men. Then, two by two, with the eldest going first, a man and a woman entered the kitchen. Each one approached his or her designated table and leaned down to whisper the name of the man he or she wanted to nominate in the ear of the preacher who sat at the table. The bishop stood in the back of the room, observing while he prayed.

"So awful," someone behind Rosanna said.

The voice was familiar, but she couldn't make out the name or place the face. Instead of responding, she stared at the open door, watching for the two people to exit so that another two might enter.

"And the responsibility is now to weigh heavy on someone else's shoulders," another voice responded.

Elizabeth Esh reached for Rosanna's hand. "Are you praying, Rosanna?"

At the sound of her name, Rosanna looked up.

"I've been praying since Tuesday that we make the right choice," Elizabeth continued nervously, still holding Rosanna's hand. "Not just for the man but for his family, too."

Someone called for Elizabeth and motioned her toward the house. It was her turn to enter and cast her vote. Rosanna suddenly realized that she would have her chance to approach the bishop in just a few short minutes. Once Elizabeth walked back through that door, it would be Rosanna's turn to vote. Her palms were sweaty, and she felt herself growing light-headed once again. *Confess your sins. Clean your soul.*

Entering the house, she glanced around and saw one of the preachers gesture to her. The bishop wasn't watching; his eyes were closed. She needed to catch his gaze and ask to speak to him afterward. But the opportunity didn't come. Instead, she shuffled across the off-white linoleum floor of the Peacheys' kitchen and stopped before the table.

"Have you decided on your choice, sister?"

Rosanna blinked twice, still looking at the bishop. Her hands were clenched into fists, the nails digging into her palms. This time it was not to keep herself awake but to keep from acting out inappropriately. She wanted to call to the bishop, to tell him she must have his counsel. But the casting of the vote outweighed her needs, no matter how insufferable her pain.

"Sister?"

She turned her eyes to look at the preacher. He was waiting for her. Swallowing her disappointment, she finally leaned over and whispered a name into his ear. Unlike Elizabeth, she had neither given it much thought nor prayed about it. She merely mumbled the first name that came to her head. The preacher nodded and wrote something down on a piece of paper, which he then folded and pushed to the side of the table.

Rosanna's vote was cast.

Another thirty minutes passed before the remaining members had entered the house and whispered their nominations to the preachers. Standing under a tree near the driveway, Rosanna paced and wrung her hands. Every once in a while she sighed and lifted her eyes to the sky, watching the sun as it slowly etched its way from east to west.

"Rosanna!" Katie called her name and, with her sister Fannie in tow, hurried over to her. "Meant to ask you about that clothing drive."

Rosanna looked up, confused. "The what?"

"The clothing drive. We're to meet next Saturday for cutting the fabric into squares," Katie reminded her. Although she was a year younger than Fannie, in their black dresses and white prayer *kapps*, the two women could have been twins. Both had large stomachs, a testimony to bearing many children and having a few too many desserts.

"Oh, *ja, ja*." Rosanna nodded as she remembered. Had Cate distributed the flyers? Rosanna's memory was fuzzy. Frowning, she tried to think back to the previous week. She recalled making the flyer with Cate after that incident with Gloria and Camille. "I asked Cate to hand out flyers last week," she said, suddenly remembering and hoping Cate had done so. "I asked for the clothes to be dropped off this week by Wednesday."

"*Gut!* I knew we could count on you," Katie said with a small smile.

Before Rosanna could respond, the gathering began to walk toward the house. Someone must have indicated that the voting was over and the leadership of the church was ready for the next part of the process: calling those nominated to the front of the room. Each man would select a Bible from a bench and, one by one, open it. If he had selected the Bible with a small slip of paper in it, then he would become a preacher—and perhaps a future bishop—of the *g'may* for the rest of his life.

Rosanna followed Katie and Fannie, searching the gathering room until she found Elizabeth among the women and assumed her place beside her.

"As you know," the bishop said, standing before the bench against the back wall, "we have asked each of you to nominate a man that you feel is worthy to lead this church. Through action, word, and silence, this man should exemplify his understanding of the Ordnung."

Rosanna barely heard what he was saying. Her thoughts drifted back to how she could get his attention after the lot was selected.

"Will the following men please step forward?" The bishop glanced around the room, once in the direction of the women, but his attention was mostly focused on the men. "Adam Mast."

A hush fell over the group at the announcement of the first name. A man stood up and walked slowly to the front of the room, his eyes downcast and a solemn expression on his face.

"Reuben Troyer."

Elizabeth reached out and clutched Rosanna's hand. Rosanna frowned and looked up just in time to see her husband stand. The color was drained from his face, and he had to steady himself against the shoulder of the man seated in front of him. Reuben? Reuben was nominated? She had never remotely considered that possibility. Only married men with family were nominated, and they usually had a lot of pull in the community. They were the go-to men when there were issues. Rosanna felt an all-too familiar tightening of her chest as she watched Reuben make his way to the front of the room. She realized that, indeed, Reuben was that man.

"John David Miller."

Rosanna didn't even bother to look for John David. Instead, she stared at her husband. He had joined Adam at the front of the room. His eyes remained fixed on the back wall, his glasses tipped down to the very edge of his nose. She knew that he couldn't see anything without his glasses. Clearly he was staring at nothing, his mind in a whirl over the nomination.

Three other men were called to the front before the bishop indicated that they should select a Bible from the bench. The room remained silent as the first man quickly selected the Bible closest to him without giving it any thought. Reuben, however, took a very deep breath, his shoulders rising before he exhaled. Although his back faced Rosanna, she knew that he was praying. He reached for one Bible then paused and moved his hand to the right to take the next one instead.

No one moved or shuffled their feet as the rest of the men stepped forward to take their Bibles. The entire congregation sat completely still, staring at the men expectantly. One of them would leave the meeting as an ordained preacher for their *g'may*. It was a job that paid no money but took up so much time for the preacher and support from his family—time that Reuben did not have to spare and support that Rosanna wasn't certain she could give.

"Are you all right?" Elizabeth whispered. An older woman seated in front of them turned her head and scowled at them.

Rosanna wasn't all right. None of this was all right. She squeezed her eyes shut and prayed that the lot would fall to another man, any man, just not Reuben.

Adam opened his Bible first. He stared at the book in his hands for a moment before he looked up at the bishop. He exhaled, most likely in relief, and shut the Bible once again.

Everyone turned their attention to Reuben. Rosanna kept her eyes shut, praying as hard as she could that God would not give her husband this cup. She heard him clear his throat and the very soft sound of a book opening. There was a moment of silence before a collective noise came from the congregation. Elizabeth squeezed her hand, and when she heard gentle weeping, Rosanna knew exactly what had happened.

She didn't need to open her eyes to see that a small slip of paper had fallen from the book in Reuben's hands, floating to the floor and now lying at his feet. She didn't need to see that Reuben had tears streaming down his cheeks, the heavy responsibility that now rested on his shoulders more than he could bear. She also knew that the other men and their wives were watching with a feeling of relief and prayers of gratitude that the lot had fallen to someone else.

Gesturing with an outstretched arm, the bishop did not delay in directing the other men to return to their seats. They walked quietly, their heads bent as they left Reuben standing next to the bishop. Silence fell over the room once again. There was no shuffling of feet, no clearing of throats.

The bishop guided Reuben to the front of the room. "Please kneel," he said in a quiet voice.

Rosanna lifted her head and stared. Her eyes were dry, but her head was spinning as she watched her husband of not even a year kneel before the bishop and accept the duty that was given to him on account of a single slip of paper between the pages of the Bible—the choosing of the lot. Her ears tuned out the words spoken by the bishop and affirmed by Reuben. She'd witnessed many ordinations over the years. The words never changed. This time, however, they directly impacted her and her family.

When the ordination was complete, the bishop placed his hands on Reuben's shoulders and helped him to his feet before giving him a holy kiss. She watched as Reuben walked back to his seat with downcast eyes and pale cheeks. Clearly he felt just as stunned at how their lives had just changed.

One of the other preachers reached out and touched his arm, nodding toward the empty seat in one of the front rows, the place where the *g'may's* leadership sat. Reuben would no longer sit on the hard bench next to his peers. He would sit in the front. As for Rosanna, she would no longer sit next to Elizabeth. Her place would be in the second row facing the men, Cate by her side.

# Chapter Fourteen

Their whispers carried in the quiet of the house. They were not intended to be overheard, yet the muffled sound reached her ears as if the walls were thinner than paper. In her mind, Rosanna saw their heads bent, their eyes staring at the bedroom door as they suppressed their voices. She knew they were talking about her. She shut her eyes and pulled up the sheet so that it covered her chest. The room was too warm for a blanket. Even with just the sheet she felt hot. The dark-green shades covering the two windows kept the room in semidarkness. She wondered if it was dawn or dusk. Or maybe, she thought, it was somewhere in-between.

"How long has she been like this?" Reuben's deep voice was easily recognizable. Rosanna couldn't hear who responded, but she knew the answer: all day. Mumbles. That's all she heard now. A voice, maybe Aaron's . . . maybe Cate's . . . mumbling. There was a delay, a moment of hesitation, before she heard Reuben again. "Best be calling the doctor."

She rolled her head to the side and exhaled. Her breath came out in a deep sigh. She didn't want to see the doctor. And she didn't want to see the bishop. Not here. Not now.

The feeling of hopelessness had begun Monday morning, just after Reuben left for the shop, before the sun rose. He hadn't slept much the previous night. He had tossed and turned for hours, eventually getting up to pace the floor before wandering into the kitchen.

For the first few hours, Rosanna had kept her eyes closed, listening to him turning in the bed, the sheets pulled away from her with each movement. Then she'd heard him moving about the kitchen and sitting rooms. Even with just his slippers on, he made noise as he paced.

When he finally returned to pull his clothing from the hooks and get dressed, obviously giving up on any sleep, she allowed herself to open her eyes. One of the shades was not closed all the way, and the light from the moon shone through, creating a glow on the floorboards. It was too early for morning chores.

"Reuben?" she whispered.

The mattress dipped under his weight as he sat beside her and placed his hand on her shoulder. "I'm afraid I've kept you awake," he said directly.

She didn't respond.

"I'm sorry, Rosanna."

Covering his hand with her own, she pressed gently against his warm flesh. "Truth be told, Reuben, I haven't slept much, either."

"I just can't wrap my head around this." He ran his hand through his hair. Even in the shadows of the room, she could see that this left it bedraggled. "Why me? I'm not a preacher!"

Reuben paused, and Rosanna remained silent. She knew that he needed time to work through this.

"A preacher! Why, I never considered such a possibility." He laughed, a soft noise under his breath. "A preacher . . ."

A preacher gave sermons on Sundays—sermons that could range from thirty minutes to well over an hour. A preacher met with the members of the congregation who were in need of spiritual guidance. A preacher needed to study the Bible, memorizing verses and talking about them in the context of how to live a life true to the Ordnung, the unwritten rules governing each church district. In some cases, a preacher helped modify the Ordnung by providing Biblical references and interpretations of specific verses either for or against suggested changes.

"Why, just yesterday morning," Reuben said, "I was a simple Amish man, taught all my life to be quiet and not express my opinions. Now I'm expected to lead the church?" He stood up and paced a few steps. "All of this while maintaining the shop?"

"People will help you," Rosanna said, but her offer of comfort sounded meek the moment the words slipped from her lips.

"Help me?" He spun around and stared at her. He looked annoyed. "With the sermons?"

"With the shop." She knew that her voice sounded terse. His tone had hurt her, wounded her already fragile feelings. *This is about him,* she reminded herself. *Not me.*

"Oh, Rosanna, you just don't understand. It's so busy, and I don't have enough help as it is! These men keep coming in from all sorts of towns, and I can hardly keep up with their repairs." He pressed his palm against the wall and leaned into it. "I'm already working sixty-plus hours a week. Now I'm to be a church leader? Counsel people? Write sermons? Develop my own theology to deliver to the *g'may*?" He turned his head to look at her. In the blue-gray light of morning, he looked tired and worn out. "It's too much to bear."

"God will help you," she offered, hoping that her words would soothe his nerves. "And so will I."

"Rosanna . . ."

She knew what that tone meant. But she wasn't going to give up so quickly. Not this time. "Listen to me, Reuben," she said. "Recruit farms in different areas where the people can drop their goods and have a driver bring them to you. That saves them the trip to the shop and saves you from having to visit them."

He didn't respond, but his silence was an indication that she should continue.

"Martin and Daniel have worked with you for a long time," said Rosanna. "Let them lead the program. Ask both of them to find three drop points in three specific towns. The logistics would run so much smoother. And give them the chance to lead it—not Nan, who has only been there a few weeks. You'll make it easier on them and have more time for studying Scripture. And Cate will have to help Aaron, whether she likes it or not. I'll manage . . ." She pushed the thought of the garden out of her mind. She couldn't go back there, not even for Reuben. She hadn't been there since the day Elias Beiler died. Just the thought of going there made her feel sick and caused her heart to race.

"I reckon I have more pressing things to do today," he said, staring at the wall. "This is a time that requires prayer and patience, Rosanna, not reorganizing the structure and logistics of my business."

The reprimand stung, and she recoiled. She had prayed for him; she had prayed most of the night for him, indeed! The fact that her idea was so easily dismissed—again—wounded her. She offered no further comments or suggestions. It didn't matter. Shortly after their discussion, he left the house. Alone in the bedroom, she fought the urge to cry. She knew that tears would do the situation no good.

For the rest of that day she had felt like a ghost, barely making her way through her daily routine. After breakfast she spent almost two hours at the sink, staring into the soapy water as she washed and rewashed the breakfast dishes. She just wasn't certain if they were clean enough, and the warm water, which she refreshed three times, felt good on her skin. Once or twice she caught Cate staring at her, but her daughter never asked if there was something wrong.

She always washed their Sunday outfits on Monday, but when it was time to do the laundry, Rosanna had lifted her hand and motioned to Cate that she should do it without her. For a moment Cate appeared as if she might talk back, but after a long pause she changed her mind and marched out of the room—insolent but without a complaint.

For the rest of the morning Rosanna had focused on sweeping the house. Her mind wandered. When she grew tired, she sat down in the reclining chair and stared out the window. She had to be reminded when it was the dinner hour, and afterward she repeated the same dishwashing routine as the morning. By this time Cate had realized that her mother was too deep in thought to notice anything, especially her. She happily slipped outside, disappearing for a few hours with the dogs.

Suppertime crept up on her, but without being reminded, she managed to slice some bread and put out cold cuts, butter, reheated corn, and applesauce. She barely ate anything. Neither Aaron nor Cate noticed.

At six o'clock, Reuben finally returned. He set his hat on the counter and walked to the sink to wash his hands and face. He looked weary after a long day that had started over fourteen hours earlier. As he dried his hands and face, he noticed the covered plate of food that Rosanna had set aside for him. Setting the towel next to it, he commented that he had visited with one of the other preachers and ate some supper with him. Then he sighed and walked away.

Rosanna didn't respond. She merely sat on the sofa, her hands resting on her lap. She had watched him enter, wash his hands, and push aside the covered plate. And then she had watched him retreat to his recliner with his Bible and a notebook. He never noticed that she hadn't spoken, nor did he notice the lifeless look in her eyes.

For the rest of the evening, he devoured the Word of God and made notations in the margins of his Bible. Occasionally he wrote something in the notebook, but for the most part he read. Twice he scolded Cate for making too much noise. His sharp words and cutting tone indicated that he wanted complete silence in the room.

Annoyed, Cate made a face and quickly left the house, choosing to play with the dogs rather than be reprimanded again. When she slipped through the screen door, she let it slam shut. The noise caused Reuben to look up and scowl.

"You have to do something about her," he snapped. His irritation was aimed at Rosanna this time. "She's far too willful!"

Rosanna did not comment.

For a while, quiet returned to the room. Rosanna sighed and lifted her eyes, noticing that Aaron still sat at the table, observing his stepfather. Clearly he was not quite sure what to make of this change in Reuben. Usually so even-tempered and thoughtful, his stepfather no longer exhibited those traits.

Rosanna glanced from Aaron to Reuben, now more worried by the concerned look on her son's face than about herself. She knew that he was just as tired as Reuben. While Daniel helped with the early morning and late evening chores, Aaron had been left to manage the farm by himself. From Cate's chatter earlier, Rosanna knew that she had used her kick scooter, dragging one of the dogs on a leash, to go visit a friend at a neighboring farm. Her daughter was resilient; her father had taught her survival. But Aaron was different. Rosanna felt a wave of guilt for having abandoned him that day. She made a quiet promise to help him more in the future.

As if reading her mind, Aaron met her gaze. His blue eyes studied her face, and she thought she saw them narrow, as if noticing something for the first time. His gaze flickered to Reuben's head, just barely visible over the back of the recliner. Then he took a deep breath and met Rosanna's eyes again, but just for a moment. He stood up, quietly pushed the chair back under the table, and left the kitchen.

For the rest of the evening, Reuben pored over the Bible, sometimes reading aloud and other times mumbling to himself. Rosanna sat at the small desk in the corner and wrote some correspondence by the soft glow of a lantern.

The next two days weren't any better. Reuben barely slept and left before Rosanna awoke, which meant that she needed to help Aaron with his chores. Cate didn't go to the shop. Not only because she hadn't been invited but, Rosanna suspected, because she wanted to avoid the bitter sting of her stepfather's increasingly short temper.

To make matters worse, the Englische neighbors had begun to drop off clothing donations. Black and white garbage bags full of used clothing started to accumulate by the side of the barn. The neighbors—mostly women—would wave to Rosanna if she were outside. Some stopped to visit for a few minutes. As the pile of bags increased, Rosanna began to feel overwhelmed. She had expected a few donations. From the looks of it, the generosity of her neighbors had far exceeded her expectations.

"How many clothes can Englische have?" Cate quipped, staring out the window as yet another car pulled into the driveway.

Rosanna sat at the table, her head in her hands. She knew she would have to sort through those bags and—if her experience with the first bag was a telling sign—half of the clothing would need to be washed and the other half thrown away. Although Rosanna and Cate had been fairly specific, given the old, worn sheets, towels, and even shoes they were finding, their neighbors apparently hadn't realized that it was a clothing drive for making quilts.

"One shoe?" Aaron laughed as he dug through a bag that he'd brought inside. "Who donates one shoe?"

"Englische, that's who!" said Cate.

Rosanna frowned, but didn't have the energy to reprimand her daughter. Her arms felt heavy and her head hurt.

"Would you two post a sign out there? At the end of the drive-way? No more donations, *ja*?" Rosanna stood up, supporting herself for a moment by holding onto the back of the kitchen chair. "And Aaron, you go with Cate to the garden. Needs some weeding, but I don't want her alone out there."

"You feeling all right, *Maem*?" Aaron asked.

Leave it to Aaron to pick up on her pain, she thought. She tried to force a smile, but the muscles in her face refused to move. *"Nee,"* she finally admitted. "I need to lie down for a spell."

Rosanna caught the look that passed between her two children: a look of concern. Even when she was sick with a cold, she rarely went to her bedroom to rest during the day. She usually worked right through her illnesses.

Not today.

That had been six hours ago. Now, as she lay in bed staring at the dancing shadows on the wall, she realized that it must be dusk. Reuben must have returned home. With no supper on the table and Lord knows what state the kitchen was in, he had obviously realized that something was wrong. She vaguely remembered hearing someone at the door, most likely peeking into the bedroom to check on her. She pretended to be asleep and, to her relief, no one had disturbed her.

She watched as the room grew darker, the sun gone at last from the sky. It comforted her, the darkness. She felt as if she could breathe again. Darkness hid the pain along with the endless amount of work and the infinite requests for help. From baked goods to cleaning bees, from sewing circles to canning parties, Rosanna couldn't handle the constant expectation of giving. It made her feel as if she were drowning, gasping for air as her body sank lower into a dark abyss, the circle of light above her slowly growing smaller and smaller as she disappeared into the bottomless pit.

She had no idea how much time had passed when she finally heard the door open, slowly at first. A beam of light flooded the room as it opened wider. Refusing to turn her head, she stared at the wall and focused on her breathing.

"Rosanna?" Reuben's voice. She recognized it, but he sounded so far away.

"Rosanna, I have a doctor here," she heard him say.

Only one set of footsteps entered the room. She suspected it was the doctor.

"Mrs. Troyer . . ." An Englische doctor. Of course it was an Englischer. After all, most Amish practiced holistic medicine, relying on herbs that could be grown in the garden. He clearly had little experience around the Amish. Otherwise he would have known that the Amish didn't use titles like Mr. or Mrs. Only the bishop, deacon, and preachers were sometimes called by their titles.

He moved across the room and set a bag on the floor. "Mrs. Troyer, can you hear me?"

She felt weak and didn't respond. Her lips were dry and her mouth parched. The bright light shone in her eyes, and she winced.

"Mrs. Troyer? Can you tell me what's bothering you?"

She turned and studied him for a moment. A balding man with gray hair over his ears, he looked like a typical Englischer. He had narrow shoulders and a paunch belly, but the wrinkles on his tanned face indicated that he spent time outdoors. To her surprise, he was dressed modestly. His white shirt was crisp and clean, and his black slacks had a crease down the middle.

"Both Aaron and Cate say she's been like this all day," Reuben said from the doorway.

The doctor shone a small pen-shaped flashlight into her eyes. She winced again. Using a stethoscope, he listened to her heart and lungs, asking her to breathe slowly. She already was. When he asked her to take a deep breath, she couldn't. Her chest was too tight.

She felt a slight pressure on her arm as he slid on a blood pressure cuff. The sound of the Velcro was loud in her ears. His warm fingers touched her wrist, feeling for her pulse as he pumped the cuff, the band on her arm tightening. When he released the air, the band loosened, and a soft hissing noise filled the room. Finally, she felt him place a tight band on her arm and then a slight pinprick.

When the doctor finished examining her, she heard him putting away his instruments. She glanced at him and saw him staring down at her. He scratched at his neck; there was a perplexed look on his face.

"There doesn't appear to be anything wrong," he finally said, more to Reuben than to her. "At least not physically. I drew some blood and will have it analyzed. However, I suspect that the issue might be something else."

"What's wrong with *Maem*?" Rosanna heard Cate ask from the kitchen.

Still standing in the doorway, Reuben shushed Cate and ordered her to go outside.

"I'm suspecting depression," the doctor said.

"Depression?" Reuben sounded surprised.

"It's more common than you think, and you did mention that she has been through quite a bit of change in her life."

"That was three years ago!" Reuben stumbled over his words. "Well, then we were married last October." A long pause. "And then the lot . . ." His voice trailed off, and he remained silent for a few long moments.

"I'm going to suggest an antidepressant," the doctor said as he picked up his bag and walked toward Reuben. "We'll start it at a low dose and gradually increase it over the next few . . ." The door shut, and the room was instantly black again. She couldn't hear the doctor's voice anymore, and she was glad for the silence. It helped her concentrate on nothing. Nothing meant *no worries*. Nothing meant *no cleaning*. Nothing meant *no cooking*. Nothing meant *peace and quiet*.

Peace.

Quiet.

She shut her eyes and listened to the sound of nothing.

It was the only thing that made her happy.

# Chapter Fifteen

Reuben sat on a chair by her bed, the worn Bible on his lap as he studied Scripture. His glasses slipped to the edge of his nose, and he reached up automatically to push them back so that he could see properly. The onionskin paper made a gentle whooshing sound each time he flipped to the next page.

Quietly and without detection, Rosanna watched him. Five minutes passed, maybe more. Time seemed to stand still while she stared at her husband as he read the Bible. At first, it intrigued her. He barely moved, appearing almost like a statue. The only motion that proved he was real and not a mirage or an image was the motion of his finger turning the page.

Sunshine came through the open window. The green shades had been rolled back to let in the light. Rosanna's head felt heavy and light at the same time, as if it were filled with giant cotton balls. It took time to shift her gaze away from Reuben and focus on the window. The light hurt her eyes, and she winced, waiting for them to adjust to the brightness. When she could finally see properly, Rosanna noticed small dust particles floating through the rays. She watched them fall toward the floor and sighed, knowing that she'd have to dust mop the floor.

Reuben startled at the noise of her breath. Quickly he shut the Bible, his thumb keeping his place as he reached for a bookmark on the nightstand. He set the book on the bed next to her legs and leaned forward. His tired blue eyes, bleary from lack of sleep, stared into her face.

"You're awake."

It was as much a question as a statement, and she detected genuine concern in his gentle voice. The expression on his face mirrored his tone.

"Why did you let me sleep late?" she asked.

He smiled, a soft smile that contained a hint of sorrow.

Did something happen? Rosanna tried to think back to the previous night. Her mind was blank. The last thing she remembered was a car in the driveway. And the bags of clothing. She groaned. Too many bags of clothing. She lifted her body and sat up in the bed, noticing how quick Reuben was to place a second pillow between her back and the headboard.

"It's Saturday," he said. "You've been sleeping for two days."

"Days?"

He nodded. "Doctor put you on a strong medicine, Rosanna. A sedative."

She didn't understand. "Why? Is something wrong?"

The door burst open, and Cate ran into the room, interrupting their conversation without a second thought. She raced to the bed and threw her arms around her mother's shoulders, nestling her head into her neck. "Oh, *Maem*! We were all so worried!" she cried. "Especially me!"

"Cate! Leave your *maem* be!" Reuben said.

Cate ignored him as she hugged her mother, an unusual display of emotion from the usually stubborn and independent girl. Rosanna hesitated before she lifted her arms and put them around Cate's shoulders and held her tightly. When she realized that Cate was crying, her tears falling against Rosanna's skin, she lifted her eyes and stared at her husband.

She didn't want to hear any more about what Reuben had to tell her. At least not while Cate was in the room. There were some things best not shared with the children. A sedative sounded serious. After all, sedatives were to calm people. For her entire life Rosanna had been taught to rely more on nature and less on pharmaceuticals. Her mother had practiced holistic medicine, using herbs to cure ailments. She had even called Englische medicine "toxic" and "poison." While Rosanna didn't really believe that, she had never felt the inclination to use man-made drugs rather than God-given ones.

But she knew what a sedative was, and clearly whatever this doctor had prescribed had knocked her out. Even if she didn't feel that she needed a sleep-inducing medicine, it was obvious that the doctor was concerned enough to prescribe something, and Reuben, while knowing her preference for holistic cures, was concerned enough to administer it to her.

When Cate finally released her, she wiped at her eyes and held her mother's hand. "Are you going to stop washing dishes and sweeping the floor now?"

"Cate . . ." Reuben said the single word as a warning.

Rosanna felt confused. She looked at her daughter and noticed that her eyes were wide and full of fear. The only other time she had seen such fright on Cate's face was the day that Gloria and Camille verbally attacked them. What had caused her daughter to be so fearful? And what was Cate talking about?

"I . . . I don't understand," Rosanna said.

"Never you mind now, Rosanna." Reuben tried to soften his voice, but despite his best efforts, it sounded strained. "Cate, why don't you run out to the garden and tell your *bruder* the good news, *ja*?"

Cate glanced in his direction but never looked directly at him. Rosanna noticed that something akin to anger flashed in her daughter's eyes. That, too, surprised her. Obviously Cate did not want to leave her mother's side. However, she knew better than to argue with Reuben. Reluctantly she slid off the bed and moved toward the door. Lingering there, her hand on the knob, she cast one last look over her shoulder at her mother before she shut the door behind her.

"What is going on?" Rosanna asked, her mind foggy. Her head felt heavy, and she lifted her hand to her forehead. A few stray strands of hair were stuck to her skin. Her hair was down, a single braid over her shoulder. She wondered who had done that. "I don't understand any of this, Reuben."

Reuben moved his chair closer to the side of the bed and reached for her hand. The gesture startled her almost as much as Cate's embrace had. Neither of them were overly affectionate. She let him lift her hand, and clutching it, he squeezed it gently. To her further surprise, he leaned forward and pressed his lips against the back of her fingers. His beard whiskers tickled her skin.

"Doctor thinks you've been depressed, Rosanna," he said slowly. "Everything else seems just fine. Even your blood work."

"He took my blood?"

Reuben pursed his lips and studied her with his eyes. "You don't remember, then?"

She shook her head, too aware that it was uncovered. She felt naked sitting before him without her prayer *kapp*. In fact, she felt even more uncomfortable that she was in bed during daylight hours. Try as she could, she couldn't remember what her last memory *was*. The ride home from worship? Reuben's sleepless night? His cutting tone in the morning? "*Nee*, Reuben," she admitted. "I don't."

"You were catatonic, Rosanna." Reuben shifted his eyes away from hers, and she felt the color flood to her cheeks. "You barely spoke. You repeated the same chores over and over. And then you just laid there in bed, staring at the wall."

Despite his words, she didn't feel the familiar pounding of her heart. She pulled her hand free from his and pressed it against her chest. No tightening either.

Reuben didn't seem to notice. "Doctor said you've been through a lot." He still didn't look at her, and she wondered if he was ashamed of her. Just a week after being chosen to be a preacher, his wife was put on medicine for depression! She knew that he'd have to tell other people. If not, the Amish grapevine would speculate, and imaginations would run wild. "He asked a lot of questions," Reuben admitted. "When I told him about how much you've been through, he compared it to something called post-traumatic stress."

This was a new term to her. She raised her eyebrows. "Traumatic stress?"

Reuben nodded. The serious expression on his face indicated that he was not teasing her or making this up. "The hard life with Timothy. His sudden death. The years of struggling." He paused before he added, "Our sudden marriage. I'm sure that was an adjustment for you. I haven't always been the most cooperative."

She exhaled sharply, her breath escaping her lips like a soft puff of air, and shifted her weight.

"Even that awful neighbor woman." This last part he added with restrained fury in his voice, his eyes blazing with hostility as he looked at Rosanna. "I should have addressed *that* situation from the very first time she said something to you."

Rosanna had never heard Reuben sound so angry, not even the other week when she had contradicted him. "Turn the other cheek," she whispered, a gentle reminder to both her husband and herself.

There was no visible reaction from Reuben at first, and she wondered if he had heard her.

"*Ja*, Rosanna," he finally said, breaking the silence. "That doesn't mean she couldn't have heard a word or two from me. Now . . ." His voice trailed off and his shoulders fell, just a little, as if defeated. "*Ja, vell*, it's never too late to deal with her kind."

Reuben took a deep breath and struggled for a moment to find the right words. As she waited for him to continue, she looked at him—really looked at him. He looked as though he hadn't slept in days, and his clothes were disheveled. It dawned on her that Reuben might have stayed by her side since Thursday.

"Everything just built up inside you. I'm sure that the vote and lot didn't help." He kissed her hand again. "That's a shocking change of life for both of us, *ja*?"

She didn't respond. She was still trying to digest what Reuben had said. Post-traumatic stress? That sounded like a made-up term, typical of the Englische, who wanted to label everything. She wondered what type of label people would give her now that she was diagnosed with depression. Even the Amish were not immune from tittering behind their hands about mental health issues.

"He put you on two medicines." Nervously, Reuben reached out for the orange bottles sitting on the nightstand. When he shook one, the sound of pills rattling startled her. "This one to help you sleep. This other one," he said, shaking it, too, "*ja, vell*, this one is an antidepressant."

Rosanna sat up straight and stared at the bottles in his hand. "You know how I feel about taking Englische medicine! They take pills for every little thing."

He shook the bottles again. "I know your aversion to medicines and all. But I had to make a decision, Rosanna. And the doctor assured me that these medicines are safe for you. The one, the antidepressant, takes a few weeks to feel the effect. He stopped by this morning to check on you. Said your blood work came back and that everything is normal. Gave me another prescription. I haven't filled it yet."

"What is it?" Rosanna asked.

Reuben reached into his front pocket and pulled out a small piece of blue paper. He squinted as he looked at it. "*Ja, vell,* I can't read his handwriting." He passed it to her. "Said it's for anxiety. I wanted to talk to you a spell about that one first."

She looked at the small blue lettering. She couldn't read it, either. "Anxiety?"

He nodded, retrieving the paper from her. "If you feel anxious or overly upset over something." His fingers fumbled as he slipped it back into his pocket. When it was safely tucked away, he finally lifted his eyes to look directly at her. She thought she saw tears along his eyelids. Once again he leaned forward and lowered his voice as he asked, "Have you felt anxious, Rosanna?"

Not wanting to answer, she looked away.

Reuben reached out to cup her chin in his hand and tilt her head so that she had no choice but to look at him. His eyes flickered back and forth, searching for an answer. When none came, he took a deep breath and released his hold on her. Leaning back in his seat, he nodded his head. "I thought so." Once again he ran his fingers through his hair. "This is my doing. I knew it."

Alarmed, she reached out, touching his knee. "*Nee,* Reuben! It's not your fault—"

He interrupted her so abruptly that she withdrew her hand. "*Ja, ja,* it is. I've been awful busy at the shop." He shook his head, working extra hard at fighting the buildup of tears. "And irritable, I reckon." Standing up, he began to pace the floor. It reminded her of the previous Sunday night. "And now this whole preacher thing."

It took him five steps to reach the wall and turn around and begin pacing the other way. "It's a blessing, I understand that. The lot fell upon me. But it's such a burden!" The word rolled off his lips with a ferocity that startled her. He clenched his hand into a fist and pressed his lips together. "We have to set examples now. All of us, and that includes your *dochder*."

"Reuben . . ." Rosanna started.

He held up his hand to stop her before she could speak. "I know that's a pressure. On all of you."

"That's not it."

Whirling around, he stared at her, a wild expression on his face. Although he had already decided he was the one accountable for her breakdown, he wanted answers. "Then what is it?" Hurrying to the bed, he knelt beside her and grabbed her hands. "Please tell me, Rosanna. For the thought that I am an awful husband just tears me apart. I can't eat. I can't sleep." The tears fell freely down his cheeks. "I'd never harm you, Rosanna. You are more than a *fraa*." He forced a smile, a tear lingering just above his lip. "You are my friend."

His words moved her, and she knew that she, too, had tears in her eyes. "You are not a neglectful husband, Reuben, but I am an ungodly wife."

He reached out to wipe her eyes. "Don't say such a thing. That's the depression speaking."

She shook her head, softly at first. "You don't understand . . . I haven't told you about the night Timothy died. I could have prevented it!" She shook her head more vehemently now. "I saw the car coming up the hill, and I knew his buggy was just over the crest." She pulled her hands free from his grasp. She felt a new sense of calm as she finally admitted the truth. "I could have stopped the accident. I could have signaled the driver to slow down." She paused, searching for the strength to finish what she had started.

He waited, watching her with no expression on his face.

Finally she leveled her gaze at him as she spoke the words that she had denied, even to herself, for the past three years. "But I didn't."

No sooner had she spoken the words than someone knocked softly at the bedroom door. Reuben cleared his throat and stood up, his knees creaking. He averted his eyes, refusing to look at her, and backed away from the bed. Before she could speak further, the door opened, slowly this time.

Aaron entered with Cate following close on his heels. Rosanna forced a smile at her children, too aware of her husband's back as he moved to the window and, lifting the shade so that more light could shine into the room, looked outside, deep in thought. Quietly, Aaron sat on the edge of the bed while Cate vaulted into the room, landing next to her mother. She rested her head on Rosanna's shoulder.

While she answered Aaron's questions of concern and listened to Cate begging her to get better soon, Rosanna kept an eye on Reuben. He didn't move. His hands were behind his back, and his body was motionless. She wondered what he was thinking as he stared outside and contemplated what she had confessed moments before. A tugging at her arm interrupted her private musings, and she returned her attention to her children. Cate's clinginess and Aaron's concern required more from her than Reuben's reaction did. After all, her children came first.

# Chapter Sixteen

At first Rosanna couldn't tell whether he was treating her differently because of her illness or because of her confession. Reuben seemed to tread ever so cautiously around her, speaking in soft tones as if trying his best not to upset her. It caught Rosanna off guard. Even when entering the bedroom during the day, he would knock gently on the door before opening it. This change, such a contrast from how he used to act, made her wonder about the depths of his disappointment in her.

Sometimes in the early morning hours she awoke to find him in a chair by the bedroom window, the shade lifted just enough so that a beam of light cascaded onto his legs. Even though the Bible lay open on his lap, he merely stared at it, a lifeless look in his eyes.

In those early morning hours when he didn't know that she was watching him, Rosanna studied his profile. She really looked at him. Despite the wrinkle in his brow and the tired look in his eyes, he had a kind face, one that had weathered many storms and earned a lot of respect within the community. Now, however, she saw a hint of sorrow that had previously been hidden.

"You're not at work again?" Rosanna asked softly.

Startled from his thoughts, Reuben looked at her. His blue eyes were bloodshot and tired. Without his hat on, and with his hair yet to be brushed, the wrinkles near his temples were more noticeable. He seemed to have aged in the span of just a few days, and Rosanna knew that her illness had caused him much grief in that time.

He shifted his weight on the chair and cleared his throat. "You're awake, then."

She nodded and sat up in bed.

There was a moment of hesitation, as if both of them were waiting for the other's next move. Rosanna watched him, not knowing what to say. He watched her as if wondering what to do. Finally, he set the opened Bible on the table and pulled the chair beside the bed. When he leaned forward, he took her hand in his, a gesture that once again surprised her.

"How are you feeling, Rosanna?"

The touch of his skin on her hand combined with the question caused the color to flood to her cheeks. When was the last time someone had asked her that question? When was the last time anyone had noticed that she, too, had feelings and emotions that needed nourishing and attention? The truth was that she wasn't certain how she felt.

When it was clear that he was waiting for a response, she finally managed to find a word, the only word that seemed to fit her current state of mind: "Foolish."

He almost smiled, but she could tell that it was strained and forced.

"I'm sorry, Reuben." The words popped out of her mouth before she was really certain why she was apologizing. Was it the buildup of emotions? Was it the breakdown of a protective wall? Or was it her inability to keep giving of herself any longer?

"Rosanna . . ."

She didn't let him say anything else. "I . . . I never meant for any of this to happen, Reuben. I had only the best intentions when I married you." She stared at the blanket that covered her legs. "It just kept building and building, a feeling of wanting to please everyone and feeling as if I could please no one."

"That's not true, Rosanna."

She shook her head, adamant that she spoke the truth. "Everyone always seems to want something from me: Cate with her clinginess, the women from the *gmay*, even Gloria with her silly property line dispute. I feel like a shell of a person, filled with little broken pieces."

"You are not broken."

"And then the lot . . ." She lifted her eyes to meet Reuben's. She began to feel despondent again. She felt panicked for a moment over the memory of her husband being chosen, not just from the *gmay* but from God. "With my ill thoughts and short temper, how can I ever live up to being a preacher's *fraa*?" A tear fell from her eye and slowly trickled down her cheek. "I'm sure you are most disappointed in this." A pause. "In me."

"Now Rosanna," Reuben said. There was a firmness to his voice. "You need to rest and get better. Stop thinking about these things. You heard what the doctor said: rest and give the medicine time to help you feel better."

She didn't remember seeing a doctor. She wondered if any of her family had come to visit while she was sleeping. The doctor's sedative had been a godsend to help her regain her physical strength while the antidepressants worked on her mental needs. If only someone would help her with her spiritual distress. Now that Reuben was a preacher, she knew she couldn't go to the bishop. It would be embarrassing for Reuben and the family.

"Why aren't you at work?" she asked.

He shook his head. "Nan is taking care of things at the shop." There was a curtness in his voice, a distance that hinged on unhappiness. It made her wonder if her confession might have been the final straw.

Perhaps, she thought, this is too much for him . . . more than he signed up for.

By Wednesday afternoon Rosanna felt well enough to get out of the bed for the first time since she had fallen ill.

Just the previous evening, the doctor had stopped by and declared that she should be weaned off the sedative. In some ways, Rosanna knew she would miss it. Sleeping made her life easier. Reuben was too quiet, and she worried that her confession had shocked him into silence.

When she walked out of the bedroom, her hair pulled back in a bun and her dress properly pinned down the front, Reuben looked up from the table and lifted an eyebrow. It was an unspoken question, an inquiry as to whether or not she was certain about getting out of bed. She had thought that her coming out of the bedroom would be a sign for Reuben to stop worrying and return to his shop. Normalcy was needed in the house, she thought, and despite still feeling tired and drained, she knew that getting back into a routine would help her heal, both mentally and spiritually.

To her surprise, Reuben still showed no intention of leaving the house.

"I'm feeling a bit better," she said, despite not believing her own words. "I'm sure you've much to do at the shop."

"Nan's handling everything," he replied. He was focusing on the Bible again, studying Scripture and making notations on a piece of paper. "It's better if I'm home, *ja*?"

Silence fell over the room.

He had always claimed that he wanted to be home more, even talked about taking her to Pinecraft during the winter months. Now, however, she couldn't help but wonder if he was home because he wanted to be there or because he felt obligated to watch her. Either way, she wondered at the amount of confidence that he placed in Nan.

Sighing, Rosanna lingered near the counter, trying to assess where to get started. Everything looked orderly. She couldn't help but wonder who had been cooking and cleaning. "Reckon I'll make some bread today."

He looked up from the Bible and gestured toward the bread bin. "Mary and Barbara dropped off some bread just yesterday."

"Have there been other visitors, then?"

"Just the women from the *g'may*."

In a time of need, Rosanna had always been the first to help others. Now, apparently, she was on the receiving end. She wasn't certain how she felt about that shift in her position.

"Where's *Maem*?"

Rosanna heard Cate's voice from the other room followed by the slam of the screen door. Cringing at the noise, she waited to hear Reuben's rebuke to her daughter. Besides his aversion to loud noise and unruliness, she knew he'd want to keep Cate from waking her. He had noticed that Rosanna was growing weary after the noon meal and insisted that she lie down for an hour. His concern had touched her, and she had acquiesced without argument. Although she had initially fretted over his attention to her care, she now accepted it freely, allowing herself to receive the very love she so often gave to others.

"She's lying down now," came his soft response.

"I want her to see it!"

Rosanna heard his chair scrape against the floor as he pushed it away from the table. Holding her breath, she waited. Would he chastise Cate for speaking so sharply? Straining to hear, Rosanna could only make out a soft mumbling followed by a giggle from Cate. Moments later the door shut again, and Rosanna heard Cate whistling for the dogs.

Curiosity got the best of Rosanna.

Quietly, she stole across the bedroom floor and slowly opened the door. The kitchen was quiet again. Reuben sat at the table with the Bible open before him. His glasses had slipped down to the edge of his nose, and his head was tilted down as he read passages. He paused to make a note in his journal.

Rosanna must have made a sound, because he looked up and, upon seeing her, smiled. "I thought you were resting a spell."

"I heard Cate."

"Ah." Removing his glasses, he set them next to the Bible. "She's back from the produce auction with Aaron. Wanted to share her stories, no doubt."

"Produce auction?"

With a hint of pride, Reuben nodded. "*Ja*, that's correct. Twenty pecks of tomatoes and twelve pecks of eggplants were sold. But I'll let Aaron and Cate tell you the rest."

Normally Rosanna canned all of their produce and gave the extra containers to the elderly women who no longer had gardens, or else donated them to the Mennonite church.

As if reading her mind, Reuben stood up and laid his hands on her shoulders. "And there's enough for Mary King and your other women friends, Rosanna."

"Am I that transparent?" she asked.

He laughed. She liked the sound of it. The stress from work-ing so hard and the worry over his new role in the community had stolen laughter from her house. "*Nee*, Rosanna. Just a creature of habit and, when it comes to taking care of others before yourself, predictable."

She wasn't certain whether he meant that as a compliment or not. However, the levity of his mood quickly eliminated her concern.

"Let's go outside and find the *kinner*," he said. "I know they are both rather excited with their news."

Obediently she followed Reuben. He held the door open for her, and as she stepped across the threshold, she paused. The yard was freshly clipped, the flower beds were weeded, and the fence along the driveway had been freshly painted. But that wasn't what caught her attention. It was the stockade-style wooden fence that lined a large section of the property behind her garden. Six feet high and made of fresh pine, she couldn't miss it.

"Oh!" Her hand went to her throat, and she took a step onto the porch.

In front of the new fence were twelve large evergreen trees that covered most of the fencing so that it wasn't so shocking to see. With the exception of the peak of the roof and chimney, she could barely see the Smiths' house or property.

Immediately she knew that Reuben had arranged for this surprise.

"What . . . what is this?" she asked.

Reuben's hand pressed gently on the small of her back as he encouraged her to leave the shade of the porch. "I'll let the *kinner* explain," he replied, guiding her down the steps and toward the barn.

They found Aaron grooming his horse. Cate was stretched out atop a bale of hay playing with an orange kitten. Silently Rosanna stood in the doorway, enjoying the opportunity to observe her two children before they detected her presence. For the first time in longer than she could remember, she felt an emotion akin to joy. Aaron had turned into a young man, resembling his father in build but his mother in temperament, for which she was most grateful. As for Cate, whose dirty feet pressed against the barn wall as she dangled a piece of straw for the kitten to grasp, she was a miniature version of Rosanna.

How remarkable they are, Rosanna thought. Gifts from God.

Swallowing the emotions that rose to her throat, she took a step inside the barn. Both children looked up at the same moment. Cate immediately scrambled to her feet and ran to throw her arms around Rosanna's waist. More reserved with his affection, Aaron smiled and set down the grooming tool before opening the stall door.

"Did you see it? Did you see it?" Cate practically jumped up and down with excitement.

"If you mean the fence," Rosanna laughed, trying to contain her enthusiastic daughter, "*ja*, I couldn't help but see it."

"It was my idea!"

"Cate . . ." Reuben said, and at the sound of her name, Cate made a face and rolled her eyes.

"And Aaron, too." The overly dramatic reluctance to share credit with her brother made even her stepfather chuckle.

As a family, they walked out of the barn to the edge of the garden. Cate practically pranced as she pointed out each tree. She acknowledged that Aaron and Daniel had planted most of them, but was quick to add that she helped with watering them every morning and evening.

"I'm not quite certain what to say," Rosanna said. "Whatever made you think of doing such a thing? And the expense!"

This time it was Aaron who spoke up. "Don't you worry none about that, *Maem*. Daniel and I put in the posts, and Reuben nailed the fencing."

Cate poked her brother's arm. "I helped, too!" She looked at her mother. "I held the fencing while Reuben hit the nails."

Aaron strapped his thumbs under his black suspenders and tugged at them gently. The smile on his face showed his delight at having surprised his mother. "We all agreed that sometimes good fences make better neighbors."

"We may be told to love thy neighbor, but the Bible also says 'And I will give peace in the land, and you shall lie down, and none shall make you afraid.'" Reuben paused. "No one should live in fear of abuse, Rosanna, especially a woman who sacrifices so much of herself for the good of others." His voice caught, especially when he said the word "abused." "Living in fear drives people to dark places. We want you to only see light."

Darkness and light. She was only now realizing how long her life had been surrounded in darkness. The clouds seemed to be slowly lifting from her vision, and while she knew that it would take a long time until her darkest days were behind her, she felt strong enough to face the journey.

"Spoken like a true preacher," she managed to say. With a soft smile and tears in her eyes that she fought hard not to spill, she reached out and touched her husband's arm. It was a gentle touch that said what she really thought. When he nodded his head, she knew he understood. Forgiveness had been granted, not just by Reuben, but by herself.

It was time to move on from the past and to embrace the future.

# CHAPTER SEVENTEEN

S omething just isn't adding up here," Reuben said as he lifted his hands, receipts falling from his fingertips. They scattered like large snowflakes across the tabletop. He didn't move to pick them up. "Mayhaps it's me," he sighed, talking more to himself than to her. Frustrated, he ran his fingers through his hair, causing his graying curls to stand up in a wild mess atop his head.

Two weeks had passed since Rosanna had left her bed, and a new sense of calm had fallen over the house. Although Rosanna didn't feel completely better, and moments of darkness still snuck into her life, she could sense that the medicine was beginning to work. The doctor had explained that it could take up to six weeks for her to feel the full effect. Rosanna was just glad that the tremors in her hands and palpitations in her heart seemed to have disappeared.

With autumn just around the corner and his first sermon on the horizon, Reuben had quietly turned over the management of order fulfillment to Daniel and assigned Martin to visit remote farms to pick up and drop off items each Saturday. His decision to involve the two men came after much reflection—and after hearing a whisper or two about Nan's behavior at the youth gatherings.

Reuben hadn't shared his decisions about these changes with Rosanna. Instead, she learned this information from Aaron. And at night, Daniel often talked about the items that he made for different customers. She noticed a new vivaciousness to his conversation contributions, especially when he talked about the Englischer man from Vermont who came into the store for a brand-new harness, complete with fancy studding to dress it up for the holidays.

Several days a week, Daniel brought home the order log, accounting book, and customer receipts. Reuben liked to review them after supper, and tonight was one of those nights.

The look of concern on Reuben's face worried Rosanna. She knew that his books were always in order. He was meticulous with his accounting. If something was a problem, the error was certainly not his fault.

"What's wrong?" She peered over his shoulder, trying to look at the pieces of paper.

"Petersheim's order," he said, tapping his finger on the tabletop. "I can't find it, Rosanna." He explored the papers again, shoving some aside as he looked through the pile. When he still didn't find it, he slapped his palm against the table. "I know that I took that order from him. Why, it was just two weeks ago!" Frustrated, he turned to look at Rosanna. "Just after Elias Beiler passed and the lot . . ."

He didn't have to finish his sentence. Life had been chaotic since then. What with Reuben becoming a preacher and Rosanna's illness, he certainly had enough on his mind. It could have gotten lost. However, Rosanna knew it was highly unlikely that Reuben would lose an order. His attention to detail was well known, which was likely one of the reasons why the members of the *g'may* had voted for him.

"You have been rather busy," she said softly.

"But I've never lost an order."

She smiled. "You've never been a preacher, either."

Her comment made him chuckle. He removed his glasses and set them on top of the papers. She watched as he rubbed his eyes. She saw a weariness in his somber expression and downtrodden posture, but the mask that he wore demonstrated his strength in dealing with stress. Rosanna wished that she could mirror that strength, but she also knew that her protective shell had been chipped away during the last few years. It was not so easy to hide her vulnerability, even with the medicine from the doctor.

Still, she tried to put on a brave face for Reuben. His willingness to stand by her side during her mental breakdown gave her the courage to support him. "Mayhaps I could look through your order book, Reuben," she offered. "Sometimes a fresh set of eyes . . ."

Without hesitation, he pushed the papers aside and picked up the small journal where he recorded his orders. He handed it to her and sighed. "It's just not there, but have a look."

She opened the journal and looked at the first page. She immediately recognized Reuben's neat handwriting: small letters that looped elegantly but evenly across each page. There was an occasional black smudge where he must have erased something. Flipping through the pages, she looked down the date column, searching for two weeks ago. It didn't take her long to see a pattern. Slowly but surely the orders had increased over the past two months. She also noticed that Reuben's neat handwriting had been replaced with small, childish penmanship.

"Is that Nan's handwriting, then?" She pointed to a row and tilted the book so that Reuben could see.

He squinted as he tried to focus on the ledger. Without his asking, Rosanna handed him his glasses, and he slipped them on. He nodded. "*Ja*, Nan's."

Rosanna fought the urge to clench her teeth. She used the calming techniques the doctor had taught her. Slowly she inhaled and exhaled. Her eyes skimmed the page, and when she came to the end, she turned to the next one.

That was when she saw it. The smudge was barely visible, but it was there.

Rosanna lifted the ledger and peered closely at the row. Sure enough, something had been erased and written over in pen. Scanning the row, she looked for the date. It coincided with the time frame when Reuben believed Kenneth Petersheim had placed his order. But instead of an $800 harness, the line documented a small order for leather lead shanks.

"Do you remember Eli Yoder ordering four lead shanks?" she asked.

Reuben frowned. "Four lead shanks?"

She nodded. "Made of leather."

He frowned as he tried to recall. "His cousin came in just a few days ago asking for a few lead shanks. Was going to sell them at his own store. I didn't pay much attention to it."

Rosanna took another slow, deep breath, and then asked, "Did Nan take the order?"

"I do believe she did."

Quietly Rosanna flipped a few pages in the ledger and looked for any indication of another Yoder request for lead shanks . . . or anyone, for that matter. There was definitely no record of the Petersheim order. Without it being in the book, no one would fulfill it. Ken would wait for a long time, thinking that the Troyer Harness Shop was backlogged. Everyone knew how busy they were, especially with Reuben's new role in the church. Then Ken would probably just go to another harness store rather than bother Reuben. But he'd certainly remember the fact that his order had been forgotten. At least, that's the scenario that played out in Rosanna's head.

But she knew that was only the end of the story. What was the beginning? An idea began to formulate in Rosanna's mind.

Someone had deliberately erased the order and replaced it with one that was less significant. There was only one reason someone would do that—to sabotage the business.

"Oh help," she muttered.

Even if what she suspected had happened, Rosanna didn't want to be the one who said it aloud.

Reuben saw how still she had become and reached out to touch her hand. "What is it?"

Shutting the book, Rosanna handed it back to him. She shook her head. "It's nothing, really."

His eyes drilled into hers. "What did you see, Rosanna?"

Only when she saw how serious he had become—and how worn out he looked—did she sigh and reopen the book. "There's no listing for any other lead shanks in the book except here . . ." She pointed to a line on the page that had been entered over two weeks ago. "If you look closely, it was written over something else that was erased."

She watched him read and then reread the same line. Then, as if he didn't believe her, he turned the next two pages and read the entries. If he was trying to find another Yoder order, it wasn't there.

"The copies of customer receipts are correct and match with the accounting book. This doesn't make sense," he admitted, peering up at her from over the rim of his eyeglasses. "What does this mean? Why would Nan erase an older order?" he asked more to himself than to Rosanna.

Rosanna didn't want to remind Reuben that Daniel had made a comment just two nights before about Nan sending Martin to the wrong farm the previous Saturday. According to Daniel, when Martin confronted Nan, she hadn't apologized for the mistake, which was costly in both money and time. Instead, she had acted nonchalant and even defensive.

At that time, Reuben hadn't seemed concerned about the story. But now he appeared to be slowly realizing that the missing order indicated deception by someone at his shop. "Are you suggesting . . . ?"

Rosanna lifted her hands as if warding off danger. "I'm not suggesting anything, Reuben," she said quickly. "I am not partial to Nan Keel. You know that. Therefore, I'm not in any position to speculate about her actions . . . or the reasons behind them."

Reuben took a deep breath. As he exhaled, he wrapped his hand around hers in a gesture of comfort. "I know that, Rosanna. You'd sooner take the Lord's name in vain than talk negative about another." He forced a small smile. "I need to wrap my head around this, I reckon. It just doesn't make sense."

Silently, Rosanna agreed with that statement. If Nan had deliberately erased Reuben's writing, it could mean only one thing: she wanted Reuben to forget the Petersheim order on purpose. Had Nan thought that Ken Petersheim would not speak with Reuben about his order next time they met? Could she possibly believe that no one would discover such duplicity? Regardless of her reasons for doing it, Reuben had discovered what Nan had done, and the fact that she had purposefully erased the order did not make her appear honest.

For a long time Reuben sat in the chair, stunned by the possibility that Nan had deceived him. Rosanna could see it on his face. He was completely unprepared for such a dishonest action from one of his employees. Having his trust shaken like that must be breaking his heart. Seeing Reuben in such pain pained her.

"I . . . I need to go outside for a spell," he mumbled. "Mayhaps see if Aaron needs some help in the barn."

As Reuben left the house with his head hung down, he passed Cate in the doorway. His arm brushed against hers, but he didn't seem to notice. Cate turned aside so that he could pass. When he didn't even acknowledge her presence, she frowned and watched after him. Rosanna walked to the door and placed her hand on Cate's shoulder, following her daughter's gaze.

"What's wrong with Reuben?" Cate asked, her eyes big and concerned.

"Nothing that you need to worry about," Rosanna responded softly, a gentle reminder for Cate to mind her own business.

But Cate's interest in her stepfather's solemnity was stronger than her sense of obedience. "Something happen at the shop?"

"Cate," Rosanna said; the single word was spoken as a firm warning. Her eyes shifted back toward the barn, and she watched as Reuben disappeared through the doorway to where Aaron and Daniel were working. "What do you say we go pick some fresh zucchini from the garden?"

Defiantly, Cate lifted an eyebrow. "I'm not going out there alone."

"Cate!" This time Rosanna's voice scolded rather than warned. At the hurt look on her face, Rosanna softened her tone and added, "And I said 'we,' Cate."

Relief replaced Cate's pained expression. "That old woman scares me, *Maem*," Cate said. "She's just the meanest person in the world."

Even if she secretly agreed with her daughter, Rosanna tried to downplay Gloria's malevolence. "Not so scary anymore, I reckon. We have that fence to give us privacy from her."

Cate added, "And the trees! Don't forget the trees."

"*Ja*, the trees, too," Rosanna said, smiling.

While the fence blocked her view of the Smiths' house and yard, their voices still carried to her ears. They were constantly complaining, yelling, and sometimes even swearing. Gradually, however, their presence on the other side of the fence seemed to diminish. Rosanna wasn't certain whether the two women had lost interest in her because they couldn't witness a reaction, or that she simply couldn't hear them over the fence and the new foliage. Either way, Rosanna had begun to find the strength and courage to walk out the kitchen door and work in her own garden.

Although the stockade fence hid Gloria's house from view, in the beginning, Rosanna found it unattractive. The freshly cut pine wood looked too obvious, even with the evergreen trees. Once, when the bishop visited, both Rosanna and Reuben noticed him looking curiously at the new addition to their property.

"A neighbor issue," Reuben had admitted.

"Ah." The bishop pursed his lips and nodded his head as if understanding the situation without any further explanation.

Nothing else had been said about the fence.

But now the fence seemed as if it had always been there. Rosanna appreciated the expense of erecting it, and she knew that the peace of mind that it offered her was invaluable.

Together, Cate and Rosanna walked out to the garden. Their bare feet left soft footprints in the dirt. The plastic bucket on Rosanna's arm was quickly filled with green zucchinis and yellow squash. The cucumbers were plentiful, too, and Rosanna made a mental note to pickle some for the winter. She had a lot of work ahead of her. Beets needed to be canned, chowchow needed to be made, and, at some point, she needed to see about getting beef to can for the winter. The summer seemed to have flown by, and too much time had been wasted.

Still, she could breathe easier knowing that she was finally sharing her burden with others, allowing them to help lift her when in the past she had tried too hard to carry the weight by herself.

# CHAPTER EIGHTEEN

The shop was eerily quiet when Rosanna opened the door. The bell, a joyful noise in the past, didn't sound nearly so cheerful when the front office was empty. Carefully she shut the door and, as Reuben had instructed, made sure it was locked to any customers who might miss the Closed sign in the front window. It was Saturday afternoon, and Reuben had let everyone leave early. Everyone, that is, except Nan. He had told Nan that he needed to meet with her.

"Back here, Rosanna," Reuben called out.

Even standing on her toes, she couldn't see him; he stood near his narrow desk behind the large machinery. Usually the desk was covered with papers. He referred to it as his organized chaos. While Rosanna preferred orderliness, Reuben worked better with papers to shift around. He also had a habit of keeping too many catalogs, many of them outdated, in a wire bin on the back corner of his desk. Today, however, there was nothing on his desk . . . no papers, no catalogs, no bin. There was nothing there except a single manila folder.

"Why hello there, Rosanna!" Nan jumped up from her seat and held out her hand. The smile on her face was not reflected in her eyes. "I heard you weren't well. I trust things are better now?"

Deep breath, Rosanna told herself. She knew full well that Nan had more than just *heard* she was *not well*. After all, Reuben had stayed home for almost a week to tend to Rosanna's needs. The women from the church had organized sending over meals. Like most other things worth discussing in the *g'may*, Rosanna's illness had certainly hit the Amish grapevine. Nan's nonchalant comment, so clear in its transparency, would have unnerved her if she hadn't been prepared for it.

"I'm feeling better, *danke*," she said, trying to force a smile as Nan returned to her seat. "The *g'may* women were quite helpful in bringing food for the family. Their generosity was a true blessing."

At the mention of help from the church, Nan looked uncomfortable. She shifted her weight on the chair and uncrossed her feet. "I hope Daniel brought home the casserole I made," she said, too quickly for Rosanna to believe there was ever a casserole.

"*Nee*, Nan," she said slowly. "He did not."

"He's so forgetful sometimes!" Nan laughed, but there was an edge to her voice. The pointed attempt to criticize Daniel was far too obvious.

Clearing his throat, Reuben leaned forward, an indication that it was time to talk business. Rosanna sat down in the free chair, and Reuben put his hands on the folder, his eyes boring into Nan's. "Now that Rosanna is here, I suggest we get started with this meeting."

Nan glanced at Rosanna, a confused expression on her face. Clearly she wanted to ask why Rosanna needed to be there for the meeting, but she did not.

"It's been over two months since you began working here, Nan." Reuben spoke slowly and cautiously. "Things in the shop have changed since that time."

Relief replaced confusion, and Nan lifted her shoulders, smiling. "They have, *ja*. More orders, happier customers, even the mobile pickup program is a great success!"

Feeling tension in the pit of her stomach, Rosanna couldn't look at the younger woman. She knew where the conversation was headed.

Oblivious to Rosanna's reaction and Reuben's ambivalence, Nan continued talking. "I knew that new program would be a success, Reuben. It was just the logical next step. Now, if we could only get a fax line in here . . . There are more ideas that I want to implement."

"Let's focus on the orders for the moment," Reuben said, redirecting Nan to the conversation. He opened the manila folder and lifted a piece of paper. "Ken Petersheim. He stopped in the shop mid-July and ordered a new driving harness. Custom made for eight hundred dollars." Setting the paper down, Reuben looked at Nan. "There's no record of it."

Nan's only indication of concern was the slightest flicker of a frown on her face. Otherwise she remained completely unruffled, a fact that did not escape Rosanna's notice. Her reaction caused Rosanna a moment of irritation. Reuben had not slept at all the previous two nights, tossing and turning almost as much as he had during those first sleepless nights following the lot. The pain he felt was deep and more than just emotional misery; he felt a spiritual suffering that broke Rosanna's heart.

Nan, however, seemed completely unaware of the undercurrent of distress emanating from her employer. With hooded eyes, she stared at Reuben as she pursed her lips. "Who took the order?" she asked calmly.

The bluntness of her question coupled with her tone caught both Reuben and Rosanna off guard. Rosanna glanced at Reuben, noticing that he was studying Nan with a mixture of surprise and curiosity in his expression. "I did," he admitted.

For a long moment Nan remained silent, her eyes downcast and her finger tracing the edge of the chair's armrest. She exhaled slowly, with just enough exaggeration for Rosanna to realize that she was striving for dramatics, that she was overplaying her response on purpose. It dawned on Rosanna that many of Nan's reactions were contrived in such a manner, the subtleness most likely undetectable by anyone who was not anticipating the manipulation.

"What is it, Nan?" Rosanna asked, maintaining a gentle tone. She suspected that Nan was waiting for her question. The wheels of the younger woman's mind were clearly spinning, and Rosanna found herself curious as to where this conversation would lead.

"*Ach vell*, I didn't want to say anything," Nan started, speaking deliberately slowly and enunciating each syllable. She ran a finger along the edge of the desk. There was a softness in her tone that Rosanna had not heard before. Usually she was loud and direct, commanding the center of attention. This humble side was out of character for Nan and only further convinced Rosanna of how cunning and conniving she truly was, a fact further confirmed when Nan continued. "It's not really my place to say anything . . ." she said.

Neither Reuben nor Rosanna spoke, a captive audience to Nan's confession. Surely she would admit her guilt and plead for forgiveness. Like a dutiful preacher and wife, they waited expectantly for her next words.

To their mutual surprise, rather than an admission of guilt, an accusation of blame slipped from Nan's lips as she turned to face Rosanna. "Reuben has become more forgetful recently. I'm sure it's the pressure of all that has happened in the past few weeks," Nan said. "What with you being so sick and all."

Rosanna blinked her eyes, incredulous. She repeated Nan's words in her head. Reuben forgetful?

As if reading her mind, Nan nodded. "*Ja*, Reuben's been forgetting to log orders and even gave Martin the wrong directions to pick up items from farmers. No one wanted to say anything," she said softly. "But everyone is concerned and talking about it. Daniel, Martin, even Rebecca."

"I . . . I'm stunned," Rosanna managed to whisper, unable to look away from the young woman who sat before her so nonchalantly deflecting the guilt away from herself.

"I've been doing so much cleaning up after him," Nan continued, waving her hand dismissively in Reuben's direction. "Even the brusque way in which he speaks to customers, telling them that he's too busy to talk to them or stomping out of the front area."

Rosanna frowned. She glanced at Reuben, who appeared completely astonished by Nan's accusations. His cheeks were flushed red—whether from humiliation or from anger, Rosanna did not know, and she wasn't certain she wanted to find out.

"Why, your own *dochder* won't come down here to work anymore," Nan said, once again directing her words to Rosanna as if Reuben were not seated less than two feet in front of them. "It's an abusive work environment with too long hours and very little appreciation for our efforts. We all feel that it's time for him to retire before things get even worse."

When Nan finally stopped talking, the room was silent. Rosanna couldn't think of one thing to say, and she was certain that Reuben was also at a loss for words. They sat without moving, waiting for Nan to continue with her unexpected assault on Reuben's character. Thankfully she didn't. Instead, she sat there as calm as could be, as though it were an everyday event to rip out someone's heart and stomp on it—for surely that was what she had just done to Reuben.

The satisfied look upon her face, however, indicated that she was either unaware of, or simply didn't care about, the pain her words had caused. Then it dawned on Rosanna: The woman truly believed that she had spoken the truth and was doing them a favor by sharing her lies with them. Even worse, she appeared proud to have done so.

How *unusual*, Rosanna thought as she stared at Nan. It was the only word she could think of that did not border on breaking one of the commandments. Nan actually believed her fabrication. The realization shocked Rosanna as much as Nan's assertions had.

There was something about Nan that made Rosanna uneasy. It was more than just her bluntness at the farm or that she didn't help clear plates after dinner. It even went beyond her reluctance to help Rosanna clean the house or her behavior at the youth gatherings. "A fool's mouth is his destruction, and his lips are the snare of his soul," Rosanna thought, realizing how true this verse was. Not only was Nan a fool, she was also in need of powerful prayer to help her soul.

Rosanna managed to swallow. Her throat had suddenly become unbearably dry. "Nan," she began. "You know that is not true."

"You don't work down here." Short and to the point, Nan showed no compassion.

"I know that Reuben has been most kind to both you and your *bruder*," Rosanna said. "All of his workers are rewarded generously and with great appreciation."

"Oh really, then?" Nan's voice started to slip, a tightness behind her words. "Why, I didn't hear one single word of gratitude for my idea for the mobile harness program!"

Rosanna fought the urge to point out that it was actually her own idea. Thankfully, she didn't have to. Reuben slammed his hand down on the top of the desk, his blue eyes hinting at the rage he had hidden. Both Nan and Rosanna jumped at the noise.

His voice boomed as he shouted, "That's enough! I've heard enough!" He shut his eyes quickly, as if taking a moment to compose himself. When he opened them again, he stared at Nan with an intensity that made Rosanna feel uncomfortable. "I will not let you take credit for an idea that was not yours."

Nan started to respond, but Reuben held up his hand, the gesture strong and swift. "What I want to know is why the Petersheim order was erased from the log book?" He spun the book around and shoved it across the desk. Nan glanced at it, paling for just one moment. "It was deliberately erased, Nan."

"Someone else must have done that, then," she said.

"No one else has reason to access the order log," Reuben said.

Nan shrugged, trying to appear unconcerned. "Daniel looks at it, *ja*? Mayhaps he did it."

Reuben pointed to the line in the logbook. "If that was true, why would you write over it with another entry days later? Why wouldn't you question the missing order?" His voice rose as he continued speaking. "This shop does not value selfish ambition but hard work that contributes to the collective welfare of our community. This missing order leads me to believe that the person who did it was trying to make someone else look inept in order to inflate her own importance!"

At his words, Nan gasped.

Refusing to let her speak, Reuben pulled the order book from her hands and slammed it shut. "I will not have someone working here who values personal achievement over humility and obedience—not just to our way but to God!" He spoke sternly to her. Lifting his hand, he began to count off with his fingers. "God, church, community, family." He paused, his four fingers still in the air. "There is no self in the order of things. Not in our family, church, and community. And if you study God's word, He, too, requires self-denial for the greater good."

It took a solid minute for Reuben's words to sink in, in which time Nan's composure transformed. Slowly her demeanor shifted from overly confident to bewilderment. Rosanna averted her gaze when she noticed tears welling up in Nan's eyes. She finally understood where the conversation was going.

Reuben did not waste any more time delivering his final determination. "It's best that we part company at this point, Nan, before more words are said that will be regretted later."

Nan stood up and leaned against the desk, staring down at Reuben. To his credit, he remained calm.

"This is an outrage!" Nan's eyes narrowed, and she pressed her lips together, fighting the flow of tears that threatened to fall down her cheeks. "The bishop will hear about this, how you treat your employees. And from a preacher, no less!"

When neither Reuben nor Rosanna responded, Nan huffed and crossed her arms over her chest. Clearly she had not expected their lack of reaction. That incited her temper even more. With silence as her cue, Nan turned on her heel and spun around, storming across the worn wooden floor to the office door. Moments later, the front bell jingled, sounding a bit happier to Rosanna than it had when she first entered.

Alone, Reuben looked up at Rosanna apologetically. While his shoulders seemed lighter, as if a burden had been lifted just a little, he still looked worn and unhappy. "I'm sorry you had to witness that," he said.

"*Nee*, Reuben, it's right *gut* I came." She meant it, too. Nan's reaction proved one thing to Rosanna: mental illness was not as uncommon as she had previously thought. "She's very troubled, wouldn't you say?"

"Troubled?" He leaned back in his chair and ran his hands over his face. "I'd say a little more than troubled." He sighed and shook his head. "She needs our prayers. Her walk with God has great need of realignment."

Rosanna wondered if there was anything her husband could do to help Nan. After all, he was a preacher now. But Nan had not officially joined their church. While she had been baptized in her former community in New York, she had not presented a letter from her bishop requesting the transfer of her church membership to the new *g'may*. It dawned on Rosanna that the letter may not have been presented because Nan knew that it might be more telling than she wanted.

"What about the bishop?" Rosanna asked.

"I've already taken counsel from him," Reuben admitted. "He's aware of what has transpired."

She didn't press the issue, knowing that whatever Reuben discussed with the bishop was not her business. Besides, she didn't want the burden of knowing. Her focus was on healing herself and supporting her family. Slowly she was beginning to recognize the difference between self-denial and self-discipline. Her ability to help everyone was limited—not by her desire but by her inability to handle too much at once.

"What will you do about the house, then?" It was a question that Rosanna knew would be on his mind.

"She'll have to pay rent, I reckon. That was part of our agreement. No rent, but reduced pay while working for the shop."

The solution sounded simple enough, but Rosanna wondered what Nan's brother would think of this agreement. Samuel—the elusive younger brother Rosanna had met only once. Would he be willing to pick up Nan's share until she found another job? Would Nan even stay in the area, or might she return to New York? Rosanna didn't ask those questions out loud, not wanting to place additional stress on Reuben.

She knew the burden of stress weighed heavily on a person's soul, the pressure eventually taking its toll on the body. Only time could answer what remained unspoken. In the meantime, she would support Reuben just as he had supported her during her dark days. Quietly she excused herself and went outside to wait for him. Her husband needed a few minutes alone to pray and reflect.

Outside, Rosanna stood by the buggy and did the same, asking the Lord to give Reuben the strength to make the right decisions in how to approach Samuel about his sister's termination and, quite possibly, mental issues. Rosanna also prayed that the Lord would provide her the wisdom to know how to best support her husband.

# Chapter Nineteen

The banging on the front door startled Rosanna from a deep sleep. At first she thought she was dreaming. It was well after midnight, and no one visited that late. When the noise continued, however, she heard Reuben groan and roll over before sitting up. The windows were open, and she heard a male voice shout Reuben's name. In the quiet of the night, it sounded as if the person was standing beside their bed. Whoever was outside had walked around the back of the house.

"Something must have happened," Reuben mumbled, the sound of sleep still thick in his voice. He slid his legs out from beneath the sheet and fumbled in the darkness for a flashlight.

"Oh dear!" She rubbed at her eyes as the beam of light illuminated the room. "Can't be good, then."

He responded with a grunt as he slipped on a pair of black pants. "You stay here, Rosanna."

Sitting up, she leaned against the headboard and watched his dark frame moving toward the door. Nothing good ever happened after ten o'clock, she thought.

Once he left the room, she was shrouded in darkness again. A wave of fear washed over her, and she said a prayer that nothing had happened to Aaron. After supper, he and Daniel had gone out with some friends. Now that she was awake, she realized that she hadn't heard him return. Panic set in as she entertained these thoughts. Her heart began to pound, and she started to pray fervently, knowing that she must put her trust in God.

Seconds seemed like minutes as she waited. Despite Reuben's instructions, she finally slipped out from underneath the sheet and hurried through the darkness to the open door of their room. The voices of two men cut through the silence of the night. Quietly she crossed to the front door and stood in the shadows so she could hear without interrupting.

". . . letters to several girls and even one to Daniel. He's the one who called us. No one read the notes until long after she left, but it sure didn't sound good. Daniel wanted to alert you."

In the soft glow from the flashlights, Reuben nodded his head. "I'll go check on her, then."

"The police are on their way, too," the other male voice said.

At the mention of the police, Rosanna couldn't contain herself anymore. "What's going on?"

Reuben ignored her question long enough to bid goodnight to the two men. When he shut the door and turned around, his face looked angry. She knew it wasn't just because he had been awakened at such a late hour. "Best get dressed, Rosanna," he said. "I'll be wanting you with me."

"What is it, Reuben? You're scaring me."

"It's Nan." Rosanna knew by the way he said her name, low and without emotion, that whatever she had done must have been awful.

"What did she do?"

Reuben shook his head as he walked back to the bedroom to change his nightshirt for a regular white-collared button-down one. Rosanna followed his example and changed into a dress. "Not *gut*," he mumbled. "She joined up with the youth gathering tonight and handed out letters to some of the girls. Said it was her good-bye letter." He talked as he dressed. "Told everyone she was fired and going away."

"So why are police involved?" Rosanna asked.

He gestured for her to hurry. "One of the girls opened the letter about two hours later." He paused and shook his head. "Nan . . . she told everyone that she's going to . . ." His voice drifted away. He couldn't speak the words, but from the look on his face, Rosanna immediately understood. "Said that she couldn't continue living like this, the pain is too much."

"Oh dear Lord!"

"I'll get the buggy ready." He didn't wait for Rosanna's reply as he disappeared into the darkness of the kitchen.

Twenty minutes later, they pulled into the driveway at the shop. Leaving the buggy tied to the hitching post, Reuben ran toward the house. Without even knocking, he burst through the door. Rosanna followed him inside.

Nan was on the kitchen floor, leaning against a cabinet with her hands on her lap, palms up. Her head lolled forward, her chin pressed against her chest. Scattered on the floor were pill bottles and a box—an assortment of over-the-counter medicine. Reuben froze inside the doorway, staring at the woman. Rosanna, however, rushed to Nan's side.

Kneeling beside her, Rosanna reached for Nan's hand and held it as she tried to awaken her. "Nan, can you hear me? Nan?"

"Is she breathing?" Reuben asked.

Rosanna shook Nan, just a little, and called her name one more time. The younger woman's eyes fluttered open. Through narrow slits, she tried to focus on Rosanna.

"Nan, what did you take?" Rosanna asked.

Weakly, Nan attempted to point toward the floor. Her eyes drooped shut, and her hand fell back onto her lap.

"How many?" Rosanna gave her another shake. "Answer me. How many did you take?"

Nan took a deep breath and tried to open her eyes again. "Fif—fifteen."

Reuben leaned down and picked up the medicine. Rosanna stared at him expectantly, waiting for him to identify the pills. With his lips pressed together, he shook his head. He looked annoyed. "Allergy medicine." He met Rosanna's eyes. "She'll sleep, but she'll be fine."

"I . . . I took a lot," Nan whispered, her eyes rolling slightly to the right. "I should have taken more."

Rubbing Nan's hand, Rosanna quieted her. "Hush now. None of that."

The sound of a siren interrupted the silence, and red lights flashed against the wall. Reuben glanced out the window. "Police are here."

Rosanna remained by Nan's side, still holding her hand. Regardless of her feelings for the woman, Rosanna wanted to offer as much comfort as she could. It wasn't that long ago that she, too, had felt desperate and worthless and as if she were at the bottom of a dark pit that was caving in, burying her in its blackness. While suicide had never actually crossed her mind, she certainly could understand the despair and depression that could lead someone down that path.

Two police officers entered the kitchen, and Rosanna immediately recognized the one officer who had been at her farm to investigate Gloria's complaint a few weeks earlier. He knelt down beside Nan.

"Ma'am? Can you hear me?"

It took all of Nan's effort to respond with a small nod.

"Can you tell me what happened here?"

Nan managed to point to the pills.

"Did you take those?" He glanced over his shoulder at his partner and made a gesture. Immediately the second officer disappeared outside while the first officer returned his attention to Nan. "Ma'am, how many pills did you take?"

"Twenty."

Rosanna frowned and shook her head. "That's not what she said when we arrived," she told him. "She said she took fifteen."

The officer acknowledged her information and turned back to Nan. "Was it twenty? Or was it fifteen?" he asked.

"A lot," Nan mumbled. "I took a lot."

When the officer didn't ask another question, Rosanna took the opportunity to ask her own. "Is she going to be all right, then?"

"We have an ambulance coming." He stood up, his knees cracking. "They'll take her to the hospital. Are you family?"

Reuben cleared his throat and stepped forward. Rosanna knew he felt uncomfortable, but she was having a hard time reading his reaction. He looked concerned and irritated at the same time. "*Nee*, but she has a *bruder* that lives here," Reuben said. "He's apparently not home."

"And no way to contact him?"

"Does he have a cell phone, Reuben?" Rosanna asked in Deitsch. When he shook his head, she looked back at the officer. "*Nee*, but we can stay until he returns to the *haus* and tell him what's happened," Rosanna offered. She noticed the sharp look that Reuben gave her, and she immediately knew what he was thinking: don't get involved. Clearly he thought her offer to wait for Samuel was just one more indication of how generous and selfless she was, and he didn't approve. After all, hadn't her devotion to helping others without any thought of herself nearly landed her in the hospital?

Her thoughts were interrupted by the siren of an approaching ambulance. It stopped right in front of the house, eerie circles of red strobe lights illuminating the room. Two EMTs pushed a wheeled stretcher through the doorway while a third one, a stethoscope around his neck and a medical bag hanging from his shoulder, shone a bright handheld flashlight ahead of them.

"Over here!" One of the policemen directed them into the kitchen where Nan still lay.

After checking her pulse and verifying that her breathing was not overly strained, one of the medics asked the police officer about the nature and quantity of the pills she had ingested. Using a walkie-talkie attached to his belt, he shared the information with an emergency room physician at the hospital, nodding from time to time.

"There's no need to empty her stomach at this point," the medic finally announced, quickly adding, "but we'll take her to Lancaster General for further examination and to run some tests." He looked first at Rosanna and then at Reuben. "Will one of you want to accompany her?"

An awkward silence filled the kitchen as he waited expectantly. The other two EMTs picked up Nan in unison, obviously a well-rehearsed movement, then gently set her upon the stretcher. Without waiting, they rolled it out of the kitchen, carefully maneuvering through the narrow doorway.

Taking a deep breath, Rosanna opened her mouth to volunteer, but Reuben, sensing that she was, once again, about to sacrifice her own well-being and much-needed rest for the benefit of someone else—someone who would neither be aware of nor appreciate the gesture—stopped her from speaking.

"Her *bruder*, Samuel, should return home in a short while, and we will make sure we have a driver on call so that he can immediately visit his *schwester* at the hospital."

For a long while after the red strobe lights of both vehicles faded into the dark of night, Reuben and Rosanna stood in the kitchen in silence. Reuben paced the floor, his hands clasped behind his back. Rosanna, however, remained standing where she had found Nan, staring at the pill bottles, now neatly lined up on the counter.

She wondered why the police or medical people hadn't taken the bottles. It was the sole thought that raced through her mind. She didn't reflect on what could have pushed Nan to do something so selfish and hurtful to the people around her. She didn't question Nan's real motives for such a thoughtless display of histrionics. Instead, Rosanna focused on the bottles.

"Best go call the driver," Reuben finally said, his voice husky and rough. He disappeared through the doorway; Rosanna did not look up when he left. She could hear his footsteps on the gravel, the crunching noise echoing in the quiet night. If she concentrated, she thought she could hear the crickets chirping in the field behind the shop.

Five minutes later, Reuben returned. "Driver said he'd be on call for Samuel."

"That's *gut*," she said.

"Rosanna . . ."

She looked up and stared at her husband.

The color was drained from his face, and his blue eyes, so tired and weary, watered at the corners. "I . . . I need to know . . ." He couldn't finish the sentence.

"Know what?"

"Nan's demons," he whispered. "They are real, and they are dangerous. I need to know if you ever thought about . . ." Again his voice faltered.

Her heart sped up, the rapid beating hurting her chest. Seeing Nan on the floor and realizing what she had done, or at least attempted to do, had shocked Rosanna. To throw away one's life? What Rosanna had earlier thought was manipulation on Nan's part was clearly an indication of her pain, a way of trying to garner attention and cry out for help. But to actually be so emotionally distraught as to consider suicide?

Turning away from the pill bottles, Rosanna faced him and shook her head. "*Nee*, Reuben," she whispered. "I could never do such a thing as Nan did."

He shut his eyes. A lone tear escaped and fell gently down his cheek. He nodded his head, as if thanking her for reassuring him. Before he could say anything, the sound of a horse's hooves approaching the house interrupted the quiet. Listening to the rhythmic beat, Rosanna glanced at the clock and prayed that it was Samuel.

When they heard the buggy pull into the driveway, Reuben straightened his shoulders and walked to the door with firm resolve. There he waited in silence for Samuel to enter the house. Rosanna watched her husband's back, his broad shoulders blocking her view. She couldn't help but wonder about Samuel's reaction. Had he noticed their horse and buggy in the driveway? Did he notice that, despite the late hour, the kitchen light was still on?

Reuben opened the door for him. "Samuel . . . ?"

As the young man entered, he looked around, and his eyes— almost coal black in color—landed on Rosanna. Unlike Nan, who was broad in the shoulders and a bit thicker around the waist, Samuel was tall and willowy with a thick shock of wavy black hair. Rosanna had forgotten how attractive he was, his skin deeply tanned from working outside all summer at various construction sites under Jonathan's guidance. Rosanna had initially presumed that Samuel had been out with friends, but it was clear from his appearance that he was only just now returning from work.

He tilted his head in silent greeting to Rosanna and then focused his attention on Reuben. "What's happened?"

"Your sister's been taken to the hospital," Reuben said.

Samuel maintained a surprising sense of calm. Instead of reacting with shock or worry, he merely raised an eyebrow and took a long, deep breath. Rosanna wasn't expecting that. She had envisioned him receiving the news with panic. After all, his parents had died, and Nan was his only family.

After removing his hat and setting it on the kitchen table, Samuel spoke. "Is she hurt?"

His choice of words furthered Rosanna's uneasiness. He didn't ask *what happened* or *is she all right*, but *is she hurt?* She knew that Amish—especially the men—were masters at masking emotions, but she had certainly expected more concern than that.

"She took medications, Samuel," Reuben said, his voice calm and steady. He reached out and placed his hand on Samuel's shoulder. "She tried to harm herself."

The young man made a soft noise that sounded almost like a quick sigh of exasperation and nodded his head. "I see."

"I'll have my driver pick you up in a few minutes, if you'd like," Reuben said.

Samuel crossed his arms over his chest and leaned against the edge of the counter. "*Danke*, Reuben, *nee*."

Rosanna felt as if she had to reassure him. She offered him the only hope she could. "She's going to be all right. The medical people said she didn't take enough to hurt herself."

Samuel lifted an eyebrow and stared at her. There was a glazed-over look on his face, as if her words meant nothing to him. Instead of looking relieved, he looked indifferent. "She never does," he finally said.

At first she didn't understand what he said. But as the meaning became apparent, Rosanna caught her breath and lifted her hand to her chest, pressing it against her heart. The idea that Samuel was not surprised shocked Rosanna almost as much as his words, but suddenly everything began to make sense. Pieces of the puzzle fell into place, and Rosanna understood. The clarity of the moment seemed to hang in the air between the three of them.

"This . . . this has happened before?"

Samuel maintained his composure. His solemn expression remained stoic and unaffected, not the type of reaction that Rosanna would expect from a kind, loving brother.

"Has she done this before?" Samuel sighed as he repeated Rosanna's question. From the expression on his face, Rosanna could tell he didn't need to answer. But he did. "Several times, *ja*. It's for attention. That's why our *daed* didn't want her to run the business. She couldn't handle the pressure. If she made suggestions and he disagreed with her, she'd do something like this."

"You should have informed us," Reuben said sharply.

"She was taking her medicine. She is fine when she takes her medicine."

Rosanna glanced at Reuben. Medicine?

"Depression medicine," Samuel added, apparently noticing the look they exchanged. "She likes to please people, and if she thinks she's failed, she gets depressed."

Rosanna lowered her eyes. She knew what he meant. Hadn't she, too, recently gone through the same hardship of trying to please everyone until the pressure built up and her mind shut down? Her cup had been depleted—first by Timothy and then by Gloria, never mind the constant demands of her family, friends, and community.

"*Maem* used to be the one to administer her medicine. When she died and *Daed* was in the hospital, Nan really stayed strong." He stared at the wall behind Rosanna and Reuben, his eyes glazing over as he disappeared into his memory. "She spent every day in the hospital with him. But when she found out that *Daed* signed over the business to his partner and not to her, she didn't handle it well."

Partner? Rosanna frowned. "We didn't know that."

"*Ja*, his partner was our *onkel*. I never wanted to work with leather," Samuel admitted. "Nan did, however. But *Daed* wouldn't leave the business in the care of a woman."

"That's so sad," Rosanna whispered, more to herself than to Samuel.

"All she wanted was his approval," Samuel revealed. "But he always told her that a married woman had no place working."

Rosanna wondered if that was one of the reasons Nan had never married.

Samuel paused and studied Reuben for a moment, and something changed in his expression. "She looked up to you, like a father figure."

"A replacement is really what you mean." From the tone of Reuben's voice, Rosanna knew that he was not impressed with the flattery.

Samuel must have sensed the tension behind Reuben's words. Leveling his gaze at the older man, Samuel frowned as he asked, "Has something else happened, Reuben?"

"Indeed!" Reuben glared at the younger man. "You should have told us about Nan," he repeated. "Her behavior, both professionally and personally, has been questionable. Perhaps if you had warned us, we could have intervened to help her."

Samuel frowned. "She didn't want people to know."

Reuben shook his head. "'For nothing is secret, that shall not be made manifest; neither anything hid, that shall not be known and come abroad.' I told your *schwester* today that after God comes church, community, and family. Hiding the truth is never a good idea, Samuel. It festers inside until the cup tips and the contents spill out, leaving nothing behind . . ."

"But an empty cup," Rosanna whispered, completing her husband's sentence.

"This isn't my fault," Samuel said. "She's a grown woman."

"A grown woman who needs your support," Reuben added, his disapproval of Samuel's reaction more than apparent. "You best go call a driver to take you to the hospital."

Any hint of warmth or understanding on Samuel's face disappeared. Once again he was the solemn, expressionless man who had walked into the kitchen—the man who had barely reacted to the news that his older sister had tried to kill herself.

Rosanna wondered if, indeed, that was the truth. Had Nan really tried to harm herself, or had she merely tried to get Reuben's attention?

*Father figure.* The two words rang in her ears. Clearly Nan and Samuel's parents had come from a stricter community, one that valued very rigidly defined gender roles within the church district: boys worked in their father's business and girls grew up to tend the house, garden, and family. If Nan's father had neglected her, denying her the attention that she so obviously craved, it would make sense that she would transfer that inner desire to Reuben. Unknowingly, he had fed into her deep-rooted need to feel wanted by her father. And when he had terminated her, she had lashed out the only way she knew how in order to get his attention.

# Chapter Twenty

"A nd I say unto you, the Lord has blessed each of us with a gift, a powerful gift." Reuben stood before the congregation, one hand clenched in a fist while the other hung by his side. His eyes flamed with passion as he met many of the two hundred pairs of eyes that stared back at him.

Every member of the *g'may* had showed up for Preacher Troyer's first sermon. Some of the younger men had to stand at the back of the room because there were not enough chairs. Rosanna had always suspected that they didn't really mind standing during an unusually full worship service as it afforded them the liberty of sneaking out when no one was paying attention. At the moment, however, everyone was paying attention, even the young men who might have slipped through the door.

Reuben's eyes blazed with conviction, and his deep voice carried across the room. Rosanna could barely tear her gaze from him. It was as though he had transformed before her eyes. The man who usually was quiet and reserved now spoke with a passion that could only come from the heart. His words resonated throughout the large room where the members had gathered to worship. Today, indeed, no one was sneaking out.

"This gift," he continued, lowering his voice just enough that several people in the back leaned forward to hear, "this gift from God is called life!"

He paused, letting the words sink into everyone's heads and hearts.

"Now choose life, so that you and your children may live and so that you may love the Lord your God, listen to his voice, and hold fast to him. For the Lord is your life, and he will give you many years," Reuben said, his voice becoming louder as he quoted the Book of Deuteronomy from the Bible. "Choose life," he repeated. "Life!"

Behind her, Rosanna heard a child fidget and the sound of something dropping onto the floor. The child began to fuss, but the mother quickly quieted her.

"Life on earth *and* life in eternity. Those are God's gifts to us. And like everything that God gives, life is precious." Reuben paced along the narrow aisle that separated the men's benches from the women's. "Abraham, Moses, Job, even Joseph all understood the precious value of God's gift to us. To deny this gift . . . to sacrifice it . . . is a sin, I tell you. Why should any of us die before it is our time? Is that not questioning God's plan? Does that not display our lack of faith, no matter how troubling the times might feel at the moment?"

Rosanna fought the urge to look down at her hands, which were clutching the Ausbund resting on her lap. Taking deep breaths, she willed herself to not fear Reuben's words. She had not known he was going to speak them. Reuben had prepared for this sermon in private.

"And yet . . ." Another pause. He unclenched his fist and pointed toward the heavens. "And yet there is a demon walking among us, a demon like the one cast out by Jesus when He ministered to the poor, the sick, the downtrodden. A demon that Jesus cast out, leaving it to roam the earth."

Sitting in the second row, the bench reserved for the wives of the *g'may's* leaders, Rosanna dared not look anywhere but straight ahead. She felt as if everyone was staring at her, although she knew that it was far from the truth.

"But if a demon is cast out and nothing changes, when it returns to the same man and his house is still not in order, that demon will move right back in!" He lifted his open hand into the air and quickly shut it, as if grasping at something. "If a person cannot maintain his own house, it is up to us as a community to keep it in order. *Love thy neighbor.* That is one of the greatest commandments. Help maintain their houses so that demons cannot sneak in and steal that precious God-given treasure."

Rosanna caught her breath at his words.

"Who is our neighbor anyway? Is it the person living next to you? Is it the person sitting next to you?" He cleared his throat, reaching for the small glass of water that rested on a windowsill behind him. After taking a sip, he put the glass back and turned toward the members. "Jesus says it's the one who shows mercy. When someone shows mercy upon us, we know that they are, indeed, our neighbors. And in giving mercy, it is up to us to reciprocate when we see opportunities that call for grace."

He dropped his hand to his side and sighed. "Some people might think that loving your neighbor means endless giving, a life without ever receiving." He shook his head. "Someone who takes without giving back is not a neighbor. Someone who shows scorn to your mercy, who breaks God's commandments without fear or regret, who works hard to make others suffer, or who fights for personal gain at your expense . . . *nee*, I say, this is not your neighbor. Yet . . ." He paused and lifted his hand into the air, his finger pointed upward as he emphasized his main point. "We are taught that we must continue to pray for them and continue to love them."

Seated in a chair directly opposite Rosanna and to the right of the place where Reuben had been sitting just moments before starting his sermon, the bishop suddenly sat up straight and tilted his head. Worried that he was displeased, Rosanna took several deep breaths, willing her heart to be still and forcing her mind to slow down.

Reuben, however, did not seem to notice. "While there are times when loving our neighbors might be inconvenient or our prayers might be rejected, there comes a point in time when we must follow Paul's command to 'put away from among yourselves that wicked person.'"

Reuben took a few more steps. His brow was furrowed, and he looked deep in thought. No one spoke as they watched him. Rosanna hadn't known that Reuben would preach about this, using the recent issues of her depression and Nan's mental problems as the underlying theme to his first sermon. Even the comment regarding neighbors surprised her.

"Put away the wicked," he repeated. "Put away the wicked, leaving them behind you without judgment or regrets. Leave them as our ancestors left their persecutors and sought refuge in a new country. Leave them to their own destruction, the ruination of their earthly life." Then, lifting his eyes to stare at the back of the room, he raised his hand as if in greeting to a friend. "But always offer a hand of forgiveness . . . if it is sought." He glanced at Rosanna, his hand still in the air. For a second she thought she saw a hint of a smile on his lips.

After his sermon was finished, Reuben returned to his seat and lowered his head, waiting for the bishop, another preacher, and the deacon to comment on his words. Rosanna sat behind Reuben, watching his hunched shoulders as she listened to the bishop reiterate various points from her husband's sermon. When it was clear that no one had any contradictory points to add, she breathed out a sigh of relief.

After the worship service, Barbara Glick touched her arm as they set up the room for the meal. "So *gut* to see you," she said. "You were looking so tired the last time we spoke. Feeling better, then?"

Rosanna nodded. "*Ja, danke* for asking."

"And that girl?" Barbara clicked her tongue disapprovingly. "Have you heard how she is doing?"

"Nan?" Rosanna knew who Barbara meant, but she wanted time to formulate an appropriate response. Hadn't Reuben just talked about the sins of gossip and the importance of supporting those in need? Rosanna didn't want to tell Barbara about Nan's condition, how the doctors had kept her at the hospital for psychiatric evaluation for several days until they finally released her to another place better equipped for her long-term care.

"She'll be fine," Rosanna finally managed to say. "We continue to pray for her."

"Such a shame," Barbara said softly. "But so heart lifting that she's getting some help. It was right *gut* of your Reuben to take a collection for her care."

Her cheeks flushing pink, Rosanna downplayed Reuben's role. "He did what anyone would do." Or should do, she thought, aware of the irony of the *g'may* stepping forward to help Nan while her own brother had not.

"Are you two talking about the sermon?" Mary King interrupted their conversation, a broad smile on her face. With a shaky hand, Mary reached out to touch Rosanna's arm, the gesture comforting. "Your husband preached a mighty strong message today," Mary said. "He's a fine leader for the *g'may*."

Barbara nodded her head in agreement.

"I pray for him," Mary continued. "For both of you."

Emotion welled up in Rosanna's throat. She couldn't respond, uncertain of how strong her voice would be. Mary's words were so unexpected yet so full of genuine love that they caught her off guard.

"Remember," Mary said as she removed her hand from Rosanna's arm. "An empty cup cannot give." With a knowing smile—one that came from age and experience—she inclined her graying head just slightly, as if they shared a deep secret. "Keep your cup full, Rosanna. And know that God listens. Just ask, and He will refill your cup from the love that overflows His."

Mary didn't wait for a response from Rosanna. Instead, she gestured to Barbara that they should go sit at the table with the other older women for the noon meal. Rosanna stared after her, an echo in her ears as she realized the wisdom that Mary had just bestowed upon her. In moments of worry or stress, her faith in God could restore her peace of mind as well as replenish her when she felt depleted.

She did not need to drain herself dry for the sake of others. Instead, she just needed to rely on God and have faith that He would guide her—if not carry her—through times of strife and stress.

Lifting her eyes, she looked across the room to see Reuben watching her as he prepared to sit at the men's table. His blue eyes shone, and there was a smile on his face as if he could read her mind. She wanted to share her thoughts with him, but she knew it would be another hour before they left for home, perhaps longer if the older men lingered. She felt as if she were bursting at the seams, wanting to share the overwhelming emotions of knowing, at last, that her house was finally in order. However, from the joyous expression on his own face, she suspected that he already knew.

Peace flowed through her, a sense of calm and composure that she hadn't felt in many years. At long last, her cup was no longer empty.

# Epilogue

The leaves on the trees rustled in the evening breeze, their vibrant colors in stark contrast to the dark gray of the autumn sky. The clouds rolled in, and the scent of rain pervaded the air. A storm was brewing off the coast, or so the papers said. Still, it was a beautiful evening and a welcomed delay of the cold of winter that was just around the corner.

Rosanna sat in the rocking chair, a blanket covering her lap. Using the weight of her body, not her feet, she moved the chair back and forth, the gentle swaying motion calming her as she stared at the tree line. Orange, red, yellow, and brown. The colors comforted her. She was tired of green: green grass, green fields, green trees. It was time for a change, she thought, and not just of the seasons.

"Rosanna," Reuben called out through the open kitchen window, "want some tea?"

She rolled her head against the back of the rocking chair and tried to see the window. She couldn't. But she smiled anyway. "*Ja*, that would be right *gut*, Reuben," she responded, hoping that he heard her.

A few minutes later the door opened, and Reuben's footsteps sounded on the porch. He leaned down and handed her a mug of tea, steam rising from the hot liquid. As she lifted it to her lips, she shut her eyes and inhaled. Mint. How she loved the sweet aroma of mint!

"Feeling all right, then?" he asked as he sat in the empty rocking chair beside her. He stared at his wife, his eyes showing the same concern that she heard in his voice.

She hesitated before answering. How *was* she feeling? She realized that she felt steadier than usual. The tightness in her chest had abated over the past few months, and the heavy fog that used to occupy her head had disappeared long ago. Still, she felt a heaviness on her shoulders, one that didn't seem to want to leave.

"Tired," she finally admitted. "Tired, but a little better, I reckon."

"That's to be expected," he said. "You worked hard clearing that garden today."

The kitchen door opened, and Rosanna heard Daniel's and Aaron's footsteps behind her chair. "Heading out, then?" she asked. It was Saturday evening. She should have known better than to ask the question. Neither young man responded directly, but from their sheepish smiles, she knew the answer.

"Taking the horse for a drive," Aaron offered as an excuse for leaving the farm.

Rosanna tried to hide her tired smile. Neither young man had to tell her that they were meeting up with Rebecca and her younger sister. It was over the holidays that Reuben had noticed the growing attraction between his two employees. When Aaron began to drop by the shop, eager to give Daniel and Rebecca a ride home, Rosanna began to suspect that they were double-dating the sisters.

"Don't be late now," she called after them. "Tomorrow's a worship day."

Aaron waved his hand in the air. "*Ja, ja,* I know, *Maem.*"

"Where they going, then?"

Rosanna jumped at the sound of her daughter's voice. "Cate! Where did you come from?"

Laughing, Cate plopped down on the porch at her mother's feet. She leaned her head against Rosanna's knees. "Scared you, did I?" She watched as the gray-topped buggy pulled out of the driveway. "They going calling on those two girls again, ain't so?"

"Never you mind, *dochder!*"

But Cate didn't react to the rebuke. Instead, she laughed and glanced up at her mother. "By the time that baby comes, I reckon one of them will be getting married anyhow!"

At the mention of the baby, Rosanna dropped her hand protectively to her expanding belly. She had only told the children the previous week that they would soon have a little brother or sister. While her pregnancy had come as a surprise to her, Rosanna was elated to see that both Aaron and Cate seemed genuinely overjoyed—although Cate seemed most concerned about where the baby would sleep.

"In that case, it best be Daniel getting married, then," Rosanna teased back. "Otherwise you'll be sharing your room with the *boppli!*"

Groaning, Cate buried her face in Rosanna's dress. Both Reuben and Rosanna laughed at her reaction.

They watched the buggy start down the driveway, the horse excited to leave the confinement of his stall. Aaron and Daniel looked to be engaged in an agitated yet friendly conversation, and Rosanna could not help but consider how blessed she was to have the support of her family. Just as trees and flowers needed to receive plenty of light and rain to mature, thrive, and provide shade and joy to the world, she had finally realized that in order to give of herself, she had to be able to receive as well.

There was a reason for all the give and take. It was how He had designed His creation. Flowers gave honey, pollen, beauty, and fragrance, but only if they were watered sufficiently. Horses gave themselves generously to farm chores and transportation needs, but their hooves had to be shod regularly and good care provided to them daily. Why would people be any different?

"Give and it shall be given to you," He had commanded. But there were two parts to this commandment: giving must precede receiving. Simply put, one action could not exist without the other. Otherwise, the balance was offset and the cycle would be incomplete—she would be incomplete.

And now with a blessed new life growing in her womb, Rosanna understood that it was time for a renewal. She returned her attention to the rustling leaves, enjoying the vibrant colors of the new season. Inhaling a deep breath of the fresh air, she silently thanked the Lord for all His blessings.

# GLOSSARY OF PENNSYLVANIA DUTCH

| | |
|---|---|
| *ach vell* | an expression similar to *oh well* |
| *aendi* | aunt |
| Ausbund | Amish hymnal |
| *boppli* | baby |
| *bruder* | brother |
| *Daed*, or her *daed* | Father |
| *danke* | thank you |
| Deitsch | Dutch |
| *dochder* | daughter |
| Englische | non-Amish people |
| Englischer | a non-Amish person |
| *fraa* | wife |
| *g'may* | church district |
| *grossdaadi* | grandfather |
| *grossdaadihaus* | small house attached to the main house |
| *gut* | good |
| *gut mariye* | good morning |
| *haus* | house |
| *ja* | yes |
| *kapp* | cap |

| | |
|---|---|
| *kinner* | children |
| *kum* | come |
| *maedel* | a single woman |
| *Maem*, or her *maem* | Mother |
| *nee* | no |
| *onkel* | uncle |
| Ordnung | unwritten rules of the *g'may* |
| *rumschpringe* | period of "fun" time for youths |
| *schwester* | sister |
| *vell* | well |
| *wie gehts?* | what's going on? |
| *wunderbar* | wonderful |

# ONE MORE THING . . .

If you enjoyed this book, I'd be very grateful if you'd post a short review on Amazon.com. Your support really does make a difference. Not only do I read all the reviews in order to see what you liked and how I can improve, but they are also a great source of motivation. When I hear from my readers and fans, it really makes me want to keep writing . . . just for you.

If you'd like to leave a review or see a list of my books on Amazon, simply join my blog at www.sarahpriceauthor.com. And don't forget to follow me on Facebook at www.facebook.com /fansofsarahprice so that you can hear firsthand about new, upcoming releases.

With blessings,
Sarah Price

# About the Author

The Preiss family emigrated from Europe in 1705, settling in Pennsylvania as part of the area's first wave of Mennonite families. Sarah Price has always respected and honored her ancestors through exploration and research about her family's Anabaptist history and their religion. For over twenty-five years, she has been actively involved in an Amish community in Pennsylvania. The author of over thirty novels, Sarah is finally doing what she always wanted to do: write about the religion and culture that she loves so dearly.

Contact the author at sarahprice.author@gmail.com.

Visit her blog at www.sarahpriceauthor.com or on Facebook at www.facebook.com/fansofsarahprice.